THE
SANTA CLAUS
GIRL

A NOVEL INSPIRED BY
TRUE EVENTS.

PATRICIA P GOODIN

www.thesantaclausgirl.com

cover design: ebook launch

Author photo: Gina Logan Photography

Ebook ISBN: 978-0-578-77635-4
Softcover Print ISBN: 978-0-578-77636-1
Hardcover Print ISBN: 978-0-578-99547-2

To my son, Alex,
my daughter, Johnny,
and my husband, Doug.

There was a time when the "we"
was more important than the "I."

TABLE OF CONTENTS

PREFACE

Epidemic Virus Outbreak; No Vaccine Available

Presidential Candidates Spar in Election Year

Sweeping Immigration Reform Bill Passed

Defendants Jailed for Conspiring With Russians

Hottest Month on Record for New York

Headlines ripped from 2020 news stories? Actually—the year was 1952.

The year 1952 was also a presidential election year and it too was filled with headlines about the controversial McCarran-Walter Immigration Act and its sweeping reform. In New York, July 1952 set a new record for the hottest month ever recorded in the state.

That same year a more ominous record-setting statistic emerged as America faced a perilous epidemic viral outbreak for which there was no known vaccine, and no cure: poliomyelitis, commonly known as polio. When the virus swept across the country it was the most feared disease in American culture. The year 1952 marked the height of the polio epidemic in the United States, with more than 58,000 reported cases of the disease, resulting in 21,000 cases of paralysis and 3,000 deaths. When paralysis impacted the diaphragm, the foreboding iron lung was a last hope for patients unable to breathe on their own—*if* one was available.

And through it all, America moved forward. With grit and determination, missteps and magnificent achievements, America moved forward. The perseverance and collective goodwill of the everyman and the everywoman pushed America to find its way.

CHAPTER 1

THE SURPRISE

It wasn't as though she was ignoring the teacher—not intentionally, anyway. Miss Thompson's voice was there, somewhere in the background, swirling around the fuzzy softness of monotone sounds. It crisscrossed the air that February afternoon in a nondescript classroom of semi-engaged sophomores at Lincoln High School in New York City. Megan wasn't ignoring it. It was just that an image of Megan's father had suddenly emerged in the forefront of her mind, and lingered. There he was, all smiles and saying goodbye, standing on the tarmac in front of that plane that seemed so huge. He was so tall, and she was so little. Megan was only five back in 1942, but she remembered so clearly how he looked in his crisp army uniform. Though ten years had passed, she could still see his starched khaki shirt with its stiff pointed collar and the matching khaki tie, tight at his neck. There was that funny little rectangular hat. Not a hat, really. More like a cloth envelope, opened and turned upside down, sitting at a tilted angle on his head. And that dry wind that blows in late summer seemed to swallow the heat as it swept

1

across the sunbaked concrete. She could feel its warmth rising across her face, prickling her cheeks.

And then it vanished. Replaced by a nudge, a slight jar, from inside her forehead. That first little signal Megan hoped wasn't accurate. Nope. She turned her head quickly and there it was again. Ugh! Just over her right eyebrow. How much longer before class was over? Thirty minutes. Thank God it was the last class. She could go to the nurse's office, maybe ask for an aspirin. Though they always made such a big deal out of this stuff lately. She'd promised her friend Peggy and the other girls she'd help decorate for tomorrow's Valentine's dance. She'd been excited about helping. Would the nurse want to call her mother? If her mom thought Megan was sick, getting ready for the dance could become problematic. Maybe one of the girls had aspirin. Toughing it out seemed the best option for now.

New York General Hospital in Brooklyn wasn't particularly different from any other city hospital. Its walls were beige and that unfortunate green color that wasn't quite the color of pea soup but not quite sage, either. More like a blend of the two, which didn't help anybody. There were doctors walking briskly down hallways and busy nurses in white uniform dresses with bright white hats and even brighter white shoes. Orderlies pushed patients to and fro on gurneys and in wheelchairs. And, as in some of the other city hospitals, New York General had a public schoolroom on its third floor, P.S. 401, a school for chronically ill and crippled children. The hospital schools were run by Virginia

Douglas, 63, a veteran of the New York City public school system. Her assistant was Valerie Jackson, 45, a Black woman. Both women were alumni of Hunter College, where Valerie had earned an undergraduate degree in teaching and a graduate degree in English. She'd supported herself through school by working as a waitress in a restaurant that served only whites. Virginia earned an undergraduate degree at Hunter, an MA at Columbia, and later a PhD at Fordham. The two women understood that, together, they really co-managed the hospital schools, and they liked it that way.

Valerie was a quiet, polite woman of average height. The metal and leather brace on her lower right leg was a surprise to some. Her slight frame, feminine features, and demure style of dress might give someone the impression she could be a pushover, which would be a fatal mistake. One didn't acquire the grace and strength Valerie possessed without navigating some of life's toughest challenges—successfully.

Virginia's impressive teaching career spanned several decades. It was her choice to teach in some of the city's most disadvantaged districts. She felt she had been blessed, after all. Not that she was particularly privileged. She'd earned every step along the way herself. She had the foresight and purpose to bring her energy and vision to where she felt it would be useful. After earning her doctorate at Fordham, she became a junior principal. She had been at the helm of P.S. 31 in Manhattan's lower east side for several years and had chosen to take the reins at the hospital school when the opportunity had presented itself.

Like Valerie, Virginia's petite frame, silver hair, and standard pearl necklace might cause some to prematurely underestimate her character, to cast her in the sweet-little-old-lady persona. And, as with Valerie, that would be a mistake. Because it takes one tough woman to deal with a doctor too busy to answer questions, a nurse unwilling to bend visiting rules, a parent refusing to advocate for their child, or a student who has lost hope.

Yup, Virginia and Valerie were the right team. A force to be reckoned with, as more than one school and hospital administrator had discovered. The two women knew each other well. How each other thought. How each other felt.

Virginia's desk had been around for a while. Its light oak was yellowed with age, and the squatty, solid legs were dotted with nicks from brooms and vacuum cleaners. The desktop's thin veneer had chipped off around the corner edges long ago. The grain and small cracks were filled with fine gray lines where dust and soot had settled in, too stubborn for the janitor's rag to remove. Among the stacks of papers and files on top was a crystal flower vase given to Virginia by her colleagues when she left her former position to come to the hospital school. In a more obvious position were two simple handmade items: a pencil cup and a carved wooden apple. The craftsmanship of the apple was far from perfect, but that didn't matter to Virginia. The pencil cup was an empty tin can, its sides wrapped in a faded fabric of small red-and-white checks, held in place by rudimentary stitches of blue thread. As a decorative addition, buttons in assorted colors and sizes were attached with the same blue thread and sewn in a circle around the middle of the can. Both the apple and the pencil cup were unexpected gifts from students to Virginia. It had been the holiday season, the year at the height of the Great Depression. Virginia realized her young students would have no means to buy a Christmas gift for a parent or sibling, and she understood how that fact weighed on them. She wanted to empower her students to experience the joy of giving and to appreciate the importance of generosity, particularly in harsh economic times. As a morale booster, she had brought two boxes of assorted scrap materials to class—odd pieces of costume jewelry, fabric remnants, empty jars, lumber waste, string, discarded books—and guided the children through ideas to create a gift. A lace applique on a glass jar became a vase; a piece of fabric became a decorative book cover. Feeling the experience was as valuable as traditional studies, she'd set aside an hour each day for the children to work on their gift projects. She'd blocked out the final hour before holiday break as time for the students to wrap their presents to take home. After seeing the last student out the door that year, Virginia returned to her desk, where she discovered the carved apple and pencil cup, each with a handwritten note: "Thank you, Mrs. Douglas. Merry Christmas." For the past twenty years, both items had accompanied her to different schools where she'd taught throughout the district and to the hospital school, where each continued to occupy a place of prominence on her desk.

The broad blackboard on the wall behind the desk looked freshly washed. Its blank charcoal canvas was punctuated only by today's date written in chalky white script: February 8, 1952. And there she was, Public School 401 principal Virginia O'Hanlon Douglas, seated purposefully at her desk, facing an empty classroom and—daydreaming.

"Virginia?"

In the haze of drifting thoughts, Virginia heard the distant voice of her teacher from so long ago. Was she yelling at Virginia? For a split second she remembered the time when those prissy girls ratted her out, and she hadn't even done anything to that girl.

"Virginia? I'm thinking we can get out of here early for once. You ready to go?"

Oh. *Thank God.* It was Valerie.

"Valerie! I'm sorry. Guess I'm guilty. Of daydreaming," Virginia confessed. "Don't tell the kids."

"Your secret's safe with me. Tomorrow's calendar is in your box. Do you need anything else before I go?"

"No. No thanks, Val. I'll see you tomorrow."

"Tomorrow." Valerie nodded and headed out the door.

Virginia took a moment to collect her thoughts and bring herself into the present. She even allowed herself the luxury of feeling that bounce of joy that comes from knowing you're leaving work a little early. She grabbed her purse from her desk drawer, gathered her wool coat and scarf from the coatrack near the door, and headed out of the classroom. She'd used the daily walk to the elevator to perfect the art of balancing her purse from arm to arm while placing the left hand and then the right in each sleeve of her coat. By the time the elevator reached her floor and its doors opened, she appeared effortlessly composed, with scarf wrapped, coat buttoned, gloves on, and purse neatly hanging from her forearm. No contest, a strong candidate for Eleanor Lambert's Best-Dressed List.

Outside, the cold February wind buffeted her face. Thankfully, the bus was just pulling into the stop in front of the hospital. She wouldn't have to run. Not that she couldn't, but it wouldn't be smart. Not with a chance of ice on the sidewalk. The ground was still covered in snow, and Virginia noticed a few of the fresh, powdery flakes had begun falling as she made her way toward the bus.

Its accordion door was stubborn, the rubber rim refusing to budge in the bitter cold. After a few good vibrations, it finally gave in and opened fully, allowing the few passengers getting off to exit and new passengers to step aboard. Virginia found an open seat next to a window, all of which were fogged up from the humid air inside pushing against the cold glass. She was happy to be headed home before the snowplows became necessary. The bus lurched forward and then found its pace, making its way onto the street, passing storefronts and busy sidewalks where pedestrians bundled up to their necks in coats and scarves tried valiantly to overcome the cold wind. A few minutes later, the bus turned another corner, revealing the snow-covered lawn of Lincoln High School. It was late in the afternoon; most of the students had gone home and the teachers' parking lot was nearly empty. The weathered two-story building sat quietly in the snow behind several dark, crooked, bare trees.

Inside the empty school hallways, the faint sound of teenage voices echoed off metal lockers and linoleum floors. A student-made poster advertising the upcoming

Valentine's dance was taped on the wall next to a door with the sign, "Administration Offices." Farther down the hall and past the corridor near the locked science lab, Megan McGuire, her friend Peggy Tugucci, and three of their friends were headed to their respective lockers. They needed to dump their books before tackling the invigorating task of decorating for the dance. Their excited chatter grew louder as they made their way around a corner and down a dim hallway, the light overhead flickering from a faulty bulb. Megan welcomed the subdued light.

"I'm so excited I can't stand it!" Peggy's shrill voice bounced off the walls and ceiling and floor. "I can't wait 'til tomorrow night!"

Megan managed a forced smile as the girls headed down the hall, passing a March of Dimes "Fight Infantile Paralysis" poster hanging on the upper half of the wall on the left. The young poster girl, adorned in a picture-perfect starched white dress and wearing metal braces on her legs, seemed to be looking down at them. The girls reached the alcove where long rows of gray lockers stood tightly against a wall. After stowing her books, Peggy finally noticed the void that was usually filled by her friend's bubbly personality. And then she noticed something else.

"Megan. You don't look so well. Are you okay?"

Peggy's sober tone caught Megan off guard.

"I—I'll be all right. I—think I'm getting a cold," Megan said feebly.

"Meg, you *really* don't look so well. Maybe you shouldn't stay and try to help us. We'll manage."

The way Megan was feeling, her disappointment quickly dissolved into relief.

"Yeah. Okay," Megan said—rather easily, Peggy noticed. "If you're sure."

"You want me to call your mom?"

Megan didn't want that. Megan knew that would seal it with her mom. Going to the dance would be out of the question.

"No. And she's at work," Megan quickly replied. "If she thinks I'm sick, she won't let me go tomorrow. I'll be okay. I'll go straight home. And get in bed."

"Promise?"

"Promise," Megan said, mustering her rapidly depleting energy to convince her friend.

"All right. If you're sure."

"I'm sure. See you later."

Megan was becoming acutely aware of the growing ache inside her forehead as she pulled her coat, scarf, and knit hat from her locker. It was an effort putting the bulky coat on, but it meant she was one step closer to heading outside and home. Every decision she was about to make, regardless of how small, would be focused on one goal: getting home. Into her bed. Lying down. That's all that mattered. She hadn't realized she felt this badly. Get to her house. Her bed. Lie down.

Outside, the cold air felt good. The gray clouds were quiet. The puffs of snowflakes were sticking together and looked like tiny weightless planets floating through the air.

The block seemed to take longer. Cross the street. Another block. *I can walk this*, Megan thought to herself. Was she drifting? Was she doing this? She felt a little fuzzy, almost kind of fun. Was she smiling? No. That ache above her eyebrow, the nailhead, reminded her with a jolt that smiling was not a part of this. It reminded Megan of her goal.

Falling snow quieted the stoops and sidewalks in the residential area Megan had entered. What was that twinge in her right thigh? There. There it was again.

Are my legs acting rubbery? Megan wondered to herself, but there wasn't time or energy to consider anything other than attaining her goal. Megan's will gave way to the directives of her brain messaging every nerve, every cell, every impulse to propel her home, to her bed, head on pillow—before everything was short-circuited by something else.

The dull nailhead kept pressing, pushing harder and harder, bringing with it a surge of nausea. Followed by a wave, a flush that bubbled to the surface of Megan's face as fever overcame her. All at once, her head throbbed and her neck felt stiff and tender. Megan's legs gave out from underneath her and she slumped onto the snow-covered sidewalk. She allowed herself to lie there, motionless, for a moment. It actually felt better to be horizontal and have the weight taken off her legs. Relief. And the icy snow felt good against her warm cheek. Heavenly. She could see her breath rise over the snow as she exhaled. The cool relief buoyed her and allowed a split second of self-consciousness.

What if somebody sees me?

The thought propelled her to push herself up to a sitting position. She located her books and purse and slid them toward herself in the powdery snow. She managed to stand up and continue walking. Snow was stuck to the front of her coat, but she had no spare energy to care. Each step became a purposeful effort. Just place one foot in front of the other and lean forward. Keep going. One more street to cross.

My nightgown. If I can just put that on, Megan imagined. *The old one.*

Somehow, it seemed helpful to think about her nightgown. It had been worn and washed so many times that its blue floral print was barely discernible against the white background. Its once-thick flannel was now light and airy. Easy to get on. She knew where it was. Hanging on the hook inside her bedroom closet door. Familiar.

There, just ahead, she could see her modest row house with its brick facade. She could see its steps and the white door with its little arched window on top. Megan pulled her right leg up to the first step, then her left. The next step, and then the next. Her key in her purse. The door opened. *Oh, thank you, God.*

The nightgown felt soft and light against her skin. The coolness of the pillowcase on her cheek was soothing, but being able to transfer the weight of her heavy head from her stiff neck to the welcoming pillow meant everything. She lay on her side, no strength or will left to pull the covers over herself, and closed her eyes. But in a moment, they opened wide. *Panic! This couldn't be that. Could it? No. It couldn't be.*

I just need to sleep, she instructed herself.

Megan surrendered to the fever, the pain, the exhaustion, and fell asleep.

"Megan, I'm home!" Megan's mother, Nora McGuire, announced. "Why are the lights off? Are you here? Megan?"

Megan didn't know how long she'd been asleep when she heard the sound of the front door being shut. It was dark in the house.

"Maybe she's still at school," Nora mumbled to herself, "decorating for the dance."

Even through the fuzzy haze of fever, Megan recognized the unique sound only her mother's heels could make against the floor. That tapping and rhythm, that sound, was Mom's. *But don't make a fuss tonight, Mom. And please don't turn my light on.*

Megan let out a small breath of relief when Nora turned a light on in the kitchen. Its gentle reach made its way softly around the corner and into the small hallway outside Megan's open bedroom door. *That's enough. No more. Please.* She could hear her mother doing something in the kitchen. Then her footsteps approaching.

"Megan? You're in bed?" Nora asked, leaning against the doorframe. "Why so early?"

Megan wanted to respond, but it just seemed like so much effort. A quirk instantly recognized by a mother.

"Are you okay, honey?" Nora asked as she instinctively reached to feel Megan's forehead.

Megan soaked in the seconds of her mother's comforting touch.

"You might have a fever. What's going on? When did—?"

Megan forced a dry swallow, clinging to what she had guarded as hope.

"Na—na—thing, Mom. Whew. I just—just let me sleep. Whew. I—I think—" Megan forced the words out, in between short, deliberate breaths to combat nausea. "Whew. Ate sumfin—bad—at lunch. I—be fine. Whew."

"All right," Nora allowed, not fully buying it. "I'll check on you a little later. I'm going to make dinner. But if you're not better in the morning, you're staying home. Dance or no dance."

Oddly, Megan didn't necessarily feel disappointed by what her mother had just said. Fever, exhaustion, and pain were upstaging her once closely guarded interest in the dance. The nailhead was beginning to gain the upper hand.

After finishing dinner alone at the small kitchen table, Nora brought her dishes to the sink, then tied on an apron to protect her skirt. She rinsed, washed, and placed the dripping-wet pieces in the adjacent dish rack. Ooops. That lipstick residue was tough. Why didn't it stay that well on her lips? After an aggressive redo on the rim, Nora set the glass to dry next to her other dishes. She wiped her hands on the convenient apron before taking it off, then hung it back on a hook next to the refrigerator. After stalling for what she felt was sufficient time to convince herself she wasn't being an over-worrying mother, Nora went back to check on Megan.

She turned on the small wall sconce in the short hallway that led to Megan's bedroom and to her own. The lamp cast an angle of light into Megan's darkened room, enabling Nora to make out her daughter's twin bed and nightstand. Megan appeared to be sleeping peacefully, but to appease that persistent motherly instinct, Nora walked over to Megan's bed and leaned in close to her daughter's face. Yes. Megan was breathing. Yes, that was definitely breathing. Satisfied, Nora turned to leave. She started to close the door to Megan's bedroom on her way out, but second thoughts suggested otherwise. Leave the door partially open.

CHAPTER 2

HOUSE CALL

The morning sun was determined to shine, making its presence known behind the veil of an overcast sky. An abandoned birds' nest clung to the leafless branches of a winter tree, exposing itself against the silvery clouds. The tempered sunlight seemed to soften the crimson color of the bricks on the houses below. Nora's quiet neighborhood was just beginning to show signs of life.

A few houses down the street from Nora's, a clumsy white delivery truck inched its way up the block, finally coming to a stop in front of the sidewalk that led up to her stoop. The driver reached over and pulled on a lever to the right of the steering wheel, opening the truck's side door. He stood up and peered outside, his warm breath quickly turning to fog in the cold air as he pulled on his heavy gloves—first the right, then the left. He turned back inside, grabbed a wire bottle caddy holding two bottles of milk, pulled his white cap snugly down on his forehead, and stepped down onto the sidewalk. The cap was part of a white uniform, pants and shirt, over which he wore a heavy black wool jacket buttoned up to his neck to buffer the cold. He carried the milk up the steps to Nora's house and placed the two bottles in a small insulated aluminum box that sat just to the left of the door. A youngish man, too old to be a paperboy but one nonetheless, rode past and flung a newspaper from his bag onto the stoop, skillfully missing the milkman, who was headed back down the steps to his truck. The folded newspaper landed, as hoped, near the door. Nora would retrieve it soon, along with the milk. When she brought the paper inside, she might scan the headline, "Elizabeth Takes Oath as Queen, Asks for Divine Help," and perhaps the second headline noting a fundraiser at Madison Square Garden for presidential hopeful General Dwight D. Eisenhower. On any other morning, she may have noticed a smaller headline placed below the fold, "Second Polio Case This Week, Student in Queens Played on Basketball Team," but this morning she needed to check on her daughter.

The soft curtains over Megan's bedroom window muted the light in the room. When Nora walked in, she wasn't sure if Megan had even gotten up to use the bathroom; Nora didn't remember hearing her, anyway. Realizing her daughter had slept so soundly for so long triggered a cautionary response, and Nora instinctively felt Megan's forehead.

"I'm going to take your temperature. You're burning up. And I'm calling the doctor."

Megan tried to tell her mother something but couldn't form the right sounds. Not words, really. She could barely force an audible moan. For a second, Megan thought she could hear her mother in the hallway just outside her door, at the little alcove for the telephone. Was her mother turning pages in the phone book? Megan was trying to connect actions to thoughts, but thoughts came so slowly. It was hard to think. Why was she so tired? Why did her legs and her arms feel so heavy? She was so thirsty, but there was no way she could gather the strength to try to sit up, let alone consider standing up, to get a drink of water.

Megan wanted to speak, but she could barely whisper. Something had depleted all her strength. She tried, again, but could summon only a faint murmur. "Ma-ah-om?"

There was her mother's voice again, coming from the hallway. The sound of it carried a sense of urgency Megan seemed to remember from long ago. Oddly, it didn't alarm Megan; it didn't really matter. Megan wanted only to get to the doctor to get the medicine to make how she felt go away. Her mother's tone was polite, but she thought she could hear something different in it. Something insistent.

"Yes, doctor, it's a hundred and four. She seems very weak. Mm-hmm. Yes. You'll be here within the hour?"

Megan didn't want to try to understand her mother's conversation, not really. Right now, that was just too difficult.

For a moment there was silence in the hallway as Nora listened on the phone to her family doctor, Bill Lessor, providing his opinion on what Megan's symptoms might suggest. And then Nora offered her own.

"Of course. You don't think it's serious, do you? I mean, it's *February*."

Nora had quickly tidied up Megan's room before Dr. Lessor arrived. She'd even opened Megan's window for just a bit, allowing the cool rush of air to freshen the room, which had seemed a little too warm. Funny, she'd walked past Megan's room every day, had often brought in folded laundry, said good morning and good night to her daughter in here daily, but for the first time in a long time, she found herself studying the surroundings of what "my room" meant to Megan.

Several years ago, she and Megan had picked out a small blonde wood dresser for the room. It had four drawers, one on top of the other, and now stood against the wall adjacent to Megan's closet. A colorful papier-mâché box covered in print flowers from pages in magazines sat on its surface next to a small pink music box. There was also a tiny glass tray filled with bobby pins and a hair bow. The dresser's matching mirror, framed in blonde wood, was attached at the back. Several wallet-sized pictures of classmates were wedged into the mirror's frame. Megan and her mother had hung a petite wooden curio cabinet on the wall in the corner and placed a tiny round table just under it. A homemade bookcase that Nora had painted white sat below the small window. The shelves were filled with those things special to a fifteen-year-old girl; paperbacks, records, shells from the beach, a family picture, and a few stuffed animals too sentimental to disown. A world globe dominated the right side of the top shelf. On the left was a magazine about movie stars as well as the new issue of *Life* magazine and a plastic statue of a horse Megan's father had given her when she was five.

Nora thought she'd emptied the wastebasket in the corner, but there it was, full to the brim and in plain view of Dr. Lessor. It felt a little awkward having him in Megan's room. There hadn't been a man in her room since—there hadn't been a man in the *house* since—but all the frivolous thoughts vanished when Nora noticed the subtle focus in Dr. Lessor's eyes. After he placed his pear-shaped black leather bag on the nightstand next to Megan's bed, he retrieved his stethoscope, a wooden spatula, and an odd-looking little mallet device. It had a small, hard, brick-red rubber triangle at one end, held in place by its silver metal handle that fit in the palm of the doctor's hand. Megan barely opened her eyes when Dr. Lessor called her name. Her responses were groans, really, muffled, and seemed late. He listened to her heart with his stethoscope and then leaned close to her mouth and nose to hear her breathe. He asked Nora to help him prop Megan up and move her legs over the side of the bed and to hold her there. He explained he was going to lift up her nightgown so her knees would be exposed. Then he took the small mallet and tapped Megan's knees, just below the kneecaps. Megan wasn't having any of it and didn't respond. The doctor laid Megan back down, pulling the covers farther down so her feet and ankles were unobstructed. He used his wooden tongue depressor to scrape the bottom of Megan's feet. Her facial expression clearly indicated she didn't like the procedure but, oddly, Nora thought, Megan didn't protest with her feet. When he was finished, he placed his instruments back into his black bag. Nora pulled the covers back up to Megan's chest and thought she noticed Dr. Lessor clenching his jaw on his left side.

"How long has she had difficulty breathing?" he asked Nora.

"I—I'm not sure. She came home from school yesterday. I was at work," Nora explained.

Is he judging me?

"She was breathing fine last night," she added.

"Megan is fifteen? Sixteen?" the doctor asked.

"Fifteen. She'll be sixteen in August."

"May I use your telephone?"

"Of course," Nora responded, sensing the urgency. "There's one in the hallway."

Nora guided the doctor to the phone, then headed into the nearby kitchen. Darn! She'd left her breakfast dishes on the counter. What would he think? She began washing them without even putting on her apron. She could hear Dr. Lessor asking the operator for New York General Hospital as she rubbed the jam off the small plate, gave it a final rinse, and placed it in the dish rack.

"The patient's name is Megan McGuire, fifteen. She has no patellar reflex. Yes. Make preparations for a spinal tap."

The cold crack of a glass hitting the sink's unforgiving porcelain caused the doctor to pause momentarily from his instructions on the phone.

"Nora, just leave it. I don't want to have to give you stitches."

He finished his call with the hospital and retrieved a thick paper-napkin-like sheet from his bag as he neared the kitchen sink.

"This is how you should do that," he explained, placing the square sheet over the broken pieces of glass and gingerly scooping them up and out of the sink.

"They'll be expecting you at the hospital. Dr. Neill Friedman will examine Megan there and speak with you. May I call you a cab?"

"Thank you, doctor, I can get the cab. Here, let me put that in the trash for you. And thank you for coming."

"You're sure about the cab?"

"I'm sure. Oh, and what do I owe you?" Nora asked, reaching for her purse.

"Nora, don't worry about that now. Mrs. Peters will mail you a statement. Just get Megan to the hospital. I'll follow up with you tomorrow."

"Right," Nora responded confidently. "Calling a cab right now."

Nora heard the front door shut behind Dr. Lessor just as she located the number for Brooklyn Cabs. As she dialed the numbers, she began to feel a quickening sense of fear rise up her back. She was familiar with the sensation, even though it had been nearly ten years since she'd felt it. That foreign, concentrated power of panic that accompanies the brain processing an unexpected, irreversible loss of a loved one.

Wait. No. Not now. Press it down. Tamp it down. That's not happening. Not now. Megan's here. She's very ill, but she's here. Hospital. Doctors. Medicine. Nurses. Treatment.

Hope.

"Hello? I need a cab. I need a cab to take my daughter—we need to go to New York General Hospital. And a strong driver. She can't walk. I'll need help getting her in the cab. She's very ill. What? No, she's not able to walk. Yes, the doctor just left. Pardon? He said to get her to the hospital as soon as possible."

Why is he asking about the doctor?

"My phone number? Don't you want my address?"

Is this what cab companies do now?

"Okay. It's CLarkson 9-6647."

Why is he making this so difficult?

"You want to call me back? I don't understand."

What does he mean, "a policy"?

"She needs to go *now*, though. Okay. I'll wait for your call. But hurry, *please*."

Nora collected a few things for Megan and put them in a small blue suitcase. A fresh nightgown, underwear, bathrobe, slippers. The kind of things a person would need, Nora convinced herself. She coached herself to speak in a normal tone and pace to Megan and explained she was waiting for the cab company to call back. Then she realized waiting was not acceptable. She called another cab company and became worried when she was asked again about the doctor and her daughter's condition. She became downright angry as she dialed a third cab company. When she finally reached Gino Ruganni, dispatch manager and owner of City Cabs Company, she was afraid of sounding desperate.

"Hello? I need a cab. To New York General. For my daughter. My daughter needs to get to the hospital! *Now!* The doctor said she's *got to get to the hospital!* Please." She toned the last word down, then added, "You're the third cab company I've called. It's been nearly an hour, and no one's come. I need a driver who can help me. My daughter has a fever. *She can't walk, and I—*" Nora realized her voice was slipping into aggression.

At fifty-five, Gino was already a grandfather. He'd lived through and witnessed enough fear in his life to know the difference between desperation and aggression. Standing near his desk in the busy dispatch office of the City Cabs Company, Gino listened patiently to Nora's requests. The hardy man took the cigar out of his mouth as he answered the woman on the phone.

"Not to worry, miss, we're gonna take care of your daughter," he reassured her. "Sounds like she has a—a broken ankle, right?"

He continued listening patiently as Nora naively explained what she thought, and he knew, were more serious symptoms, while giving his young clerk, Willy, the rolling eyeballs. Gino was quite the figure of easy confidence, his white shirtsleeves rolled up to his forearms, open collar and white T-shirt underneath, suspenders holding up pants ample for his robust belly. Willy's appearance was at the other end of the spectrum. He was thin, twenty-four, and pale, with squinty eyes, shaved head, and a misshapen right ear. He usually wore a plaid flannel shirt over a long-sleeve Henley during the winter, and jeans. Willy worked from a desk next to Gino's. His quiet manner and unremarkable appearance masked his razor-sharp competence.

"Yes, dear, a broken ankle," Gino continued, guiding Nora through the playbook. "I've got a trusted driver for you. He'll be on his way in short order. What's your address?"

Willy grabbed a pad and paper and began writing.

"Four thirty-eight, Belford Avenue. Got it," Gino confirmed, getting a nod from Willy. "Our cab will be there soon. You just get your daughter ready."

Gino hung up and, without skipping a beat, he and Willy snapped the ball.

"Willy, get Bobby at LaGuardia dispatch on the phone for me," Gino asked unnecessarily. Willy was already dialing. "Ben Wilson's dropping a fare off there. He'll take this pickup in Brooklyn for New York General."

Inside the small City Cabs airport booth just outside the terminal, Bobby Nolan was craning his neck to find Ben. The phone cord wasn't that long, and besides, it was cold outside and the wind wasn't helping things.

"Yeah, I see him. He's free," Bobby assured Gino. "He just dropped his guy off. Hold on."

Ben was standing on the curb with his old grammar-school buddy, Joe Martinez, the two men obviously enjoying a fond moment together. Both men were in their mid-thirties, that wonderful time in life when they might be young fathers, and unjaded. Joe was a handsome figure with his dark head of hair, dark eyes, and bright white smile. He wore one of those smart-looking dark brown leather bomber jackets pilots wear, over a white shirt and a dark tie and dark pants. His pilot's briefcase was on the ground next to him. Ben looked like he might have grown up on a farm somewhere in the Midwest, not Brooklyn. His soft brown hair curled a bit on top; his eyes were more hazel than blue. Ben's brown leather jacket was worn and looked like he might have had it since the two men served in Europe, Ben with the Army 82nd Airborne, Joe with the US Army Air Forces.

"It was great seeing you, Joe! Glad you found me. Call me when you're coming up again. And say hi to Brenda and the girls."

"Will do. So, you never married?"

"No. Just not lucky in love."

"It's not too late, you know."

Ben wasn't so sure.

"Hey, it was good to see you too," Joe said, quickly changing the subject. "I'll keep in touch. You do the same."

Joe pulled a brand-new business card out of his shirt pocket and handed it to Ben.

"Here's my card and number. If you ever need anything, I'm your man. Don't hesitate to call me."

"Falcon Air Cargo," Ben read, impressed. "Owned and operated by Hank McGoran and Joseph Martinez. No kidding?"

"With a fleet of two planes," Joe humbly joked.

"Hank McGoran? Did we—from school?" Ben asked.

"No. He's older than us. But he's from here," Joe explained. "He was a test pilot for Republic Aviation out on Long Island—before the war. Met him when we were stationed in England. Good Guy. Damn good pilot."

"Falcon Air. Owner of your own company, Joe. That's really something."

"I'm in hock up to my neck. Mortgaged our house to the hilt just trying to get this thing up and running. Hank as well. We gotta get some business, more business, and soon."

"Joe, if anybody can make this work, you can."

"Thank God I have Brenda encouraging me on this. I don't know what I'd do without her. But, Ben, if it hadn't been for you, I wouldn't be standing here right—"

"Forget about it. Besides, you'd have done the same for me."

"I'll call you before I come up the next time. Maybe we can look up some of the old gang."

"You sure you want to go slumming with a cabbie? Now that you're a hoity-toity business owner?"

"You sure you don't want me to flatten you like I did in the eighth grade?"

"I seem to remember it was me that flattened you."

"Yeah, the memory is the second thing to go, you know."

"You should know."

The two men sparred, then enjoyed one last embrace.

"Get outta here," Ben remarked with a smile. "I gotta go to work."

"And I got a plane to fly."

Joe picked up his bag and headed toward the terminal doors, then turned to Ben and nodded. Ben returned the nod and watched Joe disappear inside the terminal.

CHAPTER 3

EPIDEMIC OF FEAR

"Ben! Yo, Wilson!"

Ben recognized the gruff voice instantly. He didn't need to turn around to know it belonged to Bobby Nolan.

"Gino needs a pickup in town," Bobby yelled, waving the small piece of paper in the air and jogging up to Ben. "Says hurry!"

When he reached Ben, Bobby held onto the address for a moment and looked at it skeptically before handing it to Ben.

"It's a mother," Bobby added, then explained. "Says her kid's broke her ankle. Can't walk. Needs a ride to the hospital."

Bobby took his time handing the address to Ben and looked at him dubiously before adding, "Lotta that goin' around."

As Ben studied the address, Bobby couldn't hold back his suspicions or his opinions.

"What's with Gino that he takes these fares? Doesn't he know these kids could be contagious?"

Ben held his tongue initially, but he'd heard Bobby's crap one time too many to let it go. And Bobby just kept pushing.

"What's he thinking, Ben? Why risk the—?"

"Because he's seen what fear can make people do," Ben said, then stopped suddenly. As he held the small piece of paper in his left hand, he started flicking it with the fingers of his right hand. The wheels inside his head started turning, pondering: Should he try to enlighten this clown?

"What—whadda you mean?" Bobby asked, baffled.

Ben studied the address on the paper, took a deep breath, and exhaled. His generosity inspired his patience.

"Listen. Gino was eighteen the last time this stuff was really bad. And I'm talking *really bad* in this town," Ben attempted to explain to his close-minded coworker. "And he remembers what fear made people do—to each other."

"Yeah, but why risk—?" Bobby interjected unsuccessfully.

"Gino talks about this agency the city had, this Board of Health agency that formed this self-appointed Sanitary Squad back at the height of the polio epidemic in 1916. Gino said they let this squad run rampant in the tenements where he lived. This squad, see, they targeted Italian immigrants, saying they brought polio into the neighborhood. Never mind that it was baseless," Ben pointed out as he began to paint Bobby a picture of the fear and panic that swept through the city that summer, turning neighbor against neighbor and tearing families apart.

"Gino remembers it was a night in July, humid, and hotter than hell. And none of this air-conditioning stuff we have now. Everybody had their windows open except those families with sick kids. Crazy!" Ben detailed, shaking his head. "Gino says he still remembers the sound of their heavy shoes stomping up the steps to his building."

In the crowded city of 1916, the nighttime noise clamored its way along narrow streets, ricocheting upward off the stone buildings until it found its way past rooftops and faded into the night sky. The aroma of spiced sauces and cooked meats spilled from open windows as the heavy, humid air pushed the scents downward. The smells would suddenly be interrupted by a sharp odor from the sweet, rancid stench of waste on the ground below.

The street lamps had come on; the one on the corner near Gino's building cast a stark shadow across the recessed stoop of the building's entrance. Three gruff men stormed up the steps to the building's front door, their faces hidden in the shadow. A woman joined them. She had a badge on her white blouse. She wore a black skirt, black stockings, and laced-up black pumps. Her hair was ash blonde and she wore a prominent dark hat. The men began pounding on the outer door to the building and started yelling, "OPEN UP! THIS IS THE SANITARY SQUAD! OPEN THE DOOR!"

The entrance inside was dimly lit. A single small lightbulb hung from the ceiling and barely illuminated the hallway. An elderly man, dressed in a tank T-shirt and pants with suspenders, inched open his apartment door and peered out toward the entrance to see what the ruckus was about. The Sanitary Squad men continued yelling as the man hobbled to the entrance door to open it. His hands shook as he unlocked the deadbolt. He was trying to turn the door's handle when the three men barged their way in, knocking the elderly man backward. One of the Sanitary Squad held a rolled-up paper, some kind of a poster, in his hand. Another carried something that looked like a club. They waited while the woman came inside. The elderly man clutched his hands in front of him, trying to control the shaking, as he backed up against the wall and watched in fear as the members of the Sanitary Squad headed down the stark hallway. The three men followed the woman, who quickly scanned the numbers next to every door, left and right, as she hurried past each apartment. She stopped when she reached a door on her right with the number six, where Gino lived with his mother and siblings. With a quick nod toward the door, the woman signaled the man with the club, who used it to pound forcefully on the door, yelling, "Open up! This is the Sanitary Squad! Open the door!"

Gino cracked the door open slightly to see who it was, but the men barged past him, knocking him to the floor. As he was getting up, he saw the three men, their worn, thick-soled shoes firmly planted on the dark plank floor. They were dressed in dark pants, sweaty shirts with sleeves rolled up to their upper arms, and suspenders. They could have been his dad, but one of the men had a club; another had something rolled up in his hand. Gino thought the men looked nervous. And there was a woman. Gino thought she looked younger than his mother and wore nice clothes and nice shoes. He noticed some kind of official badge on her blouse.

The men stared at Gino and his siblings. The woman looked around the scantily furnished room disapprovingly. Gino watched the woman eye his fourteen-year-old brother, Raphael, who was standing next to the stove, where steam rose quietly from a large pot of water bubbling away. The woman looked toward Gino's eight-year-old sister, Sophia, who was trying her best to set their table with the mismatched plates and utensils she carried in her hands. The woman did a quick study of the old sewing machine Gino's mother used. It sat on a makeshift table with mounds of cut fabric pieces for men's pants stacked on top and more nearby on the floor. The woman's gaze landed on Gino's six-year-old sister, Angelina, who sat on the floor with her tattered doll, surrounded by two empty fruit crates. Angelina's hair was messy and stringy. She was dressed only in underwear because of the intense heat. The woman turned her head toward Gino. She was the only member of the Sanitary Squad who spoke.

"Where's the baby?" she inquired.

"What?" Gino asked, surprised. "He's with—"

"When we were here two days ago, he was sick," she asserted. "Where's the baby?"

Sophia began to whimper, and Raphael looked to Gino for guidance. Gino subtly raised the palm of his hand, indicating to his brother to stay quiet, but the word "Mama!" escaped from Raphael's mouth when he saw his mother, Maria, walk out of the bedroom carrying his two-year-old brother, Anton. The toddler was perspiring from the heat as his mother tried to

31

comfort him. Maria's face, once youthful and pretty, now bore the weariness and fear of uncertainty. Her dark hair was haphazardly pinned back; her dingy clothes made her feel self-conscious in front of the woman approaching her.

"Give me the baby," the woman demanded as she extended her arms toward them.

"No! No!" Maria begged, "Per piacere non—"

"We know your husband's not around," the woman interrupted, "not anymore, is he? Give me the baby."

"My dad's gone to find work," Gino explained as he noticed little Anton becoming agitated. Gino tried to temper the situation unfolding in front of him and offered, "My mother doesn't speak English very well."

"We're taking him to the hospital. He'll be safe there. He can't get well here," the woman told Maria, sternly. "He's a danger to your children and to other children. Now give him to me!"

Maria looked to the faces of the three Sanitary Squad men for empathy but saw none. She looked at Gino and was unable to suppress a desperate plea.

"No. Gino, no. Please."

Gino took a step toward his mother, wanting to comfort her, but was abruptly shoved back with a thrust of the club across his torso.

"I just want to reassure my mom," Gino explained, "and baby brother that it will be okay."

The man looked uncomfortable, but nodded and told Gino, "Watch yourself."

Gino approached his mother cautiously and reached toward his baby brother.

"It's okay, Anton," Gino told him, gently stroking the toddler's forehead. "They're gonna take you to a nice doctor and nurses. They're gonna make you better. And I'll come and get you. I promise."

Gino kissed Anton on the forehead and stepped back. The Sanitary Squad woman wrestled the child out of Maria's arms, then passed him to one of the men with her. Gino saw his mother was about to rush toward Anton and held her back. Raphael started to cry but caught himself and closed his mouth, unable to stop his shoulders from shuddering. Gino watched as his mother surrendered to hopelessness, and he saw her humility as a mother's instincts triggered one last effort.

"Please. No! No! Per piacere non il mio Anton!" Maria begged.

"Stop it," the woman said, emotionless. "If you people took care of your children and kept your house clean, this wouldn't happen. You should be ashamed. Look at this filth."

Gino watched the woman's eyes scan their meager apartment and leer at his siblings and then his mother.

"They'll contact you when it's safe to pick him up, after they determine if he's contagious or not," the woman told Maria. "If it is polio, he'll be isolated for eight weeks."

The children's eyes followed the Sanitary Squad as one of the men handed the rolled-up poster to the woman, who opened it to reveal Gino's family had been given some type of official notice. The children stood motionless, listening to their mother whimpering in Gino's arms as the Sanitary Squad members removed Anton from the apartment. The children then watched in silence as the woman tacked the paper with the word "Quarantine" in bold letters on their front door.

"But as of today, your apartment is quarantined for two weeks. None of the children can leave until we're sure they aren't infected," the woman told them matter-of-factly, then shut the door behind her.

"Shit, man. I didn't know that stuff about Gino," Bobby commented quietly to Ben. "Quarantined? They did that shit back then? What happened to the kid?"

"That's not the half of it," Ben explained. "Two weeks later, Gino's mother gets a letter from the hospital. She can't really read English and she's embarrassed with Gino, so she waits till he's gone and asks her daughter, Sophia, to help her."

It was early afternoon when Sophia came in from the street. Maria was working briskly at the sewing machine, finishing piecemeal work for a clothing manufacturer in Brooklyn. Maria's boss let her take work home for extra money, what with her husband being gone and all. Maria caught Sophia out of the corner of her eye and took her foot off the sewing machine pedal.

"Sophia! Vieni qui, Sophia. Come."

Maria pulled an envelope from the pocket on her apron and opened it to show her daughter the letter inside. Maria's pride guided her efforts.

"Come. Practice. Read," Maria asked, then pointed to a few key words. "From hospital. What that say?"

"Pl-ea-ssse, please, pi-ck," Sophia read, then looked up at her mother with a smile.

"Good! Now this one."

"U-u-u-p. Up! Please pick up!"

"Very good!" Maria endorsed, then quickly pointed to another word. "I know. 'Anton.' Si? Anton!"

Sophia studied the word and slowly read aloud, "An-ton-s." She looked up timidly at her mother, who was rushing the process along.

"Si. Anton. I know. Grazie mille," Maria proudly told her daughter, then folded the letter up and placed it back in its envelope and into her apron pocket. She smiled assuredly at Sophia, who didn't feel quite as self-assured.

"So'd they get the kid?" Bobby asked, impatiently.

"The next day, Gino takes his mom to the hospital to pick up Anton, 'cause she told him they'd sent the letter to come get him, that Sophia helped her read it," Ben explained. "They get in there and head up to a counter, where there's a bunch of nurses."

The nurses' station consisted of a long wooden counter with a desk area on the back side. Two of the nurses were removing bottles of medicine from a cabinet against a wall behind the station. The nurses wore long, dark-colored skirts and crisp white shirts with small uppity collars. Their clothes were topped with prim white aprons with bibs and wide straps that went over their shoulders, crisscrossed in the back, and tied neatly in a bow. Each nurse wore a small stiff white hat perched prominently on her head. A third woman, who might have been office staff, was standing at the counter when Gino and his mother approached.

"Hello," the woman addressed them, looking down her nose. "May I help you?"

"I have letter," Maria answered, retrieving the letter from her purse and handing it to the woman at the counter.

The woman opened the letter gratuitously and began reading. The silence bothered Gino, who rushed to fill the void with the sound of his own friendly voice.

"We're here to pick up my baby brother, Anton Ruganni. My mother got the letter to come get him," Gino offered, pointing out the obvious and, unable to refrain from injecting a sarcastic tone, added, "Guess he didn't have polio after all."

His youthful cockiness drained away as he observed the look in the woman's eyes change from confidence to apprehension as she read through the letter.

"There—there seems to be a misunderstanding," the woman commented. "Mrs. Ruganni?"

"Si. Ruganni," Maria affirmed with a proud smile.

"My mom, her English, it's not that great," Gino interjected.

"Gino. Stop," Maria emphasized to her son. "I can read."

"Um, wait here," the woman requested. "I'm going to get a supervisor."

Gino thought the woman left rather abruptly with the letter. He thought he noticed the two nurses at the cabinet glance at each other and then quickly turn away, as if they knew something. Then he looked at his mother and instinctively tried to make light of the situation.

"It'll just be a few minutes, Mom. She's just getting her boss."

He observed his mother clutching her purse, looking around at objects and people unfamiliar to her. He sensed she felt uncomfortable—or was she just anxious to be reunited with her child? He tried again to put her at ease with what he thought was a touch of humor.

"They don't want to give away the wrong baby!"

Finally, he'd made his mother smile! If only momentarily. The woman who'd left with the letter returned with her supervisor, a man who looked to be in his early forties. He was balding and wore round tortoiseshell glasses and a striped bow tie with his white shirt. He held the letter in his hand as he approached the counter from the back side. He seemed anxious as he looked from the letter to Maria and back at the letter. And then he spoke quite rapidly.

"Mrs. Ruganni, there—there's been an accident. It—it explains it in the letter. The doctor was examining your son and—and turned away for just a second. He—your son—he rolled over so fast. They tried to contact your husband—*you,* at your apartment, but you weren't there when—"

"What?" Gino interjected. "What are you saying?"

"He—he fell off the examining table," the supervisor said quickly.

Maria, seeing Gino's reaction, started to panic.

"What?" Gino reiterated. "What do you mean, 'he fell off the examining table'? When?"

"He just moved so fast." A point the supervisor kept stressing, then turned to Maria. "They tried, but he never—they tried everything to save him, Mrs. Ruganni. But he never woke up. I'm very sorry, but there was nothing we could do."

"Che?" Maria asked, confused, as fear grew within her. "Gino?"

The devastating news hit brutally, without warning. How could they have let this happen? Gino started to inhale heavy, panic breaths, but then he looked at his mother. His mind raced ahead. He needed to take care of her. There was no time for feelings of his own. That could come later. When he was alone. He forced himself to hold it in and kept it together. Gino turned to his mother and tenderly took her by the shoulders, pulled her close to him, and spoke gently in her ear. Maria's eyes widened and darted around the room. Her shoulders heaved as her breath was taken away by the horror of what she was hearing. As Gino tried to comfort his mother, he noticed the supervisor and the woman appeared to observe them with limited patience as if, again, they were being forced to endure the inconsolable wail unique to a mother facing the death of her child.

"His body, your son's body, is at the morgue," the supervisor said flatly. "Not here."

"His name is Anton," Gino emphasized. "Anton Ruganni."

"Yes. It—that's—that's what's in the letter. That you can pick it—him, up there."

Gino slowly processed the blunt reality that had just enveloped him and his mother. And felt he had somehow failed. Failed his mother. Failed his baby brother. Why hadn't he read the letter? Had he made his mother feel ashamed? Why had God let this happen? To an innocent child? There was no recourse. No going back. This was irreversible. What to say to Raphael and Sophia? What to say to Anton? A promise unkept.

"Like I told you," Gino reiterated, "my mother doesn't read English very well."

The woman leaned forward over the counter and suggested, "Well, this is a good example of why it's important for her, and for all of you, to learn."

The cold and swift enlightenment was stunning. But Gino refused to give the woman the power of inflicting more pain upon him. Instead, he summoned the will to let it ground him. He realized the woman's callousness had betrayed her ignorance and he quickly compartmentalized her remark. He needed to focus his attention on his mother. On arrangements for Anton. He withdrew his contempt and disgust and replaced it with resolve, then directed his attention to the supervisor.

"Give me the letter," Gino instructed.

The supervisor handed the letter to Gino, who looked the man in his eyes without wavering, and said, "Come on, Mom. We're gonna go get Anton."

The sound of car horns blaring grabbed Bobby and Ben's attention. Multiple cars were jamming up behind Ben's cab. One driver mouthed off to Bobby, who, in his surly manner, waved him off with a flip of his hand and a colorful remark.

"Gino never forgot what happened and how his mother and family were treated. That's why he does this. He remembers…" Ben said, his voice trailing off as he looked into the distance.

Bobby started to say something but hesitated as he watched the brightness fade in Ben's eyes when Ben commented, "He remembers what fear can make us do to each other."

Bobby wasn't sure what to say, but why would that matter, anyway?

"Man, I didn't know all that about Gino," he admitted. "But tell me, why do *you* do it?"

"How 'bout you don't need to worry 'bout that?" Ben suggested and headed back to his cab.

Bobby's ego detected a snub, so the mouth, attempting to make up for lost ground, fired off clichés ringing with the familiar turf of old-fashioned advice.

"Well, I can't say I agree with what you're doing. You're taking big chances here," he called out, almost satisfied at having the last word, shaking his head as he walked back to his booth.

CHAPTER 4

IMPRESSIONS

Ben drove as quickly and safely as traffic and good sense would allow. The drive actually didn't take that long, as the morning commute was well over. An easy Friday morning, anyway. The snow had let up last night and the snowplows had been out since well before sunrise, even in the residential areas, so the streets weren't too bad to navigate.

He rounded the corner onto Belford Avenue, looked past the shrubs and trees, and scanned the house numbers. He guessed 438 would be just ahead on his left, and, sure enough, there it was. He pulled the cab over and stared at the small home's facade. His eyes fixated on the door. There it was, in plain view, the door to the building. A mother and child behind it. Just like before. Ben's face strained. His grip tightened on the cab's large steering wheel as his breathing became heavy and fast. Somewhere deep behind his eyes, the sounds of gun and mortar fire echoed in the distance; he heard his second lieutenant's voice off in the background yelling, "Move! Move! Move!" And finally, his own voice giving the order, "Clear the building!"

The pounding in his chest fueled the rapid, heavy breathing in his lungs.

"Hello! Are you with City Cabs?"

The urgency in the voice from across the street jarred Ben back to the moment, back to his purpose. He managed a smile and waved, then maneuvered his cab through a short U-turn to the other side of the street. He jumped out and opened the rear door, then headed up the steps to help his fare.

As Ben carried Megan to the cab, Nora rushed ahead and climbed into the backseat. Ben placed Megan into the cab next to Nora, who settled her daughter in, pulling her close. Ben quickly closed the door, checked to make sure it was secure, then ran around the back of the cab, jumped in behind the wheel, and pulled away from the curb.

"It won't be long now," Ben, somewhat out of breath, promised his customers. "It's—it's a short drive from here—and traffic's—not too bad."

Megan's fever continued to rise as she swayed through the inertia of turns and the car's acceleration and measured stops. She suddenly began murmuring indistinctly as she tried to speak words that failed to form coherently. When Ben stopped at a light, he looked in his rearview mirror to check on his passengers. He was reminded how ill Megan must feel and how worried her mother must be. The light changed and he moved the car forward, overhearing Megan's odd mumblings to her mother.

"Mmm-mmm-mah," Megan struggled to utter.

"It's okay, honey," Nora reassured her daughter. "Don't try to talk."

"Mmm-ah-omm. Yuu-yuu. Yu-rrrr. Yu-rrr har-arr-art."

"What? Oh, honey. We're almost there."

"We-eee. I don't. Haa-va. Yu-rrr harr-harr-heart."

"Don't worry about it, Megan. I'll take care of it, I promise. We're here now."

Ben's cab pulled up to the curb at the emergency entrance as two waiting orderlies, ready with a gurney, headed toward it. Ben turned around to his passengers and quickly offered Megan a few words of encouragement.

"You hang in there. It's gonna be okay."

The orderlies lifted Megan out of the cab and onto the gurney. The all-too-familiar scene was observed by Virginia Douglas and Valerie Jackson from the third-story window of P.S. 401, the classroom in the children's long-term patient wing. The two women watched as Megan was secured on the gurney by the orderlies, then exchanged a knowing glance with each other as a child in the room called out to Valerie.

"Mrs. Jackson? Can we draw now?"

"In a minute, Penny," Valerie answered, before she turned to the young girl and directed her, "Let's finish the handwriting work, then we can draw."

The class of a dozen children, ages eight to ten, some in wheelchairs, some at desks, were seated in a semicircle facing a teacher's desk and blackboard. Valerie walked among the students and checked their work.

Outside, Ben waited on the curb with Nora as the orderlies prepared to wheel Megan inside. Nora searched frantically through her purse, wanting to pay her cab fare.

"Can I call somebody for you?" Ben asked. "Your husband?"

Nora looked up from her purse for a moment and gently told Ben, "He was killed. In the war."

"I'm sorry," Ben said, stumbling. "What—what was she saying, your daughter, about 'the heart'? Your heart? Are you okay? Can I—?"

"I can't believe—with her fever—she's—it's—" Nora answered, flustered. "It's—since her father was killed, we've always given each other a little heart-shaped box of chocolates for Valentine's Day. I can't believe she's—thinking about that, in her—now. Um, what did you say I owe you?"

"Forget about it," Ben responded genuinely. "Please. Let me do this. Go take care of your daughter."

Though anxious to accompany Megan, Nora was touched by Ben's generosity and concern—surprisingly so. Impulsively, she reached for Ben's hand. His palm felt warm, despite the cold outdoor air. She squeezed it tightly; he didn't pull away.

"Thank you for coming," Nora told him as she released Ben's hand. "You were the third cab I called. I—I finally learned not to tell them that—my daughter has—anyway, *thank* you."

Ben watched Nora turn away and scurry up the sidewalk to catch up with the orderlies wheeling Megan into the hospital. He hoped he'd gotten the girl and her mother to the hospital in time. He hoped the situation wasn't perilous; that the doctors, nurses, medicine, and machines within the hospital walls would make everything right again.

Nora's hand felt so good in his.

Inside the busy hallways of the emergency wing, Nora dodged wheelchairs and doctors, nurses and frantic loved ones, all rushing to be where they were needed. She followed the orderlies wheeling Megan down a separate hallway, where an older teenage boy was being wheeled on a gurney headed in Megan's direction. Nora could hear him yelling far down the hallway and heard him swear combatively at the two orderlies wheeling him toward her daughter. The young man's dark brown tuft of hair jerked back and forth with each foul word exploding like rapid fire from his mouth.

"Get me OUT OF HERE, GODDAMNIT!" he yelled as one of the orderlies subdued him. "Let ME GO, MOTHERFUCKER!"

"Hey! That's enough!" the orderly shouted back, unfazed. "Right there! Cut it out!"

"Don't try and tell me—" the young man shot back. "I'll kick YOUR ASS, YOU STUPID—"

"HEY! I SAID KNOCK IT OFF, BUDDY!"

The bizarre loud behavior amped up the tension in the atmosphere for Nora. Megan's gurney and the young belligerent patient's gurney slowed, then came to an abrupt stop directly across from each other as both sets of orderlies exchanged hospital code talk. Nora noticed the combative patient was badly bruised under his left eye; deservedly so, she surmised. Megan's head was turned to the side, facing the young man. Nora, concerned what venom might spew from his mouth toward Megan, was about to intervene when she noticed the young man had suddenly become quiet and subdued. Nora realized he was looking straight at Megan's face, as her daughter was at him. For a moment, only a split second, Nora thought he might have looked frightened, even vulnerable. And then the orderlies pushed him away. Nora watched his gurney travel down the beige hallway until it turned a corner, out of sight.

"We're down this way," Megan's orderly told Nora. And she followed them into a small, sterile examining room, where two nurses were waiting to prepare Megan for an examination. From behind her mask and gloves, one of the nurses directed Nora, "You'll have to wait outside, Mrs. McGuire." Nora conceded. Because what choice did she have? Did she have *any*? She resigned herself to walking the nearby corridors of the hospital.

The nurses explained to Megan why they were taking off her nightgown and dressing her in a hospital gown, open in the back. They reassured her not to worry about going to the bathroom; both were experienced nurses. They'd helped many patients just like Megan many times. They detailed the procedure Megan was about to undergo; she'd receive local anesthesia first. It would sting a bit for a moment but would help make the spinal tap less painful. They were going to turn her on her side now.

If Megan could only care about all that.

Just give me something to make the pain in my head go away and let me sleep. Stop poking at me. Please just let me sleep. Is that a doctor standing in front of me? Is that a man? He's covered head to toe in cap, mask, gloves, gown. Is he telling me something? Who's he talking to? I don't care. Ouch! What was that? Oh yeah. Can I sleep now? Stop pushing.

Nora had walked every hallway, every corridor, every nook and cranny of the hospital. She'd had a cup of coffee in the cafeteria. She'd sat in a waiting room and watched the minutes and hours on the wall clock tick by, its plain black hands moving slowly over its white face. Each *tick-tick, tick-tick, tick-tick* of the thin black second hand. Each *jerk-bounce, jerk-bounce, jerk-bounce* past each tiny black bead. She'd even visited the hospital's small, simple chapel tucked quietly away inside a nearby hallway. She hadn't planned to, not at first. She'd made such a fool of herself the last time mortality arrived at her doorstep, unfamiliar and unannounced. She'd promised herself back then that she would never initiate the bargaining-with-God exercise—not again. She knew that wasn't how it worked—which, of course, it hadn't. But, then, this was different. This was her daughter. Her *daughter.* All options would be considered, pursued, sought, negotiated, and promised—if any might help. And in Nora's case, her promises were so fundamentally genuine, God, *Himself,* knew He could bank on them. For a little while, anyway. He knew also that after a few days, Nora, like most people, would then go back to living the life set before her. Just as she should.

While sitting again in the waiting room, Nora sensed another panicky thought creeping into her head and winding its way into her heart. Maybe it was the small stack of magazines on the low table in front of her, the cover of an older issue of *McCall's* sitting prominently on top. It reminded her of her own mother, and how her mother had always enjoyed reading the articles and advice columns. Had gained insight into cultural shifts and learned about the latest fashions. Even tried a few of the recipes on the family. Nora realized she was conjuring the woman her mother was when it struck her: *Who will recall who I am? If Megan dies, who will recall who I am?*

Nora thought quickly, reassuring herself that she had helped to create—to preserve who her mother, Sarah Jeanne Branson, was with Megan. When Nora baked cookies with her daughter, Nora would tell Megan stories about how Sarah made bread. About kneading the dough in flour. The smell of the kitchen when she was roasting a chicken. She told Megan how Sarah always cleaned the house thoroughly on Fridays from top to bottom. About how she loved the harp. And took Nora to museums. Her figure standing in the doorway with her long, soft brown hair pinned loosely on her head. Her hazel eyes that sparkled when she laughed. About Sarah's love for Nora's father; how she remembered seeing them so happy together. Her favorite candy was butterscotch. How she made other people feel welcome. And not just the good stuff. The time she humiliated Nora in front of Nora's friends. There was that too.

Who would do this for Nora?

Why hadn't she told Megan how—when— "In the future as you go through life, after I'm gone, you will be the person who speaks about me as your mother. Your words will create the picture of me. What I did. How I did something. What you hold in your memory and speak about me will form an image for others to understand who I was. That I lived. That I loved. The type of person I was. That my life touched others. That

I was here. And *oh, Megan, how can I be so selfish to think about this when you are lying in a hospital bed, so, so sick?* And suddenly the idea became humbling and treasured and vital for Nora.

Sitting anxiously on the edge of a chair pushed against a corridor wall, Nora looked up and saw the doctor walking toward her. When she was confident it was herself he was headed toward, Nora stood up from the chair.

"Mrs. McGuire, we've got her stabilized," Dr. Friedman told her. "She's—she's being well attended by the nurses. We'll know more in the morning. Go home and get some rest."

Inside Nora's head, the circuits were transmitting at light speed, translating, deducing, hypothesizing what his words meant. "Stabilized." Not "critical." Not "getting worse." He'd said, "well attended." He'd said, "nurses," plural. Megan wasn't alone. Trained medical staff were right there, next to her, ready to act if necessary. Nora also realized what she hadn't heard. She hadn't heard those telltale words that point to an irrevocable outcome. Things like "Do you want to see a priest or a minister?" or "You'll need to make arrangements." The surge of fear seeped back down, retreating within the sides of her neck, and slowly dispersed itself within her body, leaving her slightly sluggish and light-headed. She sat back down on the chair for a moment.

"May I see her now?" she asked, looking up at Dr. Friedman.

"She's in isolation, so I'm afraid not for a while. Like I said, go home. The nurse will go over a few things with you." And, magically, a nurse appeared behind him. She was older than the doctor and seemed at ease. Before Dr. Friedman left, he put his hand on Nora's shoulder and smiled, which Nora perceived as the kind of smile that plainly communicates, "Go home, get some rest, but—we're not out of the woods yet." The veteran nurse, on the other hand, seemed very relaxed, confident, and straightforward, all of which, Nora conjectured, could be taken as a positive sign about Megan's prognosis. Perhaps the bargaining was working after all?

"Have you had anything to eat?" the nurse asked Nora, as if she had to, but did anyway. "The cafeteria here is still open. They're serving Salisbury steak tonight, but between you and me, it looks exactly like the meat loaf they served last night. My advice would be to stick with the turkey sandwich."

"I'm not really hungry," Nora replied, rising from her seat.

"Mrs. McGuire, you'll need to keep up your strength, for Megan and for whatever comes next," the nurse told her.

Thud. Nora felt the reverberation in her stomach as loss of hope hit the floor. *What does she mean, really? Why did she say that?*

"Eat a little something. And try to get some sleep. We'll call you if anything changes," the nurse encouraged her, while gently guiding Nora toward the elevators.

The nurse pressed the elevator call button for Nora, waited with her until it arrived, and stayed until Nora was safely inside. As the doors closed in front of Nora, the nurse smiled politely, if not genuinely. Nora wasn't sure. On the ride down, Nora second-guessed her assumptions about the nurse's demeanor. In their brief encounter, Nora had seen her as an ally. Had Nora been presumptuous and imagined it? Had her instincts been wrong? Or was the nurse just an extension of the doctor's uncertainty but more adept in the subtleness of delivery? Or had Nora simply overstayed her welcome?

Why didn't I ask the doctor what's really going on? Nora questioned herself.

It was dark outside the hospital, and cold. Fortunately, there were a few cabs at the curb, looking for fares. She'd spend the money and take one, she decided. After all, that nice driver hadn't let her pay for the ride to the hospital this morning. This morning. Had it been only one day? It felt so much longer. So much had happened; so many thoughts and images had raced through her mind this day. So many emotions, rushing in like a tsunami and forcing her unwillingly to places she wasn't prepared to go. Not alone, anyway. Should she call her sister? Not yet, and it was late. She'd wait to call her friend Therese. No point in alarming people. They'd ask so many questions, and Nora would have to try to explain so many things: the whys, the wheres, the hows. She was too tired for all the effort it would take. Besides, they'd find out soon enough, if—no, not yet. Tomorrow. Go home and get some rest, yes; eat a little something. And Megan's empty room. *It's okay, she's safe. For tonight.*

The following morning, Nora couldn't help feeling anxious on the bus ride back to the hospital. The gray skies didn't help; nor did the heavy traffic. She'd woken only once during the night and remembered feeling the lightness of that brief split second between sleep and awareness when all was fine. And then the heavy assault as each boulder of reality fell down. That was when she reminded herself to temper her imagination. There had been no phone call, no knock on her door in the middle of the night. Megan was safe. Where she needed to be. *Go back to sleep. Return to the hospital first thing in the morning.*

When the bus pulled up in front of New York General, Nora was grateful it was Saturday; she wouldn't have to call her boss at work again. She wanted to get inside, to see her daughter, to speak to her, to speak to the doctor. She wanted to know. She wanted answers. How bad was it? Was the worst over or yet to come? What Nora *did* know was that she would not leave the hospital today without knowing exactly what Megan's diagnosis was. As she walked through the hospital lobby toward the elevators, Nora told herself she was not going to be timid. She was going to be assertive and ask questions. She was going to be calm and polite, but she wasn't going to be handled. She was going to get answers. She was going to fight for her daughter.

When Nora stepped out of the elevator, she spotted Dr. Friedman deep in conversation with one of the nurses. Curious to hear if they might be speaking about Megan, Nora positioned herself behind them, close enough where she could just make out what they were discussing with each other.

"No change in her since midnight. And the male patient who also came in yesterday, his name is John Williams, seventeen," the nurse told the doctor hurriedly. "His mother said his symptoms began the night before. Also, his breathing deteriorated overnight."

"You moved him into isolation, right?" the doctor asked impatiently. "How did he get the bruise on his face? Are any respirators available?"

"Only one. His mother said he fell."

Neill Friedman looked away in frustration and spotted Nora standing nearby, eyeing him rather intently.

"Mrs. McGuire, good morning. Come and sit down," he suggested, motioning to a nearby sitting area. Nora wasn't interested in sitting anywhere.

"No, I'm fine," she shot back, a little too abruptly for her own comfort, which necessitated a friendlier, "Really, I'm fine," followed by a calmer, "Tell me."

Nora braced herself when she saw the doctor reposition his feet, almost squaring off in front of her. Her mind raced to decipher the meaning, the need, for him to secure his footing before he spoke.

"Mrs. McGuire, your daughter—has polio."

The hallway around them, the smells, the voices, the sounds began to warp, in slow motion at first, then quickly increased in speed as if being drawn into a powerful whirlpool, sucking all of the oxygen from the room with it. Fear, ever waiting in the wings, surged in to fill the void.

Aware her mouth was open, the word "How?" released from Nora's throat.

"How—how bad is it? How—bad?"

In the split second it took Dr. Friedman to draw a breath, Nora's sensory receptors were attempting to decode the reasons why he would need to take a deep breath before he spoke, sparking the circuitry to accelerate her breathing, her heartbeat.

"Right now, she's having a little trouble moving—anything below her neck."

No. Not Megan. It couldn't be. *It can't be.*

A panicked "Oh God! Oh God! She's fifteen" slipped from Nora's mouth, quickly followed by an anxious "How can this happen? It's February. She—she hasn't been anywhere—"

"Polio has no absolutes. There's nothing you or Megan could have done differently. You did the best thing you could do by getting her here as quickly as you did," the doctor stated in that generous manner that tried to reassure a family member he or she is free of any culpability yet, somehow, reinforces the notion.

"But what's going to happen? If she can't move her arms or legs—she's totally vulnerable." Nora's words raced to keep up with her thoughts. "She's—she's a young woman. Sixteen this summer. Oh, please don't send her away. I'm all she's got. She lost her father in the—please don't send her away."

Neill had pegged Nora as a diffident woman; no need to worry himself about dealing with any dramatic scene from her, right there in his ward. Quickly rethinking his initial assessment, he considered she might be flirting close to one, and he gently guided Nora toward a more private area of the long hallway in front of them.

"Let's not get ahead of ourselves, Nora. Right now, her breathing is a little shallow."

"She's having trouble breathing?"

"Sometimes, with polio, the diaphragm muscle is affected. It's unable to expand and contract the chest," he explained, realizing it didn't seem as if Nora was going to crumble into a sobbing heap. *No, she's not going anywhere. Wait. She just stopped in her tracks.*

"She's having trouble *breathing*?"

"I'm putting her on oxygen and we're going to monitor it. If it gets worse, she'll need a respirator, but right now—"

"A respirator? You mean an iron lung? I heard the nurse tell you there's only one left," Nora told the doctor, putting him on the spot.

"That's only as a last resort. Megan is still breathing on her own."

"Does it really work? The iron lung? When she can't breathe?" Nora persisted. "How? How does it work?"

"Well, you've seen—you've seen pictures, I presume?" he asked Nora, no longer seeing her as a shy, timorous little lady.

"Of course."

"It manages breathing by increasing and decreasing the air pressure inside the chamber."

"But how does it *work*?" Nora asked calmly, looking the doctor directly in his eyes.

Neill quickly realized he was no longer dealing with just another patient's parent; he was now dealing with Megan's advocate and mother. He began to detail the mechanics of the iron lung, explaining how the patient's body, up to the neck, was enclosed within the cylinder chamber. The patient was placed on his or her back, with the patient's head resting outside the chamber on a small tray attached to the device. He described how each respirator was fitted with rectangular glass windows on the upper areas of each side, which allowed nurses to see inside if a patient needed—he paused for a moment and carefully chose his words, "to be attended to," and added that there were also smaller round hatches that could be opened for the nurses to insert their arms. The doctor then reached up with his hands and placed them tightly around his neck to demonstrate how a rubber collar placed around the patient's neck created a seal to the inside chamber.

"Pumps, attached to the outside, gently raise and lower the air pressure inside. When the pressure inside is high, the weight of the air on top of the chest is heavy, pushing the chest down, to contract," he explained to her, demonstrating with his hand, raising and lowering it over his chest. "When the air pressure is low, the chest is free to rise, causing the lungs to expand. Literally creating a void inside the lungs. Gravity forces air down through the mouth and into that void in the lungs. When the pressure is increased again, it pushes down on the top of the chest, forcing the air back out of the lungs. This process is repeated every few seconds—that's the noise from the pumps. You may have heard? The patient is getting oxygen, but the respirator is gently forcing the in-and-out breathing for them."

"How long?" Nora asked, then clarified. "How long would she have to be in it?"

"Each patient is different. Generally, a week or two, but sometimes it's longer—months or even—" Neill caught himself, then reminded Nora, "But let's not jump to conclusions. Megan's not there yet."

Confident he'd provided Megan's mother with sufficient information for the time being, and ever mindful of his need to adhere to his schedule, Neill guided Nora to a nearby waiting room and hoped he could soon move on to his next patient.

The small room was populated with several stiff wooden chairs with thinly padded black vinyl seats. There was a worn black leather couch against the back wall. A plain dark rectangular coffee table with several piles of neatly stacked magazines sat in front of it. An unflattering overhead light cast an uncomfortable pall over the room. Neill extended his hand toward one of the chairs and suggested that Nora sit down. He could have excused himself, hurried onward—if only he had been more aware, more strategic in where he'd positioned Nora. As he stepped aside, her eyes caught something directly across the hall from where she was about to sit down. A small sign above two double doors. Its letters were painted in red, about four inches high, and spelled out "Respirators Post-Isolation Recovery." Each of the two wooden doors had a small rectangular glass window placed just about at eye level, so persons entering or exiting through the doors would be aware if someone was on the other side. There was another sign, white with black letters, on the outside of each door, adjacent to the push plate: "Do Not Enter—Hospital Staff Only." Nora wanted to know more.

"Is that where she'll go when she can begin trying to walk again?" Nora motioned toward the doors.

"That's when a patient isn't contagious anymore. Why don't you sit down?" the doctor suggested, driven by his schedule. "A nurse will be by shortly—to go over some more things with you. I'll be back to speak with you soon."

Nora sat down as asked, appeasing the doctor, who smiled politely and left the room. Nora's eyes followed him down the hallway while she waited patiently for a nurse to "go over things." She watched as hospital staff moved with purpose up and down the hallway, passing between her and the room across the hall. She leaned forward in her chair and saw the doctor, farther away, talking with another doctor and felt compelled to stay seated. As she waited, gnawing questions began to rise and multiply. What was going to happen to Megan? What would the next day, days, weeks be like? What was the landscape awaiting her daughter? What if—? Nora's eyes returned to the double doors across the hall. *If I could just see what it looks like inside*, she thought.

Nora looked down the hallway and felt confident the doctor was sufficiently engaged. If she was fast, she told herself, she could sneak across the hall and look through the doors' small windows before anyone saw her. *But what if they stop me?* Nora asked herself, feeling her heart beginning to race. The sign on the doors clearly stated, "Hospital Staff Only." She looked up and down the hallway and spotted a lone nurse who was about to pass the double doors. If Nora could be quick enough, she convinced herself, as soon as that nurse passed—*now is the perfect time!*

Nora rose from her seat, suddenly self-conscious that her brown coat and even darker brown hat amplified her "visitor" status. She checked the hallway; no one was looking in her direction. Clutching the handles of her purse and taking a deep breath, she walked toward the doors. BANG! A shrill SLAM of metal crashing on the floor startled her and she froze. She gasped a small breath and quickly assessed the cause of the commotion. An orderly had inadvertently dropped a tray outside a patient's room down the hall, and several of the hospital staff were scurrying to help him. Nora realized that if she hurried, she might be able to get a glimpse inside the room before anyone noticed her. She approached the doors cautiously, suddenly worried that a member of staff may be on the other side. Her low-heeled pumps didn't give her much of a height advantage, but she thought that if she stood on her tiptoes, she might get a clear view of what was on the other side. She stepped close to one of the doors and braced her hand on the doorframe. *Please don't let there be anyone trying to come out.* She rose up and peered inside the small glass window. What she saw terrified her.

Inside the vast room, two tight rows of green and beige metal iron lungs stood next to each other, angled at forty-five degrees from the side walls. Toward the back of the room and along each side, there were odd-looking hospital beds, swaying head to toe, with patients in them. Down the rows of iron lungs, patients' heads stuck out at one end, resting on small trays. Nora had seen pictures of patients in iron lungs in magazines and newspapers, and the patients were smiling and seemed happy. None of the patients here were smiling. There were several nurses in the room; one was feeding a patient, and another appeared to be washing a male patient's genitals. At another respirator, two nurses had their arms inserted through small openings, one for each arm, on the sides of the machine. They were in the middle of some type of procedure on the patient. Nora thought it seemed odd that an adult patient was placed next to an adolescent, an older man next to a teenage boy.

Nora's wide, frightened eyes peering from outside the room were spotted by the nurse who was feeding a patient. The nurse set the plate of food and utensil on a small rolling cart and walked toward the doors. As the nurse pushed the door ajar, Nora quickly backed away, suddenly confronted by the unique sounds of the iron lungs' bellows as their pulsating rhythm poured into the hallway.

Sswhee-swoosh. Sswhee-swoosh. Sswhee-swoosh. Sswhee-swoosh. Sswhee-swoosh. Sswhee-swoosh. Sswhee-swoosh. Sswhee-swoosh.

"May I help you, ma'am?" the nurse asked in a soft, professional tone.

Sswhee-swoosh. Sswhee-swoosh. Sswhee-swoosh. Sswhee-swoosh. Sswhee-swoosh. Sswhee-swoosh. Sswhee-swoosh. Sswhee-swoosh.

"No. No, thank you," Nora replied, shaking her head quickly to indicate she wasn't ready, not right now, not right this minute, not this moment.

Sswhee-swoosh. Sswhee-swoosh. Sswhee-swoosh. Sswhee-swoosh. Sswhee-swoosh. Sswhee-swoosh. Sswhee-swoosh. Sswhee-swoosh.

The nurse nodded graciously and retreated into the room. As the door gradually closed, the *sswhee-swoosh, sswhee-swoosh, sswhee-swoosh* rhythm seeped hauntingly, slowly, back inside the room—and into Nora's memory.

CHAPTER 5

TEN MONTHS LATER

It had been a remarkable year for news stories. The 1952 Presidential election. A sweeping immigration reform bill passed—passed despite the sitting President's veto. The polio virus epidemic saw its worst year in U.S. history. American citizens remained incarcerated for conspiring with the Russian government. The month of July set a new record for the hottest month ever recorded in New York. Yes, a remarkable year for news and a good year for newspapers. A banner year, actually. And it was about to get better. An even bigger event was on course to impact the newspapers: the holiday season. The holiday season meant revenue to newspapers. Serious revenue. Every business that sold goods to consumers, and every competitor big or small, wanted—and needed—to advertise in the newspaper. People *read* the newspaper. But all those investigative stories, in-depth reporting, insightful opinion pieces, sports scores, stock and bond transactions, theatre critiques, fashion reviews, wedding announcements, and obituaries didn't write themselves. Then there were the photographers, secretaries, graphic designers, copyboys, typesetters, platemakers, typewriters, paper, ink, and paperboys' news bags. It cost a lot of money to report the news—impartially. The holiday season helped pay for it. When it came right down to it, it seemed the noble, respected, honored giants of the newspaper industry were really no different than the small mom-and-pop retailers who had to leverage the holiday spending phenomenon to keep things afloat.

Dan Kalman wasn't particularly keen on holiday stories but as assignment editor at the *Telegraph* he knew he needed more Christmas stories for the newspaper's upcoming holiday section. The month was rapidly slipping away, and there were only two more weekends until Christmas. Just last night his wife had reminded him, again, that Hanukkah begins on Friday. He thought about that when he woke up at 2 a.m., sitting on the edge of his bed in his striped pajama bottoms and tank undershirt. The days were flying past. He thought about it again when he got up at 4:45 a.m., rubbing the large bald spot on the back of his head and looking down at his oversized belly straining against his flimsy cotton undershirt. And it was gnawing at him now as he sat behind his desk in his newsroom office thinking, *I'm too old for this aggravation.* Dan had pretty much made the decision a few months ago that he was done with the news side of the business and was ready to move over to advertising. *That's where the money is,* Dan thought, and confidently told himself, "and I could sell the crap out of ad space."

It would be a short selling season for retailers this year. Not like last year, when there were four and a half weeks and five full weekends between Thanksgiving and Christmas. This year, there were barely four weeks and only four weekends between the two holidays. Thanksgiving's late appearance disrupted everything for party planners, retailers, Christmas tree lots, charity drives, candy cane distributors, and, more importantly to Dan, advertisers. And while he regarded the separation between the newsroom and the sales department as sacred, he also knew that his publisher expected to see Christmas stories within the paper's special holiday features section. Nope, Dan wasn't looking forward to assigning holiday stories, and he knew none of his staff wanted to be bothered with them. Writing holiday stories, particularly ones generated for a special advertising section, was considered one step up from writing obituaries—and barely that.

Dan knew several of the news reporters had already come in; the sound of typewriters clicking away filled the large open newsroom just outside his office. It was around 8:30 a.m. when Jim Ellis, one of the senior news writers, stopped at Dan's open door, holding a freshly typed story for tomorrow's paper. Dan knew that Jim always got in early before most of the news staff and that he could count on Jim for well-written stories on deadline. He respected Jim and wouldn't consider asking the seasoned reporter, or any of Jim's fellow newsmen, to write one of the holiday-themed features. He just hoped Jim could suggest someone who would.

"Morning, Dan," Jim said from the doorway. "The story—it's brief—the McCarran-Walter Act—the Immigration and Nationality Act—it's done."

"That law is a disgrace!" Dan exclaimed. "Whole damn thing. Country's going backwards! What's the deal?"

"Goes into effect in a couple weeks. Gonna be interesting at the piers," Jim commented.

"Yeah, that's sure to muck things up with the cruise ships, foreign crews and all," Dan added. "That'll come back to bite us."

"Got some good quotes in here," Jim pointed out. "There's the usual threat of calling any group opposed to it a 'communist front.'"

"For crying out loud, Jim," Dan interjected. "President-elect Eisenhower is 'opposed' to it."

"Don't think he's gonna fall for that nonsense," Jim added. "Anyway, it's done."

"Okay. Thanks," Dan replied, somewhat lackluster.

Jim leaned against the doorframe, scanning his article. The sleeves of his light-blue Oxford shirt were already rolled up, and he'd loosened his tie. He detected a reserved response from Dan, which Jim knew meant there was something distracting the assignment editor.

"So, what's goin' on?"

Dan didn't want to emphasize the mediocre aspect of his agenda, which a dramatic pause would surely do, so he cut to the chase.

"I gotta get somebody going on the holiday section content. What's that girl's name downstairs? Judy? Judy something. She writes those profile pieces—local people."

"You mean Mary?" Jim clarified. "Mary Henderson?"

"Yeah, her. When you see her, can you send her up here? I've been thinking about her for a story—something she'd be perfect for."

"Uh, she's on her honeymoon. Got married last weekend."

"Probably won't be in this week?" Dan asked.

"Wouldn't count on it."

"What about Charlie Crocker, the guy who writes the garden stuff?"

"He died last summer, Dan."

"Damn. Is there anybody else down there? This has gotta get done. I can't run another picture of kids ice skating in Central Park. I gotta have some content. The publisher's breathing down my neck. Advertising's breathing down his."

"What about the Lindsey kid?" Jim suggested. "He's been here since last June, hired for the Living section. Name's David. Been writing obituaries for the last six months. He'll jump at the chance."

"Can he write?"

"He can write. Graduated from Columbia."

"You know I hate these kids right out of college—think they know everything," Dan fired off with a look of disdain, leaning back in his chair. "They don't know shit."

"He was one of the writers on Columbia's newspaper," Jim offered, trying to bolster his candidate's prospects.

"Oh. Yeah. Real hot shots. Gonna set the world on fire."

"Just tell him what you want; he'll be all over it. He's all gung-ho. I'll send him up."

"Fine," Dan acquiesced, with the impassive look that comes from sacrificing one's credo when caught between a publisher and a deadline.

David Lindsey was ready for a story. Why the newspaper had wasted his abilities for the past six months was a mystery to him. It wasn't that David didn't have the talent—he did. It wasn't that he didn't have the reporter's drive to ask the tough questions—he did. It wasn't that he didn't have the commitment for the long hours and short pay—he had that too. What David didn't have—were connections. David had grown up in a small neighborhood town outside Gary, Indiana. His parents were hardworking people who operated a successful deli and grocery store in downtown Gary. They'd hoped David would help grow the family business, but David had other passions. One of which was getting the hell out of the steel-factory, smoke-filled city of Gary and into the bigger-than-life city of New York. He saw the world as modernizing by leaps and bounds from his parents' way of thinking, and he wanted to be part of it. He wanted to shape it. He wanted to announce it.

He had the grades in high school to get into Columbia and received a substantial scholarship to help with finances. With the money from his summer jobs and what his parents managed to set aside for college, he'd been able to make things work, financially, at Columbia. That is, for a single young man whose priorities didn't include anything extravagant, such as clothes, cars, or dating. During all four years, he worked part time in the evenings washing dishes at a small diner near the school. The owner gave him a free meal at the end of each shift, which fueled him for all-nighters when he had to complete a paper or study for exams. He didn't mind the menial labor or the hard work at school. Didn't matter. Because he wrote for the *Columbia Weekly*. He remembered the first time he experienced the small, faint rush of power he felt when an interviewee referred to him as a "reporter." The man was impressed and intimidated at the same time, David recalled. The man unwittingly handed David the upper hand, the perceived power. *Yes*, David remembered thinking, *and as it should be. I'm the one for this. I can handle it. I know how to use it.* David knew where he was headed.

On his way up to the assignment editor's office, David felt energized, invigorated. *Finally*, he assured himself, *they know I'm here. I've done my six months; now I'm gonna show them what I've got. The readers are gonna love my stories. They're gonna want more. I know how to flush out a story*, he boasted to himself, oozing with self-confidence. *I nailed it at the* Weekly. *Get the basics down, then be patient*, he recalled with arrogance. *Let them talk, and talk, and talk some more. Observe how they like the attention. Seem like I'm interested in every single irrelevant, uninteresting, boring, who-gives-a-shit thing they wanna say. Then wait. Wait. Say nothing. The silent void. People are so uncomfortable with it. They gotta fill the silence up with something. And they do, every time, guaranteed. And voila! Out of the mouths of babes—and flattered, naive interviewees. A little golden nugget of unexpected truth. Given freely, openly, without reservation. As if I were the one person in the world they've been waiting for, saving it for. The one person in the world they would trust with their secret.*

David adjusted his black-framed glasses as he rode in the elevator up to the fourth floor. He quickly swept his hand over his slicked-down crown of curly brown hair before the doors opened. *Oh yeah*, David thought, walking down the hallway, *they're gonna want my stories. Front page, above the fold. I'll show 'em how it's done. Never mind I begged for the opportunity to write obituaries. Never mind that I've been paid shit, having to live in a converted garage apartment in Queens. That's all behind me now. This time next year, foreign correspondent. Europe. After that, Pulitzer Prize. Look out, New York. David Lindsey has arrived.*

Dan looked up from his desk at the young reporter who stood in his doorway and forced a friendly smile, thinking, *God, look at him. Cocky as hell standing there in that odd-color checked shirt, with a black tie no less, under that zipped-open jacket flapping in the wind. Another Steinbeck in my midst.*

"You Lindsey?"

"Uh, yes, sir," David replied, studying Dan's meager office; he'd imagined it to be much larger, much more plush, than the modest space he was now looking at, somewhat curiously.

"Come on in. Sit down," Dan urged him, pointing to a wooden chair against a wall inside the door. "So, how'd you like to write a feature story? It's David, right?"

"Yes. Yes to both," David answered quickly, shaking his head affirmatively.

"You graduated from Columbia, wrote for the university paper, right?"

"Yes, sir."

"Very impressive, David. We're lucky to have you."

"Thank you."

"Don't know why they've had you down in obituaries all this time. Kind of a waste of your talents," Dan remarked, hoping he sounded earnest.

David couldn't help nodding and rolling his eyes, thinking he and Dan were on the same page.

"They're well done; well written. I've enjoyed reading them," Dan extolled, thinking, *The kid's buying it.*

"Thank you, Mr. Kalman."

"Lindsey, I've been thinking about you for a story—you'd be perfect for it. I'm assigning you to a story out at New York General Hospital—"

"Was there a shooting? Was somebody shot?" David blurted out.

"What? No! No, uh, no. Um, I want to do a story on the meaning of Christmas, um, in today's world."

David studied Dan's face, hoping for a sign of some deeper relevance.

"There's a school at the hospital. It's for kids who are sick or crippled or both. Kids who can't go to regular school," Dan explained with conviction. "I want you to interview the woman who runs the school. Virginia Douglas. You know, 'the Santa Claus girl'?"

"Uh, sure, right," David said quickly, hoping to hide his ignorance.

"I know she gets interviewed every year, but I'm confident you can put your own mark on it. Make it important."

"This—this is a *holiday* story?" David asked, a hint of disappointment evident to Dan.

"Lindsey, this isn't just a holiday story. I could ask anyone to do that. This is a story about *people.* About *meaning*. About the point of the holidays in today's world! Nineteen fifty-two has been a tough year! Think about it. We've got atom bombs. Now a hydrogen bomb. A new president. A war in Korea. There's China. Japan. Polio's worst year on record. The McCarran-Walter Act, a sweeping new Immigration and Nationality Act that's gonna change everything! The Russians are flexing their muscles, reaching beyond their borders. Spies. Hell, people are afraid, uncertain about their future! I want to use the opportunity the holiday season presents to help people reflect on their lives, their neighborhoods, and how we can help each other face the challenges of today. I think you're the writer who can do that for us."

David took a deep breath and exhaled.

"I am, Mr. Kalman. And you say *Virginia*?"

"Virginia O'Hanlon Douglas. She's at the hospital school—New York General. She'll be able to provide you with valuable insight."

"I'll find out more about her, don't worry. When is this due?"

"Noon tomorrow. Better get going."

"I'm on it," David replied eagerly as he rose from his chair.

A small sly smile grew on David's face after he left Dan's office. They wanted a holiday story? He'd give them a holiday story all right. How about, "Christmas in the Atomic Age"? And this Virginia woman, why was she exiled to a hospital with some school no one had ever heard of? He hadn't, anyway. He knew where his first stop would be, but it wouldn't be the hospital. He knew where to find records—marriages, divorce decrees, and more—just in case there was any bit of information, anything shady that all those other reporters before him hadn't taken the time and energy to uncover prior to interviewing Virginia "every year." He was gonna be ready for her and armed with every dirty little detail he could find. He'd be slow and patient and methodical with the interview. Just keep it going long enough and he'd find the chink in her armor.

Chapter 6

Greetings

At the intersection down the block from Virginia O'Hanlon's apartment building, morning commute traffic was well underway. Every now and then a horn would blare, but not for long. Maybe drivers were happy. The sun was shining, and all the snow had been pushed off the streets before the morning rush. Never mind the dirty black slush that stained the white snow piled on each side of the street. Up above, shiny holiday decorations hung over the busy streets and swayed gently in the morning breeze. A traffic cop held a whistle in his mouth, directing cars this way and that with his hands covered by bright white gloves. Steam swirled up through a small opening in a manhole cover as the warm air inside escaped and met the cold, fresh air above. A Salvation Army Santa had already set up his red pot near a bookstore entrance, hoping the sound of his bell would catch the attention of pedestrians hurrying off to work. Shopkeepers were rolling up gates and unlocking doors, preparing for another business day.

Virginia was happy to see the sunshine and clear skies when she came out of her building that morning. The air was cold and crisp, but she was ready for it, bundled in her winter coat, scarf, and gloves.

"Good morning, Virginia!" her neighbor Helen called to her.

"Morning, Helen!" Virginia shot back. "Morning, Bentley!"

Bentley was Helen's eight-year-old Boston terrier, and Virginia had a soft spot for him. The feeling was mutual; his tail wagged vigorously when he spotted her. Bentley was out for his morning walk; his neat black-and-white coat stood out sharply against the bright, glistening snow. A black paw, then a white, gingerly tested the snow depth. His big round eyes followed Virginia as she walked down the steps of her building, then went right back to something on the ground his nose found more interesting. Normally, she'd have stopped to give Bentley a special scratch behind the ear, but her taxi had arrived and was waiting at the curb. She'd found herself running a bit late for work this morning and decided to splurge for a cab ride.

Ben Wilson had been watching the entrance of Virginia's building, waiting to spot his passenger. As soon as he saw her walk down the steps, he hopped out and ran around the cab to open the rear door for her.

"Morning, ma'am."

"Good morning."

Once his passenger had settled inside, Ben closed the door for her, ran around to the other side, and scooted in behind the wheel.

"Where're we headed this morning?" he asked, looking in the rearview mirror.

"New York General Hospital, please."

"You got it."

Ben checked his side mirror for oncoming traffic and headed out onto the street. The cab made its way down the block, crossing through the busy intersection, and into the throngs of morning traffic. Ben managed to make three green lights before he was forced to stop for a red one.

"You can tell it's the holiday season again. The traffic's a nightmare already. I was uptown earlier, and you'd think it was the weekend before Christmas," Ben lamented.

Virginia smiled politely from the backseat.

"I hope you're not in a real hurry to get to the hospital."

Ben looked again in his rearview mirror and studied the face of his passenger.

"Uh, excuse me for saying this, but you look familiar," he commented.

"Oh?" Virginia replied graciously, not surprised.

Ben looked left and right, passing through the next intersection and onto the next block, then looked up again at his mirror to affirm Virginia's face.

"By any chance, are you Mrs. Douglas? Mrs. Virginia Douglas? The teacher?"

"Well, yes, I am."

"I knew it! I'm Ben Wilson!" Ben blared out, eyeing the traffic in front of him, searching for any opening in an adjacent lane that might give him an edge. "You were my teacher when I was in the eighth grade. P.S. 107!"

"Hmmm. Seems to me I remember a skinny Ben who ended up staying after class with me a few times to wash the blackboards. *That* Ben?"

"Uh-huh," Ben confessed, checking his rearview mirror again. "Guilty as charged."

"I had the cleanest blackboards in the school."

"Well, you took the time to straighten me out."

"You didn't need straightening out, Ben. Maybe just a little reeling in."

"Those were some good times. Who'd a known where we'd end up a few years later?"

"You were in the service, Ben?"

As the traffic light ahead changed from amber to red, Ben slowed his cab to a stop.

"Eighty-Second Airborne."

"My goodness. You were in Europe?"

"Yes, ma'am. I was."

"You had some rough goings there," Virginia offered.

"Not as rough as some," Ben replied, his voice trailing off.

Waiting at the light, Ben withdrew into himself. The noise of the traffic around him receded to the far perimeters of his mind. His brows furrowed slightly as images and sounds from the past snaked their way toward the forefront of his memory. Images, black and white, covered with powdery gray. A bombed-out village in Europe. The faint sound of mortar and gunfire echoing off stone buildings. His second lieutenant's voice coming from somewhere off in the distance: "MOVE! MOVE! MOVE!" He could still see with such clarity the young faces of two soldiers staring at him. Staring at their leader, Sergeant Ben Wilson. The young soldiers were anxious for direction. And he would give it. Sgt. Wilson nodded toward the stone building's entrance; the door was just slightly ajar. Using the tip of a rifle, one of the young soldiers gingerly nudged the door open a few more inches until Sgt. Wilson quietly raised his hand, then looked them in the eye and nodded. They quickly pulled back against the building, the two soldiers on one side of the door, Sgt. Wilson on the other, grenades in hand, amped up on adrenaline and fear, ready to pull the pins. The soldiers hesitated, then Sgt. Wilson ordered, "CLEAR THE BUILDING!" Instantly, the two soldiers pulled the grenade pins, *then hold, hold, hold,* LET THE SPOONS FLY! KICK THE DOOR OPEN! HURL THE GRENADES INSIDE! GET THE HELL AWAY FROM THE DOOR! FACES TURNED UP AGAINST THE BUILDING! EYES CLOSED! The sound waves from the explosions shuddered through their ears. Bits of flying debris pinged their helmets and jackets as a rushing cloud of smoke blasted through the entrance and encircled them. OPEN EYES! MOVE! CHARGE INSIDE THE BLOWN-OUT DOORWAY!

"The light's green," Virginia mentioned to Ben as she leaned forward and inquired, "Ben?"

Ben's hands had gripped the wheel so tightly he noticed them first before responding to Virginia's comment. He loosened his grasp, looked up, found the traffic light's bright green disc, and instinctively pressed his foot on the gas pedal. As the cab moved forward, he tried slowly, purposefully, to normalize his breathing.

"You okay, Ben?" Virginia asked, not wanting to pry but genuinely concerned.

Refocusing, Ben looked again in his rearview mirror to find Virginia's face.

"Oh, yeah. Sorry," Ben muttered, still trying to catch his breath. "Uh, you—you visiting somebody—who's sick?"

"No. I work there. P.S. 401."

Virginia briefly outlined her role as principal, emphasizing that the school was housed within New York General to serve children who weren't able to leave the hospital for regular classes. She intentionally took her time describing the scope of her role to give Ben a few more minutes to regain his composure. As the cab made its way through town and Ben focused again on his passenger, he shared that he was surprised to learn about a school within a hospital, but not that Virginia would be working there.

"That sounds like something you'd be doing, Mrs. Douglas."

"Thank you, Ben. I enjoy it."

Ben shared how he may have taken a wrong path when he was younger, but that Virginia's influence had helped him to correct his course when he found himself off track. He admitted he may not have even gone to high school—more like juvenile hall—if it hadn't been for her. She let Ben know how that made her feel very proud, and that he should feel proud as well.

"You always taught us to do the right thing. 'Take care of yourself, and help others along the way,' right?"

"That's right," Virginia affirmed good-naturedly.

"I haven't forgotten that, ma'am. In fact, I'm in charge of the company's Christmas charity drive this year."

Virginia let Ben know she was happy to hear that. She pointed out that leading something like that carried a big responsibility, but one that also came with the reward of making a difference for another human being.

"And what's the drive for?" she asked.

"Not sure yet. Salvation Army or St. Anne's Food Pantry. There's a lotta people out there that need help."

"*Who* need help."

"Yeah," Ben agreed, oblivious to the grammatical point Virginia had attempted to make.

The two chattered throughout the remainder of the ride. Virginia asked Ben how long he'd been driving with City Cabs, how he liked it, and how many drivers the company employed. Ben enjoyed her interest and revealed he'd been driving almost six years now and had also worked there for a while before he joined the army. He explained that the company was small—only about three hundred drivers.

"Small is good. You can make decisions locally," Virginia commented, almost advised, then asked, "So, how many drivers on any given day?"

"Oh, maybe two hundred fifty, two sixty, give or take."

The cab pulled into the front drive at the hospital's entrance. Before he got out to open the door for Virginia, Ben turned around and announced, "This one's on me, Mrs. Douglas."

Virginia let out a sigh of disapproval and told him directly that it wasn't necessary. Ben, however, was insistent.

"Now, Mrs. Douglas, you just gotta let me. I've never been able to repay you for everything you did for me. *Please.* It's a freebie."

Virginia was charmed by Ben's genuine attempt to show his appreciation. Wisdom reminded her to let go of a need to control and allow someone else the experience of giving to another. She reached inside her purse and retrieved a one-dollar bill.

"All right, Mr. Wilson, if you insist. Just this once. But please take this," she suggested, handing the bill toward Ben, who quickly leaned away and raised his hands with a resistive "No! No tips, Mrs. Douglas. I want to—"

"Ben, hold on," Virginia interjected. "It's not a tip. Let this be the first donation for your charity drive. Not a tip. A donation."

"A donation?"

Virginia encouraged Ben to consider the possibilities and casually asked how many fares he picked up in a typical day.

"Fifteen or twenty, depends on how far they're going. Like the airport or—"

Virginia proposed that even at ten fares a day and a fifty-cent donation per fare times 250 drivers, the tip-donation concept could bring in quite a haul. Ben did the math and agreed that his former teacher could be on to something.

"Right. Donation. Good idea," Ben concurred.

"Could make quite an impact, Ben," Virginia suggested as she started to reach for the door handle, but Ben was a pro and was up, out, and around the cab and opened her door before she was able to pull the handle. As she stepped out of the cab, Virginia reminded Ben, "But no more freebies! I mean, after all, if every former student of mine I ran into insisted on giving me a free—well, what would people say?"

"They'd say you were the best teacher they ever had!"

Ben smiled with enthusiasm as he made his way back around his cab and opened the driver's door, then looked back at his former teacher before climbing inside. Virginia smiled back as she clutched the collar of her winter coat close around her neck to shelter from the cold air. Ben called out, "Happy holidays, Mrs. Douglas!" and jumped into his cab. Virginia stood there for a moment and watched Ben pull away from the curb and head out onto the street. Under her breath, she offered an earnest, "Happy holidays to you too, Benny."

Chapter 7

Homework

The third floor of New York General Hospital was bustling with activity; food service workers wearing hair nets wheeled tall carts stacked with breakfast trays and dishes retrieved from patients' rooms. Doctors scurried down corridors to finish their morning rounds on time. The nurses' station just outside the elevators buzzed with staff signing medication reports and verifying patient room assignments. A small white synthetic Christmas tree covered in pink flocking and silver glitter had been placed with the best intentions on the nurses' counter, off to one side. David Lindsey was examining the tiny artificial tree as he leaned against the counter, unable to resist testing how prickly its stubby, bristly branches were with his thumb and forefinger. The thought occurred to him, *Somebody had to be seriously shit-faced to come up with a vision like this.*

The elevator doors opened and several hospital staff emerged, headed with purpose to their various duties. Virginia was standing at the back of the elevator and was one of the last to exit. As usual, her first stop was the nurses' station, where a small bin with the label "P.S. 401" was kept for any notices or forms pertinent to the hospital schools. Virginia or Valerie, whoever arrived first each morning, usually picked up the bin's contents. Virginia liked to stop at the counter regardless; she enjoyed speaking with one of the morning nurses, Jeanne O'Connor. Jeanne had worked at the hospital for about six years. Jeanne knew the ropes and, despite working in an environment often filled with loss and suffering, hadn't developed a calloused detachment from her work, her patients, or their issues. Virginia particularly appreciated that Jeanne was also impervious to workplace drama.

Headed from the elevator, Virginia looked past the hurried people, carts, and gurneys toward the nurses' station. She couldn't help noticing the lanky young man standing awkwardly at the counter. She recognized the reporter's notebook he clutched in his left hand and the look on his face that said, "I have to bother you this morning when you're trying to get all your work done." Virginia was glad when she spotted Jeanne standing behind the counter. The two women exchanged a knowing look of "Here we go again."

"Good morning, Mrs. Douglas," Jeanne said calmly as a wry smile emerged on her face. "This young man from the newspaper has been waiting for you."

"Uh, Mrs. Douglas? Virginia Douglas?" David inquired, looking at Virginia and thinking, *She looks like my grandmother, only nicer. More refined. Yeah, a lot more refined.*

"Good morning," Virginia replied to both. David didn't hesitate to barge right in.

"Uh, yes, Mrs. Douglas. I'm with the *Telegraph*. I'm here to get your comments, um, on the spirit of the holiday season."

Perfectly at ease with priorities, Jeanne interjected to let Virginia know that another reporter, Mike Reilly from the *Times*, was waiting for Virginia down the hallway near the multipurpose room. Jeanne also suggested that Virginia may want to check in on one of her students, patient John Williams. Virginia appreciated Jeanne running interference and attempted to postpone the inevitable with the young reporter, asking him if they could meet a little later. David felt otherwise.

"Mrs. Douglas, I've been waiting a long time. I, uh, need to get—want to get a new angle."

"Angle?"

"I mean, these being modern times and all. Atomic power. Has the spirit of Christmas changed? Does it still have significance?"

"These being 'modern times' and all," Virginia repeated, studying the rookie reporter.

"Yes, ma'am."

"Well, Mr.—Pardon me, what did you say your name was?"

"Lindsey, ma'am. David, with the *Telegraph*."

"Well, Mr. Lindsey, that might take some time to answer."

The look of disappointment kept in check by frustration was all over David's face. He launched into his case for his story as Virginia listened and graciously availed her full attention. Not quite patronizing—she wouldn't intentionally insult such a genuinely eager young man—she generously crafted a quote and guided the reporter down the hall.

"Hmmm, let's see. I believe," she began, pausing to give David time to scramble for his pen, click it repeatedly to get it functioning, and begin taking notes, "the spirit of Christmas is very much alive in these—modern times. You can see it in the faces of children everywhere, even here in the hospital. The children are preparing a holiday recital—"

"Here? In the hospital?" David blurted.

Virginia affirmed that the children in the hospital school were indeed planning a holiday recital for their parents and for each other. She began to explain the benefits of such an activity for the children when she noticed David appeared a bit anxious, a bit distracted.

"Are you uncomfortable in hospitals, Mr. Lindsey?"

"Well, they're not my favorite place to be," he revealed, unwittingly letting his guard down as yet another mother figure professed such genuine concern for his well-being. He caught himself, regrouped, and got back on track.

"I'll be—I'm fine. Now, what I want to get is *your* story, Mrs. Douglas. Wouldn't you like to see your name in print? Get the publicity?"

Virginia was intrigued by the young Mr. Lindsey and assured him she was very happy to speak with him but asked if he might be able to wait ten or fifteen minutes while she took care of an urgent matter that needed to be addressed. She suggested he take a peek in the open multipurpose room down the hall and get a preview of what the children had done. With a sincere smile, Virginia promised David she would give him everything he may need for his story and guided him toward a group of chairs outside the room. David reluctantly surrendered to the delay, seated himself in one of the chairs, and reviewed his meager notes.

Virginia caught Jeanne's eye as she neared the nurses' station. Jeanne couldn't help letting a little smile escape as she eyed the young reporter down the hall, surmising that the petite silver-haired principal had gently but masterfully handled the young know-it-all.

"So what's going on with John?" Virginia asked quietly.

"He's got a foul mouth, that one." Jeanne rolled her eyes for emphasis.

"I know it's getting a little old, Jeanne, but he thinks it's his only weapon against the outside world. He's had a rough time."

"You're right there," Jeanne agreed. "He did ask about that student, Megan McGuire. I guess you've talked about her with him?"

"It helps to know you're not the only teenager in here. I'll let Megan know. Did he have a message for her?"

"Not really, just that he was wondering how Megan was doing," Jeanne explained. She let Virginia know that the "Megan" question was the high point of her conversation with John. Jeanne suggested that even though John said he hated being in the hospital, he didn't seem to be in any hurry to go home. She revealed that John had spoken again of wanting to have his arm cut off, that he wouldn't go back to school with it withered and useless. And there was something else, Jeanne started to mention, then hesitated.

"I haven't told this to the doctors yet. I'm writing that report now," Jeanne told her. "Do you remember when he first came in last February and had that bruise, a bad bruise, on the side of his face?"

Virginia nodded affirmatively.

"He told the doctors that he'd hit his head when he fell," Jeanne recalled. "Well, yesterday he told me that the night before he came here, when he started to feel sick, he began having muscle twitches in his arm and legs. And when he asked his father if it could be polio—"

As Jeanne hesitated, Virginia could see the nurse was troubled.

"Go on, Jeanne," Virginia encouraged.

"His father hit him across the face and yelled, 'You don't have polio! Don't ever say that again! To anyone!'"

Jeanne exhaled a sigh of relief, finally able to share the young man's pain with a trusted ally. Virginia imagined what John had gone through that night. The two women shared their concerns, assessment, and support. Jeanne confessed she wanted to hug John but explained he was back in the iron lung. She also shared that John and his doctor had been trying to wean John off the respirator but hadn't been very successful, which had also been demoralizing to him.

"And when he told you about his dad hitting him like that, he probably acted like the 'tough guy,' right?" Virginia asked. "Like it didn't bother him at all."

"Yup. He just said, 'That's my dad. Well, I guess I showed him.'"

The two women discussed how young men feign such callousness, convinced they're hiding their need for love. Virginia also reminded Jeanne that not only were Jeanne, the other nurses, doctors, and researchers fighting the disease of polio, but they were also fighting the stigma of the disease, and added, "Which can be just as powerful, just as difficult to overcome." Jeanne confided in Virginia and shared how angry and sad it had made her when she'd heard how John's father treated him and, now, how she must process the realization that she had been the first and only person with whom he'd shared the experience.

"I didn't know who to tell," Jeanne admitted, "but you seemed like the right person."

"Thanks, Jeanne. I'm glad you did, but now I'm going to remind you of something you and Valerie are usually reminding me. Don't coddle him. He's nearly a grown man. Treat him like one. Because it's clearly time he started acting like one. He's going to face a different world outside this building. It can be tough and unsympathetic. No free lunches. No road maps. It's our job to help teach him how to navigate."

Jeanne took a deep breath and nodded in agreement as Virginia collected a few papers from the P.S. 401 bin tucked under the counter. Virginia informed Jeanne she planned to stop in and see John briefly this morning, which reminded Jeanne of a favor Megan McGuire had asked of her. Jeanne grabbed the book *East of Eden* from her desk area and handed it to Virginia, then told her that Megan had asked if "Mrs. Douglas would pass it on to John. If he wanted something to read."

"Happy to," Virginia let her know.

The two women playfully raised their eyebrows as Jeanne handed the novel to Virginia.

On her way to see John, Virginia stepped inside the classroom to drop off her coat, purse, and a few papers. As she headed toward the elevators and a lower floor, Virginia strategically planned the conversation she and John were about to have. After a short walk down a quiet hallway, she entered the Respirators Post-Isolation Recovery Room. The *sswhee-swoosh, sswhee-swoosh, sswhee-swoosh* whirring from the rows of iron lungs filled the room with a constant reminder of life being sustained. Virginia walked past several patients lying in the metal chambers and finally spotted the thick tuft of dark brown hair where the back of John William's head rested on a small tray attached to his iron lung.

"Hello, John!" Virginia announced in a friendly tone as she placed the book down on a metal cart near John's respirator, then added, "How's your morning going?"

"A thrill a minute," John replied, oozing sarcasm.

"I'm gonna cut to the chase, John. I hear you've been using some pretty tough language with the nurses."

John slowly turned his head in her direction, stopping short of looking at her, stared blankly at the ceiling, and answered her with a snide "Yeah. So what?"

"You think they deserve it? Why?" Virginia asked matter-of-factly.

John didn't have a lethal comeback prepared and continued staring at the ceiling as a substitute. Virginia relayed that John's reader informed her that John wasn't cooperating to complete his class assignments. She asked, "What gives?"

"Nothing. Bored. What's the point? Take your choice. What the hell do you care?"

Unruffled, Virginia picked up the book from Megan and showed the title to John.

"Oh, Megan, the McGuire girl, thought you might enjoy this new book by John Steinbeck, *East of Eden*."

"I'd say we're pretty much south of Eden in this shi—" John remarked, checking himself in time, "in this dump."

"It's got everything. Deception, in-fighting, murder, prostitution. You know, just your typical family story."

"I don't need to read about any more dumbasses," John retorted, turning toward Virginia. "Got enough in my own family."

"So, what's with the swearing at everybody?" she asked, directly. "Is it for shock value? To intimidate? Does it make you feel like you're able to bully people?"

John ignored Virginia, rolled his eyes, and turned his head away, staring back at the ceiling. Virginia placed the thick novel back on the cart and moved close to John. Bracing herself with one hand at the top of the metal chamber, near John's head, she leaned in close and began whispering in John's ear. His eyes widened as his cheeks suddenly flushed red. He pressed his chin downward, as if he were trying to shrink himself through the rubber collar circling his neck and escape downward into his iron lung. He was speechless and for a moment even afraid after seeing the stark flash of his own naiveté. Virginia rose back up and John's eyes assessed her distance.

"You think your generation invented swearing? You're amateurs," Virginia assured him. "But I'll tell you this—use foul language around the nurses again, and I'll shave your head."

John didn't say anything. His eyes spoke for him.

"And I know right where pre-ops keep all their electric shavers. They get such a nice clean cut. Oooh. They're fast too," Virginia described, motioning back and forth with her hand, as if holding a shaver while emitting "bzzz-zzz-zzz-zzz-zzz-bzzz-zzz-zzz-zzz."

John tried, too transparently, to recover his cool.

"Enjoy your morning," Virginia said encouragingly as she turned and walked away from John and headed toward the doors.

The sounds of chattering students left alone in a classroom without a teacher spilled into the hallway outside the P.S. 401 classroom as Virginia approached. She ran into her assistant, Valerie Jackson, who was in the middle of helping Megan settle back into a wheelchair. Valerie was determined to let Megan figure out how best to secure the walking sticks in a side compartment one of the janitors had jury-rigged for the chair. The three women exchanged greetings and Virginia shared that she thought Megan would have been done with her wheelchair by now. Megan lamented that she'd been "trying" but started to whine about the walking sticks being "just so, so—"

"So helpful?" Virginia suggested.

Megan resigned herself to the lack of sympathy while Valerie asked Virginia how her ride in was this morning. Virginia told Valerie and Megan about her cab driver, who had turned out to be a former pupil of hers.

"Quite a charming young man, really," Virginia recalled.

"Well, there's another charming man from your past here," Valerie said and indicated toward the nurses' station. "Mike Reilly, from the *Times*."

"Yes, Jeanne said he was here," Virginia mentioned as she looked down the hallway.

Virginia spotted the seasoned reporter, dressed in his overcoat and hat, pleasantly chatting with one of the nurses. Virginia thanked Valerie for the heads-up and let both women know there was also another reporter waiting for an interview. Megan had another priority and didn't hesitate to change the subject.

"Um, Mrs. Douglas, did you give the book to that boy? John Williams," Megan asked, quickly adding, "If he didn't want it, no big deal. I don't really care. Why are the reporters here to see you?"

Virginia and Valerie stared at each other as Virginia wryly answered, "I guess it must be a slow news day," and without skipping a beat told Megan, "He was very interested in the book."

Megan's curiosity, or hope of further delaying the start of class, sparked her to question again why the reporters wanted to talk to Mrs. Douglas. Valerie couldn't resist the opportunity to playfully annoy Virginia, and she teasingly encouraged Megan. "You mean you didn't know our Mrs. Douglas is a celebrity?"

Which drove Virginia bananas, but the two women had volleyed enough times over the years, so Virginia wasn't truly perturbed. Instead, she responded with a controlled, "Now, Valerie, there's no—" But Valerie was on her game today, determined to have some fun, and egged Megan on. "You mean she's never told you about her famous letter to the editor?" Megan bit and asked Virginia about the letter, what editor, and what its purpose was, which prompted Virginia to suggest Megan was beginning to sound like a reporter. Valerie, satisfied with a win, proposed the story would have to be told, but quickly, as she indicated now that *both* reporters were waiting for Virginia at the nurses' station. Virginia glanced down the hallway and saw that David Lindsey had joined Mike Reilly, waiting near the counter.

"Guess it's too late for me to sneak out?" Virginia asked.

"Not a chance," Valerie replied, relishing the moment with a broad smile.

CHAPTER 8

A DIFFERENT PERSPECTIVE

"Mr. Reilly, what are you doing here?" David asked. "I thought you only covered the big stories downtown. You waiting for Mrs. Douglas too?"

"Relax, kid. I'm not here to scoop you. It's your story. I'm just getting into the holiday spirit."

David seized the moment to attempt to impress the veteran reporter. After all, they'd even talked about him in the journalism class at the university.

"So, hey, I hear she was married once, but her husband's not in the picture, right?"

Mike gave Lindsey a what-the-hell look but forced himself to be patient with the young reporter.

"I may have read that. Somewhere. *Maybe ten or fifteen years ago.*"

David tried another crack at demonstrating his reporter's savvy and pressed Mike, "So how come she never remarried? But she raised the daughter. Did you know that about her?"

Annoyed but wise enough to be generous, Mike attempted to enlighten the rookie.

"What if I do know? I ain't writing her biography. *Are you?*"

David sheepishly turned his attention to his open notepad, but he knew he had to respond and mustered a chastised, "Uh, no. But, man, what's she want to work here for?"

Displeased but not surprised by how clueless his young colleague was, Mike assessed it was worth the effort to help David become a better reporter. Mike relayed he had first interviewed Virginia twenty years ago, and that he'd followed her as she moved around the New York City public school system. He told David she'd taught in some of the city's poorest neighborhoods, schools on the lower east side, Harlem and Brooklyn, and that it didn't surprise him that she was a principal at the hospital school. Mike asked David if he was aware Virginia had a master's degree and a PhD, but he could see David had no idea. David interrupted and suggested Virginia was supposed to be famous, and he added, "You'd think she'd be rich or something." Mike assured him she was famous and pointed out that her name was known to more people around the country, around the world, than just about anyone, except, perhaps, to David's generation.

"I know about her," David asserted to Mike. "They used to call her 'The Santa Claus Girl,' right? She wrote a letter to the newspaper asking if there was a Santa Claus. What's the big deal?"

Mike continued asking himself why he was letting himself suffer this fool; it would be so easy to just stop trying and step back. Let David reveal his own ineptitude in print. But it was the holiday season, Mike reminded himself; kindness and generosity to our fellow man, even when it was excruciatingly painful.

"Would you like a few more facts for your story?" Mike asked with the most carefully crafted, non-threatening guise he could concoct. "Did you ever hear the phrase 'Yes, Virginia, there is a Santa Claus'?"

"Yeah," David answered, unaware, when he suddenly connected the dots. "That's about *her*? No kidding? I just thought it was a phrase, you know, when somebody's being a chump. You know—I've got a bridge to sell you. That kind of thing."

"I'm sorry I've kept you gentlemen waiting," Virginia apologized, greeting the men. The three exchanged hellos as Virginia asked for their indulgence for one last delay while she greeted the class of children just down the hallway. Mike assured her that it was fine, and David saw no point in challenging. As Virginia walked away, David argued that there was really no story, because of course a newspaper was going to print there was a Santa Claus, and added he just didn't see the big deal here. Mike's generosity was rapidly reaching its limit, but there was enough left for one more gift.

"What did your assignment editor tell you this morning? Did he give you a copy of the editorial reply to her letter? Have you ever read it?"

David shook his head, indicating, "no," saving himself from having to admit it out loud.

Smiling, but thinking, *You dumb little shit*, Mike took out his wallet and retrieved a folded, worn copy of the editorial and handed it to David, instructing him to sit down and read it before writing a story. Mike

95

patiently explained that the piece was reprinted year after year, all over the world, more than any news article ever written. David scanned the article and said he was surprised the paper had allocated so much space for an editorial opinion about Santa Claus.

"Come on!" David suddenly exclaimed. "This says it was written in—you gotta be kidding me! In 1897! This is 1952!"

"You need to read this to understand what the public sees—what they feel and what they want," Mike told him.

"Schmaltz and sentimentality?" David suggested, thinking himself witty.

Mike took a deep breath, smiled, and exhaled through clenched teeth, telling himself, *Think tolerance, a teaching moment. You pathetic little shit.*

"No," Mike replied calmly, then suggested, "Philosophy. Beauty. Art. Intellectual distraction. Tradition. And, coincidently, a brilliant piece of evidence parents can point to for their children. They're off the hook! It's brilliant! We're all off the hook!"

His patience spent, Mike knew he needed to excuse himself immediately and told David he'd be back in a minute. He instructed him, "Don't lose that!"

David spotted a nearby chair, grabbed a seat, and began reading the article quietly to himself.

Dear Editor, I am eight years old. Some of my little friends say there is no Santa Claus.

He paused briefly, looked to his left and then right, checked to make sure he wasn't being observed, then continued reading.

Virginia, your little friends are wrong. They have been affected by the skepticism of a skeptical age.

David reflected for a moment, actually finding himself thinking about the meaning of the sentence he'd just read. He settled back into his chair and continued reading.

Virginia found Valerie waiting just outside the classroom, eager to speak with her. Megan was still hanging around in the hallway, convincingly reading a book to appear as though she were engaged in studies. Aware of John Williams's struggles, Valerie asked Virginia how the young man was faring. Virginia shared that the cocky John Williams was angry, frustrated, and troubled about what an uncertain future held for him, adding that it was nothing Valerie didn't already know.

"You didn't *scare* him, did you?" Valerie asked sarcastically. "Not with the 'shave your head' routine?"

Virginia assumed the "guilty as charged" stance.

"You're so bad," Valerie chided.

"I learned from the best," Virginia reminded her.

"Well, don't patronize him," Valerie advised. "He'll think you don't respect him."

"The new nurse supervisor, Ruth Hoffman, the one we met last week, is supposed to start down there tomorrow," Virginia recalled. "She'll give him a new perspective."

"She mentioned she was at the veterans' hospital in DC, for the past ten years. She's seen it all. Dealt with it all," Valerie mentioned, then raised her eyebrows and delivered an exaggerated, "Oh yeah. She'll give John a new perspective all right."

The two women recollected how challenging the past ten months had been for John and how none of the former basketball player's friends had visited him since being admitted, and his parents only occasionally. Part of John's treatment involved removing him from the iron lung with therapy to encourage his chest and diaphragm muscles to strengthen, which would enable him to breathe on his own. Because John's breathing was understandably shallow, he became anxious with fear, which rapidly caused his breathing to become erratic, causing him to panic, which necessitated being placed back inside the machine. The process had become a frustrating and discouraging cycle for John and had taken its toll on his morale. Valerie suddenly remembered she wanted to tell Virginia about a new polio patient admitted last night, a young girl named Rachel Hall. Valerie explained that she heard Rachel's prognosis wasn't very good, as the young girl was also having difficulty breathing.

"Every iron lung we have is being used, and it looks like we're not the only hospital in that position," Valerie explained, adding she had overheard the orderlies talking. "Which patient gets the last available iron lung? I don't envy the doctors having to make *that* decision."

Both women remarked how difficult 1952 had been for patients, doctors, and nurses, with the year seeing the highest number of polio cases ever recorded.

"Nationwide, they say we're close to reaching fifty-eight thousand cases this year," Virginia remarked, "and nearly three thousand deaths."

"I read we're looking at more than twenty-one thousand new cases of children with some form of paralysis this year alone," Valerie added.

The two women shared their hopes for the polio vaccine to be developed quickly, safely, and successfully, and that its progress would not be impeded by politics.

Megan had been waiting nearby, not exactly patiently, hoping the two women would wrap up their conversation so she could speak with Mrs. Douglas privately. Virginia noticed Megan's apparent eagerness and asked Valerie if she wouldn't mind getting things started in the classroom. Valerie got the picture and reminded Megan she would catch up with her later downstairs. With the woeful look of a forlorn sixteen-year-old, Megan wheeled herself close to Virginia, and tested the waters.

"Mrs. Douglas, I really am trying to walk. I'm doing the therapy. Really. Even though it's horrible. *Well, it is!*"

"I get it, Megan," Virginia assured her. "I know it's difficult, but all that hard work will pay off. And why wouldn't you want to get out of here as fast as you can? Even with all the drama around here, Lincoln High School is a lot more exciting than this place."

Megan wasn't so sure—or perhaps she was, and imagining the latter could be daunting for a teenage girl struggling with walking sticks. Virginia suggested Megan accompany her down the hallway for an errand and used the opportunity to encourage Megan to open up about what was troubling her. With trepidation, Megan spoke of the subject of going back to high school. She began, then hesitated and looked around to make sure no one else was in earshot. Virginia suggested they move farther down the hall to a less crowded area and gently reminded the young woman, "Megan, it's *me* you're talking to. No one else. Just us."

Megan began speaking slowly at first; then, as if the flood gates had been thrown open, the words came gushing out of her mouth. She pointed out that at her school she would be the only one using walking sticks and that everyone would be staring at her. She would have to go up and down stairs carrying all her books, she explained, with all those people wanting to go faster than her. And what if she fell? And no one would want to date her. And how could she ever go to a dance again?

"Well, we do have a lot to contend with here," Virginia said genuinely. "And let me reassure you, we can do it. One step at a time, literally."

For a moment, Megan was teetering on exasperation, but she controlled the urge to respond, knowing Virginia would be straightforward with her. Although it would have been nice to have been given a little sympathy—actually a lot of sympathy—after having just shared that everything her future represented seemed so uncertain, so uncharted. Virginia understood what Megan's concerns were and empathized with the fact that to a young woman of sixteen, those issues seemed insurmountable. She was confident Megan was ready to move forward and, like so many of Virginia's previous students, just needed a blueprint to get started. Virginia affirmed Megan's concern about navigating the school's staircases and that the task could pose a challenge, but not one that Megan couldn't overcome.

Virginia suggested that with the progress Megan had been making with the walking sticks, they wouldn't be of much use for long. She reminded Megan that friends, true friends, would support her—probably smother her with well-intentioned support. "Now, *that* concerns me," Virginia told Megan. "I don't want you taking advantage of them."

Megan couldn't help but smile, thinking about the possibility of owning even a thread of control. Virginia offered Megan another perspective around the fear one imagined regarding a dance and suggested Megan consider what the boy who has to work up the nerve to ask a girl to a dance might experience.

"Think about the anxiety *he* feels, wondering if she'll turn him down or if she already has a date with someone else."

Virginia playfully reminded Megan to be gentle with boys, as their egos were so easily bruised. Megan laughed and decided the conversation wasn't as painful as she'd anticipated. She shared with Virginia that at school, before she came down with polio, she'd never been really popular. She had friends—*has* friends—but now, all of a sudden, everyone would know she was the girl who'd had polio. Virginia was well aware that *that* news had been shared over the high school grapevine long ago but saw no benefit in pointing it out now.

"Hmmm, yes. Standing in the spotlight can be awkward. But, and this is big, it can also be very powerful."

Intrigued, Megan asked Virginia what she meant.

"Well, how one chooses to handle all the attention," Virginia explained, craning her neck and spotting

Mike Reilly farther down the hallway. Inflecting a tone of sarcastic drama in her voice, Virginia offered, "The newspaper reporters, photographers, the glamour. You can't go to parties all the time."

"It could be fun?" Megan imagined.

"Oh, I'm sure it is. But you know what's really fun?"

"What?"

"Making a difference," Virginia answered confidently. "Creating awareness. Making the world a better place."

"How can I—?" Megan asked, somewhat defeated.

"Reach up and tilt the spotlight."

Virginia could see Megan was eager to understand. She told Megan, "Point the spotlight where it's needed." She explained that a person in the spotlight could, indeed, attend a lot of parties and the newspapers would follow, and that would be fine. Virginia suggested, however, that if the same person went to a food drive or an animal shelter or an orphanage, the reporters would follow there as well. She emphasized that not only would they photograph and interview the celebrity, but they may also write about the help that was needed. Bringing that need out of the darkness and into the light.

"The spotlight," Megan remarked.

"Bingo! Think about it, Megan," Virginia encouraged. "Other young women will want to know about your experience. What did you do? How did you manage? You have so much to offer and so much to share. And you're a very good writer."

"Then she should be writing for us," Mike Reilly interjected cheerfully, standing behind Megan. "Hello, ladies!"

The three exchanged hellos and introductions. Mike explained to Megan that he couldn't stop by the hospital without saying hello to Mrs. Douglas. Megan, whose mood had changed 180 degrees since she had begun her conversation, was ready to face the world head-on, and decided she needed to be somewhere else.

"Excuse me. Mrs. Douglas, I've finished my homework. Mrs. Jackson said we could take a break before we go to the torture chamber—uh, therapy. It was nice meeting you, Mr. Reilly," Megan said with a smile.

"Likewise, miss."

Megan backed up her wheelchair, spun around, and headed down the hallway. Mike asked Virginia about Megan, commenting she seemed like a nice kid. Virginia shared that Megan had been at the hospital school since last February and that she'd done remarkably well, considering. Mike guessed polio, which Virginia confirmed, adding that Megan was very fortunate but worked hard and had a very supportive mother. Megan's father, she explained, was killed in the war, shot down over St. Lô, France. Mike revealed he'd heard that another polio case had been admitted to the hospital last night.

"That's why I'm here again. Been a rough year for this."

"They're making headway on the vaccine, right?" Virginia asked, hoping Mike might have some insight available to reporters.

"We keep hearing that, but more and more kids keep getting infected."

The two shared information on the latest news of the disease's progress. Both were familiar with the spike in cases this year and the devastating effect on the lives of children and their families. Virginia was a fan of Mike's reporting and grateful he appreciated there was a compelling and personal impact behind each number that was added to the impersonal quantifier known as statistics.

"And I did also want to stop by and wish you merry Christmas."

"Thank you, Mike."

"You take care."

Mike made his way down the hallway where he found David still pondering the editorial. He asked David if he had finished reading the piece. David didn't really answer but handed the worn copy back to Mike and reminded him, "You never did tell me. Why did *you* come to see her?" Mike looked back in the direction toward Virginia and, initially, answered that he couldn't really explain it.

"I dunno. It's a lot of things. Little things, really. Look, let's go get something to eat," Mike suggested, adding, "Let them know you'll come back this afternoon, when Mrs. Douglas isn't so busy. Trust me, you'll get a better interview."

On the way to the elevator, Mike shared that he didn't usually go in for the holiday mush stuff but told David there was something about Virginia that made people feel good just being around her. She was always upbeat. Encouraging. Mike said he couldn't put his finger on it exactly. Maybe it was because she was a teacher, maybe because she was just a decent human being.

"I don't know, but I'll tell you this," Mike told David, turning to look him directly in the eye. "Find out what it is—and *there's* your story!"

Engines rumbled inside the City Cabs garage as drivers headed in from shifts and out to pick up fares. Ben was pretty much oblivious to the background noise as he checked out the company Christmas party notice pinned on the bulletin board just outside the dispatch office. "Enrico's again. That figures," he muttered to himself, smiling. He headed over to the small window counter at the dispatch office. Willy was inside, busy fielding calls and completing paperwork. As usual, Gino was standing in the middle of the office reading from the newspaper and spouting his commentary about headlines in the news. Gino's eye caught Ben standing at the small open window to the office.

"Looks like they're gonna start getting oil, at cut-rate prices, shipped over here from Iran, despite Britain's blockade of Iranian oil sales," Gino espoused as he continued reading. "It says our government is basically telling these businessmen, 'The legal aspect is best left to the individuals or companies involved.' That could, hopefully, mean cheaper gas prices here, right?"

Ben wasn't so sure what it meant, potentially, for himself, the firms, or global politics, and asked Gino and Willy if either had a fare for him to pick up. Gino asked Ben to hold on, then checked with Willy if there was anything for Ben. Willy cradled the phone between his ear and shoulder, covered the mouthpiece with his hand, and asked Gino and Ben to give him a minute. Gino lowered the paper and walked up to the window to speak privately with Ben through the small round opening in the window.

"You doin' okay?"

"Yeah. I'm fine. All good."

"You know I'm here for you," Gino reminded Ben, "anytime you want to talk."

Ben reassured Gino that everything was fine and thanked him for the concern. Gino stepped back to the center of the office with his newspaper and returned to his oratory on another headline. He asked both men if they'd seen the story about some college kid who came down with polio on a cruise ship out in the middle of the ocean.

"Says here the dad is flying a doctor from here and—hold on—an iron lung to Nova Scotia; then the Coast Guard is gonna take 'em to the ship. Can you believe that?"

"No kiddin'?" Ben commented.

"Yeah," Gino affirmed. "Says the kid's mom is some big socialite here."

"Where did you say he was?" Ben asked.

Gino read aloud that the young man was on an ocean liner, the *Liberté*. He was returning home for the holidays from college in Europe and was stricken with polio on the voyage home. The article revealed the ship was 300 miles off the coast, and the United States Coast Guard would transport the doctor and respirator from Nova Scotia to the ship.

"I guess if you're rich enough you get whatever you need," Gino remarked, "wherever you need it."

Willy hung up the phone and passed a slip of paper through the counter window opening to Ben, explaining he had two fares for the cab driver.

"Easy. Both visiting somebody at New York General. You're taking one lady there now, then her sister at three o'clock. Both pickups at the same address."

CHAPTER 9

FAIRY TALES

The sun was still shining brightly, clearing the sidewalks of any ice residue, when Megan and Valerie met up outside the hospital's front doors. The air was crisp but fresh and welcoming. The two enjoyed this dedicated time together each day, especially if weather permitted an outside stroll. It was a treasured opportunity after lunch to review any school assignments Megan might need help with and to discuss Megan's opinion of her progress. But mostly they enjoyed discussing what life in general meant for women in the 1950s and what the cafeteria's menu had offered that day. Bundled in coats and gloves, the women made their way around the hospital grounds at their own pace. Megan wheeled herself in a measured way to stay in stride with Valerie, who refused to be impeded by her leg brace. The sun's bright reflection glared off the glistening snow, forcing the women to squint their eyes, but the lure of thousands of tiny ice crystals sparkling on the snow's surface compelled them to look anyway and admire. In the middle of the snow-covered lawn, several large, sturdy trees stood quietly; their dark, rugged trunks contrasted with the smooth white backdrop. A flock of tiny black-crested chickadees swooped down from the treetops and onto the snow crust for a brief inspection. Then, as if synchronized, one by one, each flew back up into the high branches, searching for previously hidden seeds. Closer to the hospital, a cluster of evergreen pines dusted with snow looked as if they were dressed for the holidays.

"So, Mrs. Douglas passed your book on to John Williams?" Valerie asked, knowing the answer, but also knowing how appreciative Megan was of any opportunity to talk about John.

"Yes! Well, she said she did. I guess she did."

"Um, last February, when you came in, you were really sick, but you recognized him, from school?"

"He didn't go to my school, but I knew of him. From around," Megan said timidly, "the neighbor-hood…dances. You kind of find out who someone like him is. You know."

"Mmm-hmm," Valerie answered knowingly. "The intense ones. The dangerous ones. Oooh, yes."

"*Really, Mrs. Jackson?* Did you ever date someone like that?"

"I think every girl has—or thought about it any-way. It's the Beauty and the Beast fantasy," Valerie explained, becoming overly dramatic. "We're the one special female who can tame the wild, misunderstood beast. Ha! But what does that mean, really?"

Valerie paused for a moment, then added, "Actually, that's kind of an odd power concept, to control someone else. Hmm. Maybe you'll major in psychology or anthropology in college. Study human behavior. If you do, come back and let me know what you find out."

"But it seems so romantic."

"Let's ask ourselves. Is it just the *idea* that seems so romantic? Because reality? That's something else. Beauty and the Beast? That's why it's called a fairy tale."

Valerie thought, *Let them grow up. Function in the real world. The young rebel persona doesn't really cut it there, but no point in dismissing Megan's enchantment entirely.*

The two made their way back to a bench outside the hospital entrance, where Valerie sat down. The women took a moment to enjoy the sun on their faces and to people-watch before they returned inside.

"I like your shoes. Your shoe," Megan commented awkwardly, quickly wishing she hadn't said anything. "I—I didn't mean to—" looking down at Valerie's left foot with a smart navy pump and the right shoe fitted with a dyed-to-match navy platform lift attached to the metal and leather brace on her leg.

"Thank you! Got a thing for shoes. Can't help it. Don't care to. And the husband says, 'Honey, if that's what makes you happy, then buy the shoes.' I always tell him *he* makes me happy, but I think deep down he knows the shoes run a close second, sometimes neck and neck," Valerie confessed good-naturedly and quickly added, "And Megan, no need to feel uncomfortable. We, of all people, should be able to talk about the aftermath of polio. And *openly*, especially with each other."

"Thank you, Mrs. Jackson." Megan paused for a moment and finally garnered the courage to approach the subject of polio. "I'd always thought, always heard—"

"That Negroes didn't get polio?"

"Yes."

"Guess I'm living proof there's a lot of misinformation out there. Perhaps when you get to college you can study epidemiology and research that. Help us *all* be better informed. Or maybe study engineering. Design a nicer-looking leg brace, for starters. What would you suggest for this thing?" Valerie asked, turning her leg from side to side.

"How about a prettier color and silk straps instead?"

"Oooh, like that Elsa Schiaparelli shocking pink! I'd love that! Mmm, but on the other hand, would that give the wrong message? Like this was fun? Not sure if we want to convey that."

"That's for sure. I'd like to get the message out that this isn't fun at all. But I will tell you something, Mrs. Jackson. When I was younger, think I was around ten or so, I remember watching a young girl using walking sticks and telling my mother, 'I wish I had polio; those things look like fun!' and then seeing my mother's face turn so suddenly angry. She spoke so fast, yelling at me, 'NO! DON'T EVER SAY THAT! THAT'S ABSOLUTELY STUPID! HORRIBLE! IT'S NOT FUN USING THOSE! NOT AT ALL!' and I knew from the look in her eyes not to say that ever again. And I don't know why, because I love my mother so much, but I sometimes feel resentful for how she treated me in that moment. I was just a little kid. I didn't know—"

Valerie let the words settle between them and allowed Megan time and breathing space to sense the comfort realized from finally sharing a fearful and embarrassing moment kept suppressed deep inside for so long. And knowing today, in Megan's reality, how the aftermath must weigh on her. Like anyone who's made it to adulthood, Valerie was well aware of those unpleasant moments in childhood, instances seared into the mind that when recollected seem as if the person startling us was caught off guard by a camera, flash popping, in their most unflattering expression. And years—decades later, the wretched image appears in the forefront of the mind, frozen in the moment, crisp and clear as any glossy print. Accompanied by those pesky, ugly thoughts that grow in the wake of the moment when a child's mistakes are so violently exposed by someone they trust. Awakening survival instincts Mother Nature intended, but which a child has no perspective for understanding.

"You know, Megan, it's remarkable how something that happened a long time ago is recalled so vividly, isn't it? And not just what transpired, but sometimes there's those resentful thoughts too. Don't beat yourself up for those. A child doesn't have the tools, the life experience, to understand all the variables of why someone might react in such a surprising, jarring manner. A child can't comprehend if someone had a bad day or struggles with harsh experiences of their own. Those resentful thoughts? Normal reaction for a child. Nature's way of self-protection. We all need some years, some life experience, under our belt before we can look outside ourselves and consider the predicament of others or imagine what it might be like to experience life through their eyes. I had an experience when I was a child somewhat similar to yours. I remember an aunt, my aunt Constance, whom I thought was perfect. She'd always treated me like I was perfect, which, as a six-year-old, of course I thought I was. One day, we were at a home of a friend of hers. I'd gone there with my aunt for something. Anyway, we were sitting at her small kitchen table; I remember there was a white linen tablecloth on it with a lace trim that hung down the sides just a few inches, you know, those kind with the finely crocheted little scallops, little points, that went all around the edge. The woman had made coffee or tea for herself and my aunt, and she'd given me a small bowl of cereal or something. She had milk for us in a little white pitcher. It was the first time I remember eating at another person's home, and I was somewhat nervous. I'd poured some of the milk from the pitcher into my bowl, and as I lifted the pitcher back up, I saw there was a drop of milk hanging on the spout, ready to drip, and I instinctively licked it with my tongue so that it wouldn't fall on the tablecloth. Well, my aunt went crazy on me! She called me out so vehemently in front of her friend, I wanted to run away and hide forever. And then my aunt said something about me being a Negro. I can't remember the exact words she used, but it was the first time I realized that having black skin made me feel as if it were something I had to contend with, to worry about, to suddenly be aware of—*very* aware of, going forward. I'd never felt that way before. Never even really thought about it. No one had told me about this before. I didn't remember any of my little friends telling me this. And I think that was the *goodbye* moment. Goodbye to the naive, carefree, happy-go-lucky world of a child, and hello to a world of being aware. Aware of real, not imagined, *real* obstacles the world had suddenly stacked against me. Obstacles I would have to face every day simply because of the color of my skin. Something I couldn't change. Something God had given me. Suddenly, it was an issue. An issue for a six-year-old girl to deal with. Why?" Valerie took a breath and slowly exhaled. "How does a child process that realization?"

Valerie gave Megan time to absorb the perspective. The two sat silently, the sun shining on their faces, its warmth fencing with the cold winter air, as staff and visitors passed on their way in and out of the hospital.

Megan started to say something. "I—I'd never— never thought about—" But Valerie steered her past it.

"So as we get older, gain a little life experience and insight, *grow up*, we gain the knowledge to put things like those harsh scenes we experienced as a child in perspective," Valerie suggested. "As adults, we can intellectually understand that contracting polio and having to use walking sticks isn't really fun, is it?"

"No. Not at all," Megan answered with a laugh.

"So you can understand and rationalize your mother's harsh reaction. She—the entire public—was scared to death about polio," Valerie continued, then added, "just as I can understand my aunt's reaction to me licking the milk drop as a six-year-old. She thought I'd lost all my manners. Thought her friend would think so too, and how would that make my aunt look? She had to come back at me with World War III."

Megan laughed at the remark but felt as if there was something missing. Something more. She remained silent, hoping Valerie would come back to it.

"These are little issues, really. We can let go of the childish resentment. No sense carrying it around with us. Just let it lift off our shoulders and float away," Valerie continued, then added, "but you've probably noticed others who may feel they were somehow wronged in the past, and no matter how many different ways an explanation or a rationalization of 'why' is pointed out to them, they've chosen to cling tightly to their resentment, convinced their behavior or deed was correct or appropriate. And they will defend it till the day they die. Out of fear. Fear that they may have actually been wrong. Convinced that admitting they were wrong somehow makes them appear weak or flawed. Ha! When admitting you were wrong is actually one of the strongest indicators of self-confidence. And competence, I might add. But some people will continue to justify their position, digging their heels in, grasping at straws. And all that time, all that energy that could have been channeled into something positive ends up bundled in a closed-end, boxed-in, dreamless void. Going nowhere. When you run up against that—and you will—don't be blindsided. Choose your battles wisely. There are more important problems to solve."

The two women sat quietly for a moment, allowing Valerie's words to linger in the silence between them. To soak in. But there was something, a thought, gnawing at Megan. Something Valerie had mentioned earlier that Megan wanted to come back to. Something bigger.

The two women watched as a taxicab pulled up near the curb and its driver helped an elderly woman out of the backseat and escorted her toward the hospital entrance. Megan thought the driver looked somehow familiar, and slowly the image was recalled from the murky fog of memory. A friendly cab driver turning around in his seat and telling her, "You hang in there. It's gonna be okay." She was going to mention it to Valerie, but the man had already gone inside, and Valerie preempted her with something else.

"Megan, our unique, awkward, and closely guarded experiences are, in reality, probably not as unique as we'd like to think they are. And I'd bet when you begin to share yours, you'll find that others have been in a similar boat, one time or another," Valerie suggested. "What you shared with me is exactly the kind of experience you could write about and keep in the good *and* the unpleasant, so that other young people will know they're not alone in their thoughts and concerns."

"That's what Mrs. Douglas was saying, that I should write, or talk as a speaker, about what it's been like. But I don't know, Mrs. Jackson. I wasn't one of the popular kids at school. Before—before this happened. And I'm not really looking forward to being known as the girl who had polio."

"Mmm-hmm. Well, let's examine this one element at a time. First, and if you remember one thing from our conversation today, remember this: being the most 'popular kid in high school' is not the same as being Marie Curie. You really don't have to have that much upstairs to be popular in high school; the bar can be pretty low for that. Think about it; the popular ones reach their peak in high school because they've impressed contemporaries with no experience in the real world beyond school. Any fool can do that. Most successful leaders today were probably not the most popular students in high school. Trust me on this, but why not research it? Choose a leader you admire and read his or her biography. I think you'll find very few of them were among the most popular kids in high school. Secondly, let's examine this whole 'celebrity' aspect— being the object of so much interest or attention. Sometimes it's sought after, sometimes not, but if it's headed your way, it seems to me you have several choices: you can use it, abuse it, or let it abuse you. Ignore it? There's fallout from that too. The way I see it, there's all this energy that's going to discharge somewhere. Why not direct it? Build a channel, if you will, to guide it to a destination where it will do the most good. Benefit the most people."

"But it's kind of scary for me to think about standing in front of a group of students at Lincoln and trying to speak. What if someone laughs at me or makes fun of how I walk?"

"Is it always going to be easy, perfect, and smooth sailing? No, but try this: laugh with them; tell them how many times you've heard *that* before. It'll take the wind out of their sails and put the rest of the group at ease. It will show that you're brave, unflappable, and a leader. A force to be reckoned with, not walked over. Guide them. Welcome them. Up to the high road. Not to a snobby or pretentious place, but the high road of integrity, honesty, intellect, education, joy, and enlightenment."

Megan listened, somewhat convinced, but it was a mountain she'd have to warm up to before tackling. And what about Mrs. Douglas? Megan asked. "She doesn't seem like she's in any hurry to sit down with that guy from the newspaper. Why doesn't she just answer his questions and get it over with? She probably has a hundred other things to do today."

"Megan, every experience is a teaching moment," Valerie suggested. "Now, Mrs. Douglas certainly could have answered that reporter's questions when he arrived, quickly, efficiently, and sent him on his way, and she could have gone on hers. But what if she took a different approach—created the path for him to write a better story?"

"But she keeps avoiding him," Megan pointed out. "I don't think she really wants to talk to him. Do you?"

"Oh, she does," Valerie assured Megan. "She's just guiding him to where he needs to be for the best result. For everybody. Now, Mr. Lindsey came here because he wanted something from Mrs. Douglas, right? Yet I don't believe he called ahead to ask if she would be available to meet with him or what time might be convenient for her. His first misstep. By graciously asking him to wait the first time, and then a second time, she's allowing him a learning experience. Call ahead next time. Make an appointment if someone has something you need. By giving him time to wait in the hospital, he gets an opportunity to see more of what the environment here is like. When he writes his story about the hospital school, he'll be able to do so from a better vantage point than if he just came and left. He's most likely on a deadline, so the longer she has him wait, absorbing the color and flavor of the hospital, the more eager he will be to listen to what Mrs. Douglas wants him to know. And she'll do it graciously, generously, and honestly, which will help him to write a much better story than a quick nod to the holidays filled with stale clichés. The readers will benefit, the hospital school will benefit, the newspaper will, and certainly Mr. Lindsey will. I know the process takes longer than hitting someone upside the head with a two-by-four—that's not her style, by the way—and the end result is always better. And she's a master at it. Go and observe her sometime."

Megan saw the cab driver walk out of the hospital entrance doors and was certain he was the driver who had brought her to the hospital last February. He was moving rather quickly, and she didn't hesitate.

"Hi! You—"

"Hello to you," Ben replied, pausing in his tracks.

"You—you helped me!" Megan exclaimed.

Ben was somewhat perplexed but responded politely, "I did?"

"Yes! Last February. It was almost Valentine's. You came to my house. You brought me here with my mother."

Megan watched Ben's eyes as he recalled the day and the moment from his memory. She was reassured when she saw his face brighten as the recollection emerged and his obvious joy as he realized Megan was, indeed, okay.

"Wow! You look great!" Ben gushed. "I *do* remember! You and your mother! She was—a real nice lady."

"Yeah, she is."

"I remember. But anyway, how are you doing? You look fantastic!"

"Thanks," Megan said, starting to blush and quickly adding, "Oh, let me introduce you to Mrs. Jackson. She's one of the administrators at my school here."

Megan, Ben, and Valerie exchanged introductions. Ben learned that Valerie worked with Mrs. Douglas, who, he explained, he'd driven to the hospital that morning and had been his teacher when he was in the eighth grade. He shared several fond memories, to which Valerie added a few colorful anecdotes of her own. Ben told Valerie that he'd been pretty concerned for Megan when he brought her and her mother to the hospital last February. He was amazed and delighted to see how great she was doing now. Valerie concurred that Megan had done remarkably well with therapy and determination. She added that Megan was considered one of the "lucky ones" who didn't need to be placed in an iron lung and was able to start therapy right away. Uncomfortable with the attention focused on her, Megan felt the urge to change the point of interest.

"But not everyone is so lucky," Megan interjected and told Ben, "I heard that a little girl was brought in last night with polio, just like when you brought me here, but she's worse. They were saying that she needs a respirator, but the hospital doesn't have any more."

Ben looked at Valerie, who affirmed what Megan had just said, and asked, "Won't the March of Dimes help out? Don't they provide those?"

"They can. And we've asked, believe me, but there's several dozen hospitals across the country ahead of us on that list."

Valerie explained to Ben that this year had been one of the worst for polio cases, and hospitals just couldn't keep up with the need for the device. Ben shared that he had read it had been a really bad year, but he also asked Valerie if the girl could go to another hospital nearby that might have an iron lung. Valerie shook her head, "No," and explained that the other hospitals in the area weren't equipped with respirators the way New York General was and added, "If a polio patient requires a respirator, they would be brought here. And when all of ours are in use—well, it's not like you can just walk into Gimbels and buy another one. And it'd be more a Saks Fifth Avenue price point, anyway."

"So, what does one of those things cost?"

"Around fifteen hundred dollars," Valerie pointed out.

"Whooo-weee." Ben whistled in awe, feeling somewhat surprised and at the same time somewhat disillusioned, recalling the news article Gino had read to him and Willy earlier that day. He took a deep breath, shoved his hands in his pants pockets, and shared the story with Valerie and Megan. The women were impressed with the efficiency of obtaining and transporting a respirator to a needy polio victim at sea, but their enthusiasm for the effort was subdued by the reality facing the young girl at New York General.

"How fortunate for the young man that his parents are of the financial means and political connections to make such a feat possible," Valerie commented.

"But somehow that doesn't seem, I don't know, fair." Megan added, "Not everybody has parents who can do that."

Megan's point struck a chord with Ben, which didn't go unnoticed by Valerie, who shared that young Rachel's parents were working-class people. Valerie told Ben the hospital had applied for grants to purchase another respirator, but that process would take some time.

"So where would somebody buy one of those things?" Ben asked.

"The Kerner Manufacturing Company, Philadelphia," Valerie replied without hesitating.

"Philadelphia, huh?"

"Mmm-hmm."

"I wish I could do something to help her," Megan remarked.

Ben studied Megan's face and felt a tug of empathy. He looked off toward the street and his cab parked at the curb and uttered, "Maybe you already have, Megan."

Valerie and Megan looked at Ben inquisitively. Both could see the wheels in his mind were churning. He hurriedly said goodbye and headed toward his cab at a quickened pace but turned around and shouted something back to Megan and Valerie about calling an old friend and seeing his dispatcher, then added, "But I'll be back later this afternoon. I've got another drop-off at three. I'll meet you back here!"

Megan looked at Valerie, who gave her an affirmative nod, then shouted back to Ben, "See you at three!" The women watched Ben drive away, then slowly turned toward each other with wide eyes and raised eyebrows.

"This day's becoming quite interesting," Valerie commented, and the two women, buzzing with a curious speculation they could discuss on the way to class, headed back inside the hospital lobby.

CHAPTER 10

THE SANTA CLAUS GIRL

"You say it's in Indianapolis at a nursing college? But it's all good, ready to go? Okay, hold on a minute," Gino told the Kerner Manufacturing Company representative on the phone and motioned with his left hand to Ben, who was on another phone with his army buddy, Joe Martinez. Gino covered the receiver's mouthpiece with his free hand and gave Ben the details.

"So, this guy with the respirator company says we can buy this one if we want it. They had it at a nursing college in Indianapolis. For teaching. Says it's a pediatric iron lung, but since it's for a child, it'll be fine. Says he'd let us take it now, 'cause the school ended up buying one the company's delivering in January. He said shipping by air would cost a bundle. Can your buddy help us out?"

Joe and Hank's office was located inside the cargo hangar at Gainesville Municipal Airport up in the northern part of Florida. Their office wasn't really an office per se, more like a couple of army surplus metal desks pushed up against a wall inside the hangar. A Falcon Air insignia hung on the wall above the desks along with a plaque for the US Army Air Forces. An American flag stood tilted slightly to one side in a pedestal to the right of the desks. The one phone they had sat on Hank's desk. When Joe took the call, he was surprised to hear Ben's voice on the other end, and even more surprised when Ben asked what Joe was doing the following day. Joe explained that he and his pilot, Hank McGoran, were scheduled to transport a load of produce to a broker in Cincinnati at the crack of dawn.

"It ain't much, but we'll take whatever we can get," Joe explained. "Why do you ask?"

Ben rattled off details about a young patient, critically ill from the onset of polio, who needed an iron lung, but New York General Hospital, and all the other hospitals nearby, didn't have any to spare. He explained that his cab company was raising money to pay for one, but the closest one available they could purchase was in Indianapolis.

"Yeah, Indianapolis. At a nursing college, but it's available now. It's not like these things are sitting around collecting dust in warehouses," Ben explained, then asked, "Joe, can you help us get it from where it is to where it's needed?"

"Actually, that could work," Joe replied. "Indianapolis is a stone's throw from Cincinnati."

Joe gave Ben general flight time parameters between Cincinnati and Indianapolis as well as New York City. The men discussed time frames for loading and unloading cargo, refueling, and drafting flight plans.

"Uh-huh, uh-huh." Ben could hear the sound of engines roaring on the other end of the line and responded loudly into the phone. "Oranges and grapefruit?

Cincinnati? I guess that's close—for you, anyway. Uh-huh. Okay, hold on."

Ben covered the mouthpiece on his phone and told Gino, "He's flying into Cincinnati early tomorrow morning. Says he could be in Indianapolis by 11 a.m., ready by noon. Could the Kerner guy get it to the airport by then? And, hey, Gino, can we help cover the cost of fuel for him? I know he's still struggling. I'm thinking—I don't really know, a few hundred dollars?"

Gino gave Ben a thumbs-up—okay—and returned to the Kerner representative on the phone.

"Uh, we got a air cargo company, Falcon Air, that will be at Indianapolis tomorrow by noon. Can you get it trucked to the airport by then? Uh-huh, okay. Sam Weinberg?" Gino asked, then spelled out the man's name and nodded to Willy, who had already begun taking down the details on a pad. "W-e-i-n-b-e-r-g. He'll go with it? To here? Uh-huh. Okay. That's great. A cashier's check? Kerner Manufacturing Company. Got it. When they land at LaGuardia. Before it's unloaded. You got it. Okay, hold on a minute."

Gino covered the mouthpiece again and told Ben, "He's got a salesman who lives in the area. He'll take care of getting it trucked to the airport and bring all the paraphernalia and gizmos, but he has to accompany it on the plane. Does your friend have an extra seat for him?"

"Hey, Joe, they got a sales rep who will get it trucked to the airport, but he has to come on the plane with the respirator," Ben informed Joe and asked, "You got a seat for him?"

Ben laughed after Joe explained the C-47 would most likely be empty except for the iron lung. Ben nodded affirmatively to Gino for the seat onboard and encouragingly told Joe, "Hey, not for long, buddy. People are gonna start shipping more and more by air. Everybody wants everything sooner, faster, nowadays."

Gino confirmed to the representative, "Okay for Mr. Weinberg onboard. You got a number where we can contact him, just in case? He already knows? Uh-huh. Yeah, that'd be good. CLaymore 8-6284. Got it. Uh-huh. The air cargo hangar, Weir Cook Municipal Airport. By noon tomorrow. Joe Martinez. Falcon Air. We'll tell him to be on the lookout for Mr. Weinberg. Shouldn't be too hard to miss. Only guy at the airport with an iron lung. Uh-huh. Thank you. Goodbye."

"Joe, Gino says we're gonna help with your fuel costs," Ben informed his friend. "So—so you don't have to eat the whole thing."

"Don't worry about it, Ben. Besides, I know Brenda would want us to do this. Hey, we got two little girls of our own," Joe reminded his buddy. "And Ben, thanks for asking. I mean it."

Valerie walked into the classroom to let the group of children know she'd accompany them to the multipurpose room. She asked Virginia, who was seated at her desk, if there was anything she needed. Virginia let Valerie know she was "good" and planned to catch up on a few things during the hour.

"Yeah. Like some peace and quiet," Valerie suggested.

Just as Valerie was about to make it to the door, David Lindsey stuck his head in and inquired, "Mrs. Douglas?"

Valerie looked back at Virginia and commented, "So much for quiet time," then turned and left, smiling at David.

Virginia nodded to the reporter and motioned with her hand for him to come in. She quickly placed the cap back on her pen and moved her papers off to the side. David offered a fast "thank you" to Virginia and, without hesitation, pulled up a chair to face her desk, seated himself, and dove into questions.

"Now, Mrs. Douglas, about your letter to the editor."

Virginia was suddenly distracted by someone at the door, which immediately frustrated David, particularly when he turned in his chair and saw the person maneuvering to come in the door was a teenage girl who had no qualms about interrupting David's interview.

"May I join you?" Megan asked unreservedly as she wheeled toward Virginia's desk.

"Yes, come in, Megan."

"Mrs. Douglas. I really need to get—" David started to say, attempting to plead his case.

"Of course you do. Mr. Lindsey, meet Megan McGuire. Megan, David Lindsey. And I'm going to give you my full attention. Please go ahead."

Exhaling a breath of frustration, David began again with, "So, Mrs. Douglas, when you wrote your letter to *The Sun*—"

"Yeah, when did you write it, Mrs. Douglas?" Megan asked.

"Well, it was a very long time ago—"

"Uh, 1897, if I'm correct," David commented.

"You were alive in 1897?" Megan asked, astonished.

Virginia raised an eyebrow and answered Megan in a deadpan tone. "It wasn't *that* long ago."

David's impatience mounted as Megan, having realized her faux pas, quickly averted her eyes. Virginia took a deep breath and calmly began the background story about how it came to be that a little girl of eight would write a letter to the newspaper. She explained it was in September, and the new school year had begun just a few weeks earlier. Two girls, both a grade above her, had told her Santa Claus wasn't real.

"All I wanted to do was get home and wait for my father to come home from work so I could ask him about it," Virginia recalled. "I was upstairs in my room waiting, doing homework, and waiting some more. It seemed like it took him forever to get home that day. Finally, I heard the front door close and his voice calling to my mother, telling her, 'I'm home!' I flew down the stairs and gave him a big hug. My mother came in. I can still see him standing there, just inside our front door, in the entrance."

"Virginia! To what do I owe this extravagant show of affection?" Virginia's father, Dr. Phillip O'Hanlon, asked, somewhat surprised.

Virginia's mother shrugged her shoulders and raised her arms as if it was a mystery to her as well, then announced, "I'm going back to finish dinner," and left the two to themselves.

"Nothing, Papa," Virginia answered. "I'm just happy you're home now."

"Well, so am I," Dr. O'Hanlon concurred, taking off his coat and hat and hanging them on the coatrack inside the front doors, not forgetting to fetch the newspaper from his coat pocket.

"Did you have a nice day today, Papa?"

"Yes, dear, very pleasant, thank you."

"Did you have to go to the police station today?"

"No. They had no need of my services today."

"What are you going to do now?"

"I'm going to read my paper. Like every day. Why all the questions? You're not thinking of becoming a police investigator now, are you?"

Virginia hesitated to answer. She looked down at the floor disheartened as she bobbed her back against the wall, an image that tugged at her father's heartstrings. He put his arm around Virginia's shoulder and invited her to come into the parlor with him and tell him about her day.

The parlor was a lovely room on the front of the house. It wasn't particularly formal, but its high ceiling and large window overlooking the street made the room feel open and grand to someone Virginia's age. Her father's large oak writing desk and chair sat against the wall to the left of the front window. A photograph of Virginia's grandparents in a gilded oval frame hung above the desk. A Victorian-era sofa covered in an elegant beige jacquard sat against the opposite wall. A low oval mahogany table was placed in front it. An armchair, where Dr. O'Hanlon usually sat, was anchored just to the right of the sofa. The comfortable chair was covered in maroon upholstery with tiny raised diamond shapes woven into the fabric. A small table with a frosted glass oil lamp stood between the two.

Dr. O'Hanlon sat down in the armchair, gingerly removed his reading glasses from their case, placed them properly on the bridge of his nose, and opened the newspaper onto his lap. Hoping to be close but not intrusive, Virginia climbed onto the sofa near her father's chair. She always liked the way the fabric's pattern seemed to emerge in the soft glow from the nearby lamp. Virginia had learned she could make the pattern appear, then magically disappear and reemerge by brightening or dimming the glow of the lamp; something she relished, but which instantly irritated her father. She refrained from the exercise today.

"Now then, why don't you tell me about your day, Virginia?" Dr. O'Hanlon suggested, scanning the front page.

"Well, it wasn't very good."

"I'm sorry to hear that. What happened?"

"Papa, you believe in Santa Claus, don't you?"

"Santa Claus? Of course. Everybody believes in Santa Claus."

"Well, not *everybody*. Some of the other children at school said that he was just a story. That he isn't real."

"Why, that's utter nonsense," Dr. O'Hanlon remarked, looking up from the newspaper and toward

Virginia for effect. "What do those children know? They're no authority."

"Well, they're older than me."

"That doesn't make them an authority on the subject. It doesn't make them anything except older," her father commented, turning to page 3.

Virginia asked her father what "an authority on the subject" meant and who might be one. Dr. O'Hanlon provided a few examples meaningful to an eight-year-old, such as a judge being an authority on the subject of law, a doctor being an authority on the subject of illnesses, and her teacher an authority on the subjects she's teaching. And, of course, himself.

"Take me, for instance. I might be considered an authority on the subject of medical advice."

"Is that why the police come to you when they have a question about dead bodies?"

"Virginia!" Dr. O'Hanlon remarked, abruptly looking up from the newspaper. "You don't need to worry about such things."

Virginia leaned in close toward her father and reassured him. "I'm not, Papa. I'm worried about Santa Claus!"

"Yes, that's right. And we were looking for an authority on the subject, weren't we?" her father asked, scanning another page.

"Is there, Papa? Are *you* an authority on the subject?"

"Well, no, not exactly, but I—"

"When you don't know about something, what do you do?"

With her father engrossed in an article, Virginia's question went unanswered.

"Papa?"

Virginia waited for what she believed to be an appropriately patient length of time and tried again.

"Papa, when you want to find out about something, what do you do? Papa? Paaa-pa?"

Dr. O'Hanlon lowered the newspaper, looked down over his glasses, and told Virginia, "I try to read about it in the newspaper," then returned to reading.

"Are they an authority on the subject?"

"Usually."

"And do they know about almost everything?"

"Well, yes, or they'll find out," her father explained, then looked up from his paper and emphasized, "That's their job, to investigate the facts and report them to the public. And they do a fine job of it."

"Do they always tell the truth?"

"Most newspapers do, dear."

"Papa, could you ask the newspaper if they could write about Santa Claus and tell everyone there is a Santa Claus?" Virginia asked with determination as she battled the newspaper for her father's attention. "Paa-paah?"

While scanning the stories on a new page, Dr. O'Hanlon explained he didn't need to find out if there was a Santa Claus because he already knew. Virginia countered that she knew *he* knew, but her concern was for everyone else, which became an easy out for her father as he told her that everyone *he* knew believed in Santa Claus. Virginia persisted, again pointing out that some of her friends didn't, and stated that if her father could just ask the newspaper to write something—

"Virginia, if it's *your* friends who don't believe, then it should be *you* who asks the newspaper."

"Me?"

"Yes. You."

Virginia fired off questions like a Gatling gun. How? Who? Where? Dr. O'Hanlon explained that she could write a letter to the editor at the newspaper and, hopefully, someone would reply to her in the paper. Virginia jumped up and headed to the desk, where she retrieved paper and a pen, knelt down at the low table in front of the sofa, and asked, "Papa, will you help me?" Her father was just getting to the financial page to check railroad earnings but assured his daughter he'd help her when she was ready. Virginia informed her father she *was* ready and asked if he would help her with some of the spelling. He promised her he would as he reviewed an upcoming auction of stocks and bonds. Virginia softly spelled out "D-e-a-r," then asked her father, "How do you spell 'editor'?" Dr. O'Hanlon slowly spelled out the word as Virginia wrote it down. She plugged away with her sentences while her father reviewed the stock and bond transactions of the New York Exchange. Then came a stumbling block. Virginia looked up at her father and asked him how to spell "truth." Unanswered, her question lingered in the air. "Truth?"

"Pa-pa? Truth?"

"What?"

"Truth. How do you spell truth?"

"Truth. T-r-u-t-h," her father spelled out, a bit sheepishly.

"Thank you."

Dr. O'Hanlon returned to his newspaper, seeking sense and truth in the reporting of the district's upcoming primaries. Virginia felt satisfied with her letter but soon realized she had one more hurdle and would need to pester her father again. She took a deep breath and mustered the courage to ask how she should address the envelope. He muttered something about the editor, which was of no use to Virginia. She paused, patiently, for what seemed an eternity to an eight-year-old—at least fifteen seconds—then burst out with, "Papa, please! What do I put on the envelope?" Exasperated, Dr. O'Hanlon realized he had no chance of reading his paper in peace and plopped *The Sun* on the table in front of Virginia, pointed to the masthead, and told her, "Just copy this, dear!"

Each evening for the next several days, Virginia peered anxiously out of her front window, hoping to spot her father arriving home from work, extra newspapers in hand and sporting a huge smile. After a week of disappointment, Virginia's hope had begun to wane, allowing self-doubt to creep in. Surely the newspaper had no interest in answering a little girl's letter—or worse, they didn't want to confirm publicly that the other children were correct. Virginia's mother and father had affirmed their daughter's noble intentions and attempted to assuage her disappointment with reasonable explanations for the newspaper's lack of response, explaining the editors received a large number of letters to review, the sheer size of its building and offices, and the always-reliable slowness of the mail. All logical but marginally effective in soothing the embarrassment of a young girl. Virginia was glad she hadn't told anyone at school about her letter; the fact that the newspaper chose to ignore her would only add public humiliation to the wound.

Across the New York and Brooklyn Bridge, inside *The Sun* newspaper offices in lower Manhattan, copyboys ran errands and carried pages of copy to and from reporters across the hectic open news floor. Edward P. Mitchell, a senior editor, made his way across the room to an adjacent hallway, headed in, and found his way to the office of Francis P. Church, a fellow editor. Francis's office walls were painted in a dark gray, but the generous afternoon light streamed in from a tall paned window on the far side of the room. Dressed in a neatly fitted vest, shirt, and tie, Francis, 58, was engrossed in writing at his desk and hadn't noticed Edward standing in the doorway. Edward rapped his knuckles on the wooden doorframe, garnering Francis's attention.

"May I come in?"

"Of course, Edward! Come in! Sit down." Francis's friendly face beamed with a smile as he motioned to a chair in front of his desk, then pushed the hair on his forehead to one side. "To what do I owe the pleasure of this visit?"

Edward made his way in, sat down, and proceeded to tell his fellow editor about the review he'd just read of the biography of Ulysses S. Grant written by Francis's brother, Colonel William Conant Church.

"They say Colonel Church is destined to be remembered as a great authority on the period," Edward shared, hoping to compliment.

"Well, he is destined to be remembered in history; that he has earned for himself."

"And how is Elizabeth?" Edward asked, continuing with pleasantries.

"Very well, thank you. I wish I could say the same about our publisher."

"Yes. I'm afraid the prognosis is not good for Dana."

"Hopefully he'll pull through. In the meantime—"

"In the meantime, we've got a paper to get out," Edward concurred, reaching into his breast pocket and retrieving a letter. "By the way, this has been on my assistant's desk for several days now."

Edward placed the small letter on the edge of the desk and nudged it toward Francis, who picked it up, examined it skeptically, and inquired, "What's this?"

"I think *you* would be best to answer this letter."

"This is obviously from a child. You know Elizabeth and I don't—"

"You'd be perfect."

"I don't know what to say to a child—any more than—can it wait?"

Edward suggested Francis needed respite from everything else he'd been working on lately. Hoping to enhance the appeal of the nuisance he'd just pawned off on his associate, Edward rose from his seat and suggested, "Besides, she's not asking for much."

"If, and only if, I have time."

"Good. I'm off to the press room."

"Good day, then."

Edward left, content, while Francis returned to his work at hand, shaking his head at the inconvenience created by his colleague's visit. He'd been working on his opinion piece, "Religion as America Enters a New Century," since the previous evening and was nearly ready to send it off. Just one more point here, and bring this paragraph forward. But soon, the childlike script on the envelope Edward had left on his desk became a distraction. Francis picked up the humble letter and studied the handwritten address. Charmed by the simple handwriting, he gingerly removed the small paper inside, unfolded it, and began reading to himself.

> *Dear editor, I am eight years old. Some of my little friends say there is no Santa Claus. Papa says if you see it in The Sun, it's so. Please tell me the truth. Is there a Santa Claus?*

> *Virginia O'Hanlon*

Francis set the letter down on his desk, rose from his chair to stretch his back, and walked over to the large window in his office. Gazing down into the square below, he watched as people and carriages moved about in the busy afternoon. A group of children, on their way home from school, giggled as they played around a lamp post near a grassy area of the park. Weighing the balance of religious debate versus the timeless and universal significance of Santa Claus might appear a simple task to an eight-year-old girl, and today, it seemed Francis happened to concur. He returned to his desk, sat down, and put pen to paper, speaking to himself as he wrote.

> *"Virginia, your little friends are wrong."*

For nearly a week Virginia had stopped waiting for her father to come home, hoping that he had just forgotten about the whole letter issue and wouldn't bring it up again, because *she* certainly wasn't going to, anyway. Instead, when she'd finished her school lessons, she went into the kitchen to help her mother with dinner or setting the table; anything that would keep her busy. She'd just about finished setting the utensils at each place when she heard her father call to her from the entrance. She thought she heard an exuberance in his voice she wasn't expecting, but didn't dare get her hopes up. So she waited. To be sure. For him to call her name again.

"Virginia! Virginia, where are you?"

"In here, Papa!" Virginia called back, frozen, afraid to move in that blissful moment in time where not knowing allowed the euphoria of hope.

And there, right before her eyes, Virginia's father came bounding into the room waving an open newspaper in one hand and carrying a stack of newspapers in the other. He hadn't even stopped to take his coat off, or his hat, Virginia noticed.

"Virginia, look! Your letter was printed in the newspaper! Santa *is* real! It says so right here!" Dr. O'Hanlon exclaimed, holding the editorial page in front of his daughter.

Hearing the excitement, Virginia's mother hurried into the room and joined her daughter's side. "Look at this, dear!" Dr. O'Hanlon called out, pointing to the editorial for his wife. "It's quite profound, really. Everyone's talking about it. People are saying it's the most wonderful thing they've ever read!"

Virginia wasn't quite sure what to say or how to feel. Instant notoriety can present an overwhelming reality to an eight-year-old. The editorial reply was so much bigger than what she had expected, so much larger than she'd imagined. As Virginia listened to her father reading the editorial out loud, questions arose in her mind. Why did it say that? Universe? Intellect? Fairies? Now she had to worry at school about fairies? Wait. Breathe. Wait. It said, "Yes, Virginia, there is a Santa Claus." Good. A veil covering the unseen world? Why were they talking about something like that? Just a simple "Yes, Santa Claus is real" would have been enough. She merely wanted the other children, the doubters at school to hear it from, as her father put it, "an authority on the subject."

"Thank God he lives, and he lives forever."

Thank God they said that, Virginia thought to herself.

"I'm very proud of you, Virginia," her father stated. "This is quite an accomplishment. Imagine my little girl writing a letter to the newspaper and receiving a reply on the editorial page."

"Wow! Mrs. Douglas!" Megan exclaimed. "That's incredible! So what happened when you went to school the next day? Did everybody tell you they saw it in the paper?"

"Yeah, what were their reactions?" David asked. "What'd the other kids say?"

"Well, there was a lot of fuss that first year," Virginia answered. "But, as you might imagine, it was quite a different experience when you're nine, or ten, or eleven."

"Eeew. Yeah. That must have been weird," Megan acknowledged.

Virginia knew for a fact it was weird. Oh, the anguish the following year when they had to reprint it and, even worse, include her letter again. And the whole cycle started over, and she found herself having to defend her convictions as a nine-year-old and convince her contemporaries at school that she, too, no longer believed. Yet there it was in black and white, all over town: "Please tell me the truth. Is there a Santa Claus?" And oh, the dread when she would have to go through it again, at ten and at eleven. The newspapers spread it around like thick icing and lathered it all over New York—and beyond.

"So they started reprinting it each year? It must have been quite popular with readers," David deduced, reading between the lines and interpreting the newspaper's decision, driven by increased sales potential, to reprint the editorial each year.

Virginia confirmed the editorial was reprinted in *The Sun* every year until the paper was no longer published. After that, other newspapers began picking it up.

"My parents had copies printed. They started receiving requests from people all over the country and all over the world," Virginia revealed and watched as David took notes. "It's been printed in twenty different languages."

"No kidding? I mean, that's quite remarkable," David commented.

"Well, look at you, Mr. Lindsey. Even fifty years later, in these *modern times*, you're, hopefully, still interested."

"Oh, I am."

"Mrs. Douglas?" Valerie called from the doorway. "Excuse me, you were waiting for that update? The status on the—uh, the student you were asking about? I've got that for you."

Virginia excused herself but told David the issue with Valerie would take only a minute, and she'd return promptly. David assured her, "That's fine. I'll be right here."

Virginia headed out of the door and into the hallway where Valerie was waiting. Megan whispered to David that she, too, would be "right back" and scooted her wheelchair to a spot near the door, out of sight of Virginia and Valerie but within earshot of their conversation. The two women spoke in hushed tones, which required Megan to lean closer toward the open door. She overheard Valerie telling Virginia the new polio patient, Rachel Hall, was not doing well—something about bulbs or barber, Megan couldn't quite make it out. She heard Virginia ask how old the girl was; Valerie told her, "Five," then added, "Without respirator support, she won't—it doesn't look good." Megan heard Virginia say, "Thank you," a signal for Megan to hightail it back to Virginia's desk undetected. Megan made it almost halfway when she realized she didn't have a prayer's chance in hell and paused at a nearby student desk to examine a book someone, fortunately, had left on its surface. Virginia headed toward her desk, her eyes focused on David and smiling, as if feeling grateful for his patience. As she passed Megan, Virginia calmly pointed out, "You used to be a lot faster in that thing."

As Virginia returned to her seat at her desk, Megan repositioned herself next to David and conveniently changed the subject, asking, "So who wrote it? The editorial?"

"Oh, they didn't say at first," Virginia replied.

"No, the editorial is never signed," David explained to Megan. "It's—it's just understood it's the paper's position. Not any particular individual's."

"So you don't know who wrote it?" Megan asked.

David looked to Virginia for help and immediately wished he had researched this information himself. Under most circumstances, Virginia preferred to be short and concise in her response, but for Megan's benefit an alternate course seemed best. She explained that it wasn't until several years later, 1906, when she and the general public learned who had penned the editorial.

"I was seventeen. It was in the spring, April, though I remember I was looking forward to autumn that year—excited about going to college, you know. I was at my parents' home. Nothing unusual about the day, really. It was evening, shortly before dinner."

"Virginia! Virginia, dear!" Mrs. O'Hanlon called to her daughter, who soon emerged from her room near the top of the stairs. "If you're finished with your studies, can you help me with the table?"

"Of course," Virginia answered and made her way down the stairs as her mother admired her from below.

"Virginia, you're becoming prettier every day. And growing up so fast."

"Oh, Mother, *please*," Virginia lamented. "Did I hear Father come in?"

"Yes. He's in the parlor reading his newspaper."

Virginia made her way into the dining room and began retrieving dishes from a wall cabinet. The dining room was Mrs. O'Hanlon's favorite room in the house. It was the one place where she knew her family would be together, engaged, safe, and generally happy. Its cabinets and curios housed some of her favorite things: dishes she'd selected as a young bride, her mother's tea service, a framed portrait of her parents. Even the chandelier seemed to sparkle with delight when her family gathered under its glow.

Virginia's mother busied herself searching for something in a sideboard cabinet, talking to herself while opening drawers and doors. Virginia asked if she could help her but was interrupted by an "I found it!" from her mother. Virginia went about setting a plate at each place, and followed with napkins and glasses for water. She'd just placed her own utensils on the table when her father called out to her from the parlor.

"Virginia? Virginia, there's something in the paper you should read."

His voice seemed neither sharp nor cheerful. At least not to a seventeen-year-old, whose instincts had not yet developed the sense, the antennae, to detect a subtle, underlying tone of concern. Virginia left the dining room to find her father and was a bit surprised when she saw the look on his face as he stood just inside the parlor, holding the newspaper open with both hands.

"There—there's an article in the evening's paper about—about the man who wrote to you."

What could he be talking about? What man? Who wrote to me? There's nothing in my world that matches what he's saying, raced through Virginia's mind.

"Who—who wrote the reply to your Santa letter when you were a child," Dr. O'Hanlon explained as Virginia began to feel the first small surge of a tide. "Apparently, he just died, and—they have revealed it was a—a Francis P. Church who wrote the reply to you."

And the surge washed in and covered her.

"Who? I—"

"It says here that—let me read it to you."

> *At this time, with the sense of personal loss strong upon us, we know of no better or briefer way to make the friends of The Sun feel that they, too, have lost a friend than to violate custom by indicating him as the author of the beautiful and often republished editorial article affirming the existence of Santa Claus in reply to the question of a little girl.*

Dr. O'Hanlon looked up from the newspaper, then at his daughter, and pointed out, "That—that would be you, Virginia."

As the realization set in, Virginia felt the assault of emotions hitting their mark. The highs, the lows, the hurt, the exhilaration, the embarrassment, the letting go—all shooting through the conduit of the fragile connection to childhood.

Virginia's mother came into the room and, having seen the expression on Virginia's and her husband's faces, asked what had happened. Dr. O'Hanlon explained that the editor, the author of the editorial reply to Virginia, had died and the newspaper had identified him as the one who wrote it. Mrs. O'Hanlon asked his name and how old he was. Virginia's father scanned the article to find information, explaining that it was unusual for the paper to name the author of an editorial. He read aloud that it was Francis P. Church, that he was born in 1839, which would make him sixty-seven, and that he was survived by his wife, Elizabeth.

"Hmm. That's odd," Dr. O'Hanlon commented.

"What is, dear?" Mrs. O'Hanlon asked.

"No children."

A human being. A person. Feelings. Thoughts. A life. Suddenly, all that encompassed was now attached to the growing mass of recollections. Before this moment, Virginia hadn't really considered anyone personally linked to the editorial—other than herself. It had always been just the newspaper. Now she found herself asking, "Who was he?" His wife was now alone. What did he look like? He was old enough to be a grandfather, but the editorial had been written nine years ago. Still, he seemed quite old. Why hadn't he ever wanted to meet her? Surely, he must have been nice. Why hadn't she thought of anything like this happening before—before today?

"Well, now, we'll remember Mr. Church and his widow in our prayers," Virginia's mother encouraged, and gestured for Dr. O'Hanlon and Virginia to come to the dining room for dinner. "Let's go in and sit down.

A nice dinner would be of help right now. I think everything's ready."

Dr. O'Hanlon nodded in agreement with his wife and laid his newspaper on the table near his chair in the parlor. He gave Virginia a warm, reassuring look, which she returned with a half-hearted smile, and encouraged his daughter to come with him and her mother to the dining room. Virginia started to follow her parents but stopped and looked back at the newspaper lying by itself on the small table in the parlor and was drawn back into the room.

"I'll be there in just a moment," she called to her parents and returned to the parlor, picked up the newspaper, and reread the announcement. She gingerly slid the page away from the others and carefully folded it into a neat, small square. Too personal to keep in her own room, she placed the article into a far rear corner inside the left drawer of the desk.

"So you never got to meet him," Megan asked as David realized he should have, "the man who wrote the editorial?"

"No, regretfully. You have to remember, I was very young when it was written, and as time went on—"

"Time! What time is it?" Megan asked anxiously.

David looked at his watch and told her it was almost three o'clock. Megan promptly backed up her wheelchair, explained she had to be somewhere, and zoomed like a bat out of hell into the hallway.

David attempted a feeble "Uh, goodbye."

"That young lady—" Virginia mused and shook her head.

"Megan McGuire, right?" David asked.

"Yes."

"*She* had polio?"

Virginia shared with David that Megan did indeed have polio when she was admitted last February, explaining that Megan was paralyzed from the neck down. David wasn't sure he understood Virginia correctly, and he motioned toward the door with his thumb, asking if Virginia meant *that* Megan, the teenager who'd just left. Virginia assured him it was *that* Megan she was talking about and surmised David was somewhat stunned by the young woman's level of progress. Virginia explained that Megan was fortunate, that in her specific case the nerve damage wasn't as severe as others and therefore not entirely permanent. Virginia shared with David the news about a young girl who had just been admitted and who was now going through what Megan went through, but whose condition was far worse.

"Worse? What can be worse than paralyzed from the neck down?"

"Her breathing is extremely difficult. She needs a respirator."

"An iron lung?"

Virginia confirmed the patient needed an iron lung and explained that every respirator in the hospital was already being used. She assured David that the hospital had contacted every other hospital in the area, emphasizing that all hospitals were dealing with more polio cases this year than ever before. She explained that other hospitals were not as well equipped with respirators as New York General, as it was the primary center for polio patients who were critically ill and required treatment in an iron lung. Virginia sensed from the expression on David's face that her words were getting through to the young reporter, who had stopped taking notes.

"I—I'd read that this was a record year."

"Close to fifty-eight thousand cases this year alone."

"Whew." David exhaled as he sat back in his chair and absorbed the staggering number, feeling a bit small. "But they're getting close to a vaccine, right?"

Virginia stood up from her desk to get the circulation flowing in her legs and walked toward the window as she told David, "Let's hope so, but that's not going to help her today. She needs a respirator." Virginia looked out of the window to the sidewalk below, watching people come and go toward the hospital entrance. "And she needs it right now," she whispered to herself. She gave David a moment to process the hard statistics she'd just presented, then turned to return to her desk.

"But that's not the story you came in for today, is it?"

"Uh, no, but—no—no, it's fine, but, uh, getting back to the editorial. What do you think it was about the editorial that made it so popular? I mean, and over such a long period of time. I mean—" David halted, flustered that he may have insulted Virginia, and feebly added, "Not that long—"

Virginia sat back down at her desk and relayed that she was very glad the editorial had continued to be printed—for such a very long time. She explained the reason was rather simple, actually, and suggested that when Francis P. Church wrote, "He exists as certainly as love and generosity and devotion exist, and you know that they abound and give to your life its highest beauty and joy," well, that *was* the truth, and that truth was timeless. She encouraged David to think about it, gave him another moment to do so, then asked him, in *his* life, what gave him a sense of joy.

"But isn't the editorial about Santa Claus? Santa brings presents. Who doesn't feel joy getting presents?"

"Well, of course. And I love getting presents—who doesn't? But if you had to ask yourself what *real* joy is, wouldn't you remember the times when you loved someone or were able to help someone? When you shared your love, your generosity, and made a difference in someone's life? Gave them hope?"

Virginia sensed that her words may have fallen on not necessarily deaf ears, but the ears of someone who was not yet able to relate to them. Had David never been in love? Had an opportunity to be generous? Or made a difference in someone's life? She could sense that he was trying—or was it hoping?—to relate, to understand, to appreciate. She thought she might even have detected a longing to, so she persevered.

"That feeling, that sense of 'devotion,' does 'give life its highest beauty and joy,' and it's the same today as it was in 1897. Now, Mr. Lindsey, I hope I've helped you with your story. I'm sure you've got a lot of work to do, so I'll let you get going."

Virginia rose from her seat and walked over to David, who stood up to shake her outstretched hand. She let him know she was headed to check her teachers' lesson plans for the next week and thanked him for coming, as she had enjoyed talking with him.

"Thank you, Mrs. Douglas," David replied with genuine warmth.

"The pleasure is all mine, Mr. Lindsey."

David headed out of the door and turned left into the hallway, where he spotted the elevator with open doors, made a run for it, and jumped in before the doors closed behind him. His mind occupied with the story he must craft, he stepped out with other passengers on the wrong floor. He spotted an "Exit" sign ahead and decided to take the stairs at the end of the hallway. On the way, he passed the Respirators Post-Isolation Recovery Room and noted its sign but hurried past, oblivious to events unfolding behind its double doors. Inside the room, John Williams was tensing up in his wheelchair, positioned near his iron lung, wheezing and panting and calling for help.

"He-lp. Pa—lease. He-l-pah."

Two respirator nurses rushed over to John, who was perspiring and frightened, and helped him out of the wheelchair and back into the iron lung.

"Don't panic, John," one of the nurses instructed.

"I-he I-he ca-ca-can't bree-bree-bre-athe."

"Don't panic. Breathe slowly."

"Do-n't leeh-heeh-ve-ve meh out h—hh-ere."

The nurses finished placing John inside the respirator and began sealing the rubber collar around his neck.

"It's all right. You're okay now."

The nurses locked and sealed the iron lung, and the *sswhee-swoosh* sound of the bellows resumed. John began to resume normal breathing rather quickly, not unseen by one of the nurses, who also noticed John's look of disappointment and what she thought might even be shame.

David finally navigated his way into the hospital lobby and, spotting the entrance doors, zipped up his jacket to brace himself for the outside winter chill. The late-afternoon sun was muted by a soft layer of low clouds, which cut down the glare of the snow-covered lawns on both sides of the entrance walkway. His thought was to catch a bus back to Lower Manhattan to his paper's offices, but he noticed Megan and Valerie talking to a cab driver who was leaning against his vehicle at the curb. Megan was looking in David's direction, holding her hand over her brows to better see who was coming out of the hospital. As David came closer, Megan recognized him.

"Oh! Mr. Lindsey!"

"Boy. You get around," David remarked.

"Yeah, well, I've had a lot of practice. Oh, this is Ben. He brought me here when I first came."

"Really?" David asked as he and Ben acknowledged each other with a handshake.

"That's right," Ben answered good-naturedly. "Hard to believe. Look at her now. You two know each other?"

"Uh, we just—" David began to explain, but Valerie jumped in to point out that, sooner or later,

Megan made it her business to know everybody. Megan informed Ben that David Lindsey was a reporter who was here to talk with Mrs. Douglas about the Santa Claus editorial. Ben asked David if he needed a ride and revealed that Mrs. Douglas used to be his teacher, a fact which intrigued both David and Megan.

"Yup. When I was in the eighth grade. She was something!"

A cold wind whipped past the group. Megan squinted her eyes and hunkered down into her chair. Feeling the chill, David turned up his collar and told Ben, "Maybe I will take that ride."

"Hop in," Ben told David. "Mrs. Jackson, Megan, thanks for the information. And, uh, Megan, be sure to tell your mother hello for me."

"You can tell her yourself, if you come back tomorrow evening," Megan suggested. "She's having dinner with me."

See Nora McGuire again! Soon. Tomorrow. What do I do? What do I do? What do I do? What does that mean? Should I say "Great!" No. That's too presumptuous. Who am I kidding? She doesn't know I exist. Just nod the head. Get in the car. Drive. Away. Think about this. It feels good, though.

Ben allowed himself to imagine the possibility and jumped in behind the wheel.

David climbed into the front seat of the cab to ensure he would be able to hear clearly any sidebar concerning Virginia Douglas. The cold air convinced Valerie and Megan they'd had enough of the healthy outdoor experience, and the two women left to seek a warmer environment inside the hospital lobby.

CHAPTER 11

GROWING PAINS

"So, where to?" Ben asked.

"I gotta go back to the *Telegraph* and write this up. Uh, it's on—"

"I know," Ben stated and pulled away from the curb.

David didn't waste any time and barreled right in with "So, Mrs. Douglas was your teacher? What was that like?"

Ben took it as just another casual question and answered earnestly, saying Mrs. Douglas was "The greatest!" and quickly added that she didn't put up with any monkey business. Still, he recalled, she was "Really nice, I remember that," and he confided in David that if it hadn't been for Mrs. Douglas, he could have gone down a very different, very dark, path. David put his line in the water with the ever-powerful, exquisitely simple, open-Pandora's-box hook "Oh?" and hoped Ben would share salacious stories of juvenile gangs, armed robberies, attempted burglaries, and sordid details of misspent youth.

"Ooohhh, yeah. She was great," Ben replied. "I remember when she found out me and Jimmy Kowolski were running gin to the speakeasies. Whew! She wasn't happy 'bout that."

"You were—you were running gin? To speakeasies? You guys carry guns?"

"Guns? No! No, man. It was the Depression. Nobody had guns. Well, the cops, and maybe the serious gangsters. We had bicycles. Who could afford a gun?"

"But you—you were delivering—gin? To night-clubs? A couple of thirteen-year-olds?"

"Jimmy was thirteen. I was twelve. Who's gonna suspect two kids on bikes? David—Dave, it was the Depression. Everybody did what they had to do. Nobody had jobs. There *were* no jobs. My dad lost his job at the gas company and went to find work as a tenant farmer somewhere in the Midwest. I stayed with my mom. We lived with her sister and their family, pretty much in two rooms for a couple years. Jimmy's dad lost his job and started making gin in the apartment where they lived. We got five cents for every gallon container we delivered. They put it in gas cans and Jimmy and me put 'em in our newsboy bags and strapped one on each side of the back of the bike. We each could carry two gallons. That was a pretty good deal. And it really helped out my mom."

"So how did Mrs. Douglas find out?"

"Well, one evening, me and Jimmy were on our way to a delivery here in Brooklyn. We knew the neighborhood, and we're whizzin' past our school. Heck, we figured everybody'd be gone by then.

Anyway, we're going at a good clip and *bam!* I hit a pothole. The bike flipped over, I'm head over heels in the air, and the gin cans go flying outta the bags. The lid popped off one of the containers; gin was pouring down the street. Well, here comes Mrs. Douglas down the steps of the school—right in front of us! I picked a fine place to run aground. Of course, she recognized us *and* smelled the gin, obviously. And, man, that stuff must've been ninety proof. Surprised it didn't burn a hole in the pavement. Anyway, she sees me all scuffed up, bloody nose, hands. I thought our gooses were cooked."

"She call the cops?"

"She asks if we're okay. We tell her yeah, and she tells us to pick up the container and put the lid back on and come inside and get cleaned up. We were scared shitless. But, yeah, thought for sure she was gonna call the cops on us. Instead, she takes us inside, even though the school was closed. Think she said she was there because she was grading papers or something, but anyway, she sent us on our way and told me to come see her after class the next day. We made our delivery, but we got reamed 'cause we didn't deliver all four of the gallons. Anyway, I met her after class and we talked about what I was doing with the delivery thing, and she asked me if I'd like a different job, helping clean out the stables and stuff where the mounted police officers kept their horses. It only paid five cents a day, but I could do it after school. Anyway, she convinced me of the benefits of that job over the one with Jimmy."

"She didn't offer him a job?"

"Guess she knew he couldn't say no to his own father. But anyhow, it turned out to be a really good thing. One of the policemen used to bring apples to his horse each day. Said he had a tree in his yard. So, one day he brings a whole bag of apples and tells me to take them home to my mom. I did, and, boy, my mom and aunt were really happy about that. My mom made an apple pie for me to take back to him. After that, he brought apples and flour and sugar and butter, you name it. In the summer, he brought us peaches and berries. My mom started canning the peaches and would make pies and sometimes jam for him. I remember those apple pies in the winter and peach and berry pies in the summer. And I just kept cleaning out the stalls and making sure his horse was always wiped down and groomed after he came in. He treated me really good. I can still smell that musty odor of hay and manure in those stalls. In the heat of the summer, oh man! You had to hold your nose! It was pungent! Flies everywhere. In the winter, the horse would crap and you'd see steam comin' off the manure. Hmmm. I did that for almost four years."

Ben became silent, lost in thought of a memory from a long time ago, as he made his way onto the Brooklyn Bridge. David gave Ben time to think and, a first for himself, began to realize this guy, this man, wasn't only a subject he'd interviewed but might actually be just a regular guy, a good guy who had completely trusted him, someone he'd just met, with no preconceptions. David even considered *and he's talking to me like I'm a regular guy*, but then caught himself and snapped out of it. Reminded himself he was a reporter. There's a line.

"So what happened? What'd you do after that?"

"Well, the policeman was killed. Shot in an armed robbery. I missed him. He was a good guy. I think my mom missed him too. I worked there for almost another year; then the cop who replaced him introduced me to his brother, Gino Ruganni, and I started working in the garage at City Cabs. Before I left for the army, he made me a driver. Said I'd have my job when I came back home. Been there ever since. But see, if it hadn't been for Mrs. Douglas—wouldn't have met any of those guys. Could have been very different. She really cared about ya, ya know? And she's still doin' that today. I mean, look where she works, right?"

"Yeah, but that's gotta be tough sometimes," David admitted, and then shared with Ben that he'd heard about a polio patient recently admitted to the hospital, a young girl who might not make it because she needed to be in an iron lung and the hospital didn't have any available. And David, surprisingly, found himself wondering out loud, "How many times does Mrs. Douglas have to see something like that?"

Stopped at an intersection, Ben watched for the signal light to change to green, then moved forward with the rest of the late-afternoon traffic. He shared with David that Megan had told him about the girl when he'd dropped a fare off at the hospital earlier in the day. Then he surprised David.

"And you know what? Me and my buddies are gonna do something about it."

"Oh? Like what?"

Ben told David about Joe Martinez and how the two were old friends. He shared that both he and Joe were in Mrs. Douglas's class when they were kids and that both served in the war and that Joe now lived in Florida. Ben detailed how Joe had bought a C-47 airplane a couple of years ago and started a small air cargo company, Falcon Air. Ben revealed that he'd called Joe and told him about the young girl, and that Joe had offered to help get the iron lung for her.

"He's going to pay for one?"

"No. He couldn't afford that. He's just starting out with his company, and he has a family, two little girls. No. Me and the cab drivers are gonna pay for it," Ben explained. "The hospital helped us locate one in Indianapolis. Joe is picking it up there for us and flying it here."

"But that's gotta be—where're you gonna come up with that kind of dough? And in time?"

"Tips."

"Tips? Are you serious?"

"Yeah, tips. It's all set. All our cabbies are gonna donate their tips tomorrow. Joe is gonna cover the plane and pilots, and he'll fly it in tomorrow. A guy from the iron lung company is coming with them. He'll get it set up at the hospital."

"No kidding?" David remarked, genuinely surprised as well as impressed.

As the cab pulled up to the *Telegraph* offices, David looked out of the window, checked the sky, and told Ben he hoped the threatening clouds wouldn't turn into a snowstorm. He asked Ben what he owed him for the fare and paid up. He opened the door to get out but paused as an idea began to germinate in his head.

"So, this sounds like a first. All your cabbies in the city? Tomorrow's tips, huh?"

"Yup. City Cabs."

"Have you talked with any other reporters about this?"

"Reporters? No. Why would I talk to reporters?"

"Good. Listen, no promises, but I'll see if I can get something in the morning paper. But I gotta tell you, this isn't the story I came for."

Deciding to be a decent guy or eager to write an exclusive about the cabbies' tip drive to pay for an iron lung, David typed away furiously at his desk, hoping to impress his assignment editor with a real news story rather than a holiday fluff piece. *Shit!* The time! It was well past six o'clock. Nearly seven. Finally done. Thank God the boss stayed late—today, anyway. David felt he'd skillfully crafted the story, even provided a witty headline and subhead and below, his byline. Typed, proofed, no need to change anything—he'd practically tied it up in a bow for the man. On the way up in the elevator, David rehearsed what he was going to say. Keep it short and simple, he thought—just let him know it's done, ready to go to press. Holiday content story is in progress; this is real news. Timely. And it's done. Done is key. And when he reads it, he's going to want it. He'll see what this reporter can do. Okay. There's his office. Straight ahead. Door open. Good. Damn! He wasn't expecting senior reporter Jim Ellis to be in Dan Kalman's office, but okay, he'll be impressed with the story too. Sure of it.

"Is that the Christmas spirit story?" Dan asked as David handed him the typed article.

"Uh, no. This is—" David attempted to synopsize, but Dan cut him off.

"When am I gonna get the holiday story?"

David watched his assignment editor scan the cab drivers' tips story, waiting for a sign of exuberance or perhaps interest or even—support. David explained that the holiday story was in progress and he would have it to Dan for sure by noon tomorrow.

It wasn't that Dan didn't like the article, but he seemed more concerned about the late submission rather than its content, a reaction which David didn't quite know how to process.

"Number one, you don't have the holiday story done yet. Just this. And number two, you want me—to go down to composing and tell the platemakers—to move stories around now? At this hour? Why didn't you call this in?" Dan asked, handing the article back to David. Then, with a smug smile on his face, told the young reporter, "Okay. We'll ask them."

"Really?" David responded—a little too enthusiastically, he realized too late. "I mean—great. Thank you for doing that."

"Thank *me*? I'm not going to ask them," Dan pointed out.

"You're not?" David asked, surprised.

"Not a chance in hell," Dan confirmed. "You are."

"Me?" David questioned.

"You want it in? You ask them," Dan answered, with a conviction David knew better than to challenge.

David stood frozen in front of the assignment editor's desk, then looked quickly to Jim for reassurance, or at least a few words of encouragement. None. Just an indifferent smile.

Shit. Gotta move. Show confidence. Like this is nothing.

"Why are you still here?" Dan asked, unwilling to hide his irritation.

As soon as David had passed through the doorway, Dan looked at Jim and asked, "You think I should've sent him down there? By himself?"

"The kid needs to grow some stones. He'll be fine."

"Well, I'm not fine! I need the holiday story!" Dan shouted, coming unglued. "WHY CAN'T I GET THE GODDAMNED CHRISTMAS CONTENT?"

David walked reluctantly down the long hallway and into the back of the elevator. On the ride down he attempted to convince himself that the guys downstairs would be helpful. After all, it was breaking news and not a very long article. Wouldn't take up much space. They'd rather see a young reporter than the crotchety old boss, anyway, right?

The heavy sounds from the composing room drifted far into the hallway, reaching Dan's ears as he turned the corner, relieved, briefly, that he was at least headed in the right direction. An oppressive churning and clicking filled the air as he neared the doorway, where he stopped and leaned in to look inside. The weathered, grim-faced union platemakers and composers yelled loudly to each other to be heard above the noise. Most wore their shirtsleeves rolled up above their elbows; David noticed their strong arms and stained denim aprons. He thought he could make out an Eastern European accent in two of the men's voices. He imagined the men just didn't see him as they went about their work. What David couldn't imagine was what the men *did* see when they looked at him: David was a nuisance—and worse. To these men, David was another young, privileged college kid who'd had more opportunities than they could have dreamed of in their youth. They saw David as someone who'd never had to worry about a roof over his head or where his next meal would come from. David was someone who, despite his youth, carried a higher status in the professional world than they did. Someone with new plans he thought would change the world and, in his fearless unguarded youth, might do just that. And those plans didn't include them. David was someone whose new ideas threatened their jobs and their beliefs and their goals. This person, this cocky young reporter so full of himself, so full of life, so full of promise, needed to be pushed back. He needed to be contained, controlled, held down, and manipulated to conform to the known, the familiar, the comfortable. David was something to be feared. If he were feared, he could be kept in check. If he were kept in check, they would be safe. David was something to be ignored. If he was ignored, he could be postponed. David was the future. And they'd always imagined it differently than what had just shown up at their door.

"Uh, hi! I got a late story here, uh, to get in, if possible," David called feebly to the men, hoping to make eye contact, but the men ignored him. After waiting an awkwardly long time, David took a deep breath, stepped inside the noisy room, and garnered the nerve to raise his voice.

"Uh, hey, guys! Sorry to interrupt your work. I know you're ready to go to press, but I've got an urgent story that needs to get in."

The crew continued working as if David were invisible, and the young reporter endured another embarrassingly long moment of no response. Aware that David was either too stubborn, too naive, or just too damn stupid to turn and leave, one of the leads, Victor Polotofsky, paused, looked David up and down, then slowly stated, "Pages already set."

"I understand that," David replied and, whether driven by obstinance, ego, or a newfound determination to help a worthy cause, persevered and added, "And I really regret having to ask this of you so late."

The composer looked toward Milos Polis, one of the platemakers who'd been observing the scenario at the door. This wasn't the first time a reporter had shown up at the eleventh hour, pleading for an exception. The seasoned crew knew, however, that most of the writers and editors were well aware they'd better have a damn good reason, a stop-the-presses kind of story, to venture into this territory at this hour. Feeling it couldn't hurt to see what the kid had, Milos approached David, who handed him the story.

"So, this must be pretty important for you to come in here now. So late," Milos suggested as he scanned the article. "I'm Milos. What's your name?"

"Lindsey. David Lindsey."

"So the cabbies tomorrow will donate their tips for a little girl with polio at New York General?"

"Yeah. She needs an iron lung. City Cabs Company drivers are going to—"

"City Cabs?" Victor asked, turning to David. "Gino Ruganni's outfit?"

"Yeah," David answered with conviction, desperate for a way in; he'd verify the Ruganni details later. "City Cabs."

"Gino's company. Why didn't you say so?" Victor stated loudly, nodding to his workmate. "Okay. We got this. Get outta here."

"Thanks. Really appreciate it," David acknowledged and quickly headed out of the doorway, clueless of the magnitude and scope of what he'd just accomplished because of the help and cooperation of the crew in the composing room and Gino Ruganni, a man he'd never met. David felt himself becoming lighter; the relief of heading away from the room and confrontation with the unknown, and the near assurance that his story would get in. Okay to breathe. To let go of uncertainty and allow for a smidge of elation, almost. And, oh man, the sharp, excellent taste of a tall, crisp, ice-cold beer as soon as he could get his hands on one.

CHAPTER 12

A NEW DAY

When Ed Bauer woke up in his room at the Waldorf Astoria that morning, all he could think about was getting the hell out of there and back to his home and offices in Smyrna, Georgia. These New York bankers and business sharks weren't going to put anything over on him. Not Ed Bauer, owner and founder of Bauer Manufacturing, which prided itself on making the best exhaust fans and air conditioners this side of the Mississippi. And this fancy hotel made him uncomfortable with its crystal this and gilded that. He hadn't wanted to stay there in the first place. The pretentious service and snobby staff weren't to his liking. The bankers who'd hosted him in New York had insisted on putting him up at the hotel, which Ed had agreed to, but only because he didn't want to seem like a country bumpkin to the New Yorkers. Ed was glad he'd stood his ground on paying his own airfare. It meant he could arrive and depart when he wanted, on his time and his dime. And that restaurant last night; didn't need some over-trained waiter to put a napkin in his lap, no sir. And the cigarette girls. His daughter wouldn't be doing that. Not a chance in hell. All this frou-frou nonsense hadn't impressed Ed one iota. And the silver dome cover over his breakfast on the table wheeled into his room didn't make one damn bit of difference either. They couldn't even get the eggs right. What does it take to fry an egg? His wife, Bonnie, knew how to cook his eggs perfectly, and she never went to any fancy cooking school like he kept hearing about last night. At least the coffee was hot. And they brought some newspapers.

Dan Kalman had caught the 6:40 train out of Farmingdale this morning. He preferred taking the train rather than driving. It made him feel, somehow, more authentic. He'd come to terms some time ago with the reality that the newspaper business was—a business. Back when he was a green reporter, he would get as jacked up as the next guy about a story or the opportunity to scoop another paper. And then he was blindsided. A girl. With breasts. Fell head over heels. She was shy. Next thing he knew, he was married. Before he turned around, his wife was pregnant. On a reporter's salary, the three of them squeezed into a one-bedroom apartment in Queens. His first promotion, she nagged him into moving to a two-bedroom apartment. Then it seemed like it was all about the kid. The right school. Saving for college. All about him. Ten years ago, the wife was hell-bent on getting out of an apartment. Wanted a yard for the son and his friends. Dan had just been promoted to assignment editor and the wife read about Levittown. Read about it in a damn real estate special section in the newspaper. The Colonial. Had to have it, and there would be no let-up until it was theirs. Her dream house. When the son was in high school, he thought the neighborhood was the most boring place on the planet. Kid went to college out in California, and when he graduated, landed a job in Los Angeles, and never looked back. Her dream house. *A goddamned box*, Dan remembered thinking. He also remembered thinking at the time, *at least it will get her off my back*, and he wondered why he'd never stood up to her. It was just easier not to. Dan loved the long train ride. It gave him nearly an hour to himself. Both ways.

It was customary for Dan to take a cab from Penn Station to the office; the short ride didn't take long, and he liked to get a feel for the buzz on the street from the cab driver. It also gave him a few extra minutes to stop at the newsstand that was just a half a block from the *Telegraph* building. When he came out of the station, he noticed there were quite a few Checker cabs lined up, and he didn't waste any time grabbing one. He'd have plenty of time to stop at the newsstand and check out what the competition was up to.

The cab driver had jumped out of his seat and had the cab's rear door open for Dan. A moment later, they were headed to lower Manhattan, the driver chatting away about the weather and possible snow flurries. Dan asked him how business was and he responded with, "Okay. Little slow this morning. It'll pick up this afternoon, what with people coming in for holiday shopping, and if the weather gets nasty."

As they headed down Seventh Avenue, Dan looked out of the window and watched the pedestrians scurrying to offices and coffee shops. And all those damn holiday decorations. Seemed like every store window, every lamp post, had some sort of artificial greenery, ribbon garland, and light strand wrapped, draped, or strung up, on, or around it. One schmuck even had a sign in his store window announcing "Only 15 more days till Christmas!" As if he needed to be reminded, Dan thought to himself. Gotta get that holiday section wrapped up. Use the damn ice skating photo. One of the tree at Rockefeller Center. Big images. Last year he'd wanted to run a photo of the Salvation Army red kettle and bell-ringer—public service and all that. The publisher put the kibosh on that. Said people would think twice about spending money in the department stores if they were worried about all the poor people needing help. "This is the Christmas season! This is when the stores make their year! If they don't make it now, they're out!" he'd told Dan and added, "Look, here's the deal. We'll tell advertising if they buy an ad in the holiday section—we'll give 'em some editorial—feature one of their products."

Dan had the cab driver drop him off a block early. He needed a breath of fresh air. Out on the sidewalk, there was no mistaking the smell of early winter for Dan. In the middle of the city, the cars, the traffic, the buildings, the steam rising from manhole covers, it was there. A crisp, fresh, distinct smell. The air was cold and dry but felt almost humid at the same time. The low-hanging clouds were gray and heavy, just waiting to tease the first dance of flakes. Dan looked up and reassured himself. *Yup, that's a winter snow sky.*

He almost ran into a businessman hailing a cab but looked down just in time and stopped in his tracks when he heard the man ask the cabbie, "You're from City Cabs, right? Just want to be sure before I get in." First, Dan recalled something about City Cabs in the story the Lindsey kid had given him last night. Second, he'd never heard anyone in New York City hesitate about getting in a cab after they'd actually succeeded in hailing one so quickly. When he got to the newsstand, he noticed the rack was empty where the *Telegraph* was usually stacked. The competitors were there; the *Times*, the *Wall Street Journal*, the *Herald Tribune*, and others, but no *Telegraph*. *What gives? The idiots didn't deliver the damn papers*, Dan wondered, instantly growing irritated.

"Where's our paper?" Dan asked Nick, the owner of the stand. "Didn't they deliver this morning?"

"You're sold out, buddy. Can you have them send some more down? Everybody wants the *Telegraph*," Nick explained. "The story about the cabbies. Raising the money today with their tips for that little girl. The iron lung."

"We're sold out?" Dan asked, repeating it to make sure he'd heard Nick correctly.

"Sold out. Have 'em send down some more papers. I could use the extra money. Everybody wants me to break a twenty so they can give tips to the City Cabs drivers. Doesn't even matter if they're going for a ride or not."

"No kidding?" Dan asked, somewhat stunned.

"Never seen anything like it!" Nick said. "Talk about the Christmas spirit!"

"I'll be damned," Dan uttered, barely audibly, then quietly put the money for the *Times* and the *Herald*

Tribune on the newsstand counter and stepped back, taking a few minutes to observe for himself the scenario that Nick had described. Sure enough, he saw a man in hat and overcoat walk up to a City Cabs taxi, watched as the driver rolled down the window, and saw the man hand him a ten-dollar bill. Then the man walked away. Smiling. Dan stood there in disbelief, which was shattered when two women paused in front of him, one asking the other, "Did you see what that man just did? People are giving extra tips to the City Cabs drivers today. Even people who aren't taking cabs. There was an article in the *Telegraph* today—" The other woman jumped in before her friend finished. "Yes! I read the paper on the subway coming in. Had to buy one—the newsboy was shouting all about it. Come on, let's give the driver a donation before he takes off." Dan watched as the woman's friend didn't hesitate. "Yeah! A good way to start our day," she added. "Hope they can raise enough."

Dan's skepticism evaporated and opportunity rushed in and filled the void. Engulfed the void. His mind started racing. The newsstand needed more papers. A lot more papers. Every newsboy on the corner was gonna need more papers. Their annoying little voices shouting "Read all about it!" became music to his ears. Dan's pace quickened as he neared his building. *The Lindsey kid*, he admitted to himself. *Little bastard scored a winner. Even scooped the shit out of the* Times. He'd make sure Lindsey was all over the story for tomorrow's paper as well. Milk it for all it's worth. *We're gonna sell a ton of papers. And every retailer's gonna want to be in them.*

When Ed stepped out of the elevator and made his way across the opulent lobby of the Waldorf Astoria, he really didn't care if he stood out like a sore thumb. He felt he was perfectly capable of putting on his own coat, holding his own hat, and he sure as hell was going to carry his own damn suitcase. This was one of the times—and there had been many this trip—when he was glad he hadn't brought his wife and daughter with him, even though they both had nagged him to come. He could hear his wife's voice telling him right about now to "just let these nice people do their jobs, dear."

"Everything's taken care of, Mr. Bauer. Are there any bags we can help you with? May we get you a cab?" the front desk agent asked.

"Just a cab, thank you. I've got these," Ed replied, securing his grip on both his suitcase and briefcase.

"Very good, sir," the agent responded in his well-trained, seen-it-all, heard-it all, never-show-hint-of-judgment professional tone and smiled. "The doorman will call the next cab up for you."

By the time Ed crossed the lobby, the doorman, George Furding, had the entrance door held open for him. George cut a sharp figure in his tasteful doorman's uniform. His cadet-gray wool coat was long, almost mid-calf, and double-breasted, with nickel buttons and tasteful nickel braiding on the cuffs and epaulettes. His matching cap had the same subtle braiding around the hat band, and he wore dark gray leather gloves. He had a slim silver metal whistle shaped like a small tube, which he wore on a silver chain around his neck.

"Cab, sir?" George asked.

"Yes, but—" Ed interjected quickly just before the doorman was able to blow his whistle to call the next cab in the queue. "I want a City Cabs taxi."

"City Cabs, sir," George repeated. "Yes, sir, right away. And where are we headed this morning?"

"First, Columbia University, just to pick something up, then LaGuardia airport."

"Good, sir. Give me just a moment," George answered, then quickly made his way across the carriage entrance and broad sidewalk toward the row of taxis lined up at the curb. He soon spotted Murray Dolan behind the wheel, reading a newspaper while waiting to be called up for a fare.

"Yo! Murray!" George called as he approached the cab, waiting while Murray rolled down his window. "I got a guy who's asking specifically for City Cabs. Come on up."

"What's his story?" Murray asked.

"Seems like a decent guy," George answered, looking back at Ed. "Not an asshole, but one of those types who wants to carry his own bags."

"Staying at the Waldorf?" Murray questioned.

"Go figure."

"Where's he wanna go?"

"Columbia University, quick pickup, then LaGuardia. Can't miss him. Brown coat, brown shoes. Brown suitcase. And, hey, what's going on with City Cabs? He's the second guy this morning who said he only wanted to take a City Cabs taxi."

"Yeah, we got a thing with our tips today to help a little girl with polio in the hospital. It's in the paper. Here, read about it," Murray explained, peeling off the front section of the *Telegraph* and shoving it through the window to George. Murray steered his cab onto the street, around the queued cabs in front of him, and headed up to the hotel's grand entrance. George quickly scanned the front page top to bottom and there it was, albeit well below the fold, a small one-column four-inch in the lower right-hand corner and jumping to page 11. He read the headline, "Cabbies' Tips Help Polio Victim," and the subhead, "C-47 Speeds Iron Lung to Hospital." George's eyes would never notice the byline, "By David Lindsey," but instead landed on the lead, "A five-year-old girl is in a race against time in New York General Hospital fighting the onset of polio and its tightening grip on her ability to breathe. According to hospital staff, young Rachel Hall needs to be in an iron lung, but every respirator at New York General and surrounding hospitals is in use by other patients battling the same symptoms as Hall's. The City Cabs Company of New York City—or more specifically, its drivers—are coming to the rescue by donating their tips from today's fares to purchase an iron lung and airlift it to the young patient."

Heading back to his position at the Waldorf Astoria's front entrance, George read that the respirator was being flown from Indianapolis to New York City by Falcon Air, a young cargo company operated by Joseph Martinez and Hank McGoran of Florida, and that Martinez was a World War II army buddy of one of City Cabs' drivers, Ben Wilson. He also read that Falcon Air was donating the cost of transporting the iron lung in a C-47, along with the fees for pilot and copilot. George looked up from the paper in time to see

Murray pull away with his passenger, the plainly dressed, no-nonsense, carry-his-own-bags Ed Bauer. The doorman's impressions of both men ratcheted up by several notches.

George paused for a moment to notice a few feathery snowflakes floating effortlessly in the air, their light, weightless puffs playing against the massive Waldorf Astoria facade. He watched the small white flakes drift about, taking their time to descend, then disappearing just as they met the sidewalk. George would read the remainder of the article on his lunch break, but he was glad he was now informed and prepared for the next customer asking for a City Cabs taxi.

If Gino was caught off guard to find a small crowd outside his office in the garage, he wasn't letting on— not to the lively group, anyway. He was his usual gregarious, warm, big-hearted self, welcoming the group of waitresses from Lou's Diner who had just come off their morning shift. The garage was noisy and busy, with cabs heading in from shifts and out for fares. Willy was at his desk juggling calls from two phones. Ben Wilson was at Gino's desk on a third phone. Ben and Willy had made two signs that morning announcing "TIL Day," with the words "Tips for Iron Lung, today, December 9, for Rachel Hall, 5, in New York General Hospital." The signs were taped to the glass on each side of the window counter, where Alice Simi, a waitress who'd been designated spokeswoman for the group, was talking with Gino through the small round opening.

Alice had dark brown hair, which she wore short and sassy. Her pink-and-white waitress hat, more like a tiny pleated fan tiara, sat on top. She wore bright red lipstick and spoke with a vivacious Brooklyn accent. She hadn't bothered to button her overcoat and was still wearing her waitress uniform, as were the other waitresses gathered around her. Alice retrieved a neatly tied white pouch from her coat pocket and placed it on the narrow counter in front of her, telling Gino, "Me and the girls wanted to help with what you're doin', Gino." The pouch was actually a white handkerchief with a petite red rose embroidered at each corner, which she'd tied into a knot to secure its contents. As she untied the small bounty, gobs of nickels, dimes, and quarters slid from their pile, spreading out to cover the little hanky, along with a healthy take of dollar bills. She pushed the handkerchief, change, and bills into the tray toward Gino through the small opening below the window. Gino took the cigar out of his mouth and set it on the counter next to him, telling Alice, "Thank you, ladies," as he slid the handkerchief toward him, scooped the money to his side of the tray, and gently pushed the hanky back to Alice. "Thank you very much. This is a big help."

"Every one of these gals either knows about some-body who's had polio or their kids have somebody in their class who's had it," Alice shared, "and we also know the tip thing. For you guys, it's still sort of a some-do-some-don't kind of thing. So, anyway, we wanted to show our support."

"Well, we really appreciate it, ladies," Gino stated loudly, smiling at the other waitresses, who enthusiasti-

175

cally smiled and waved back. "You girls have a great day, and know that your help means a lot to us and to that little girl!"

The other waitresses called out goodbyes to Gino as they turned to head out of the garage. Their upbeat chatter and giggles bounced off the walls and echoed down the concrete lanes. Just as the girls reached the side door, it was pulled open from the outside by Emil Stephanos, mid-forties, dark hair, and wearing a deep-violet scarf tucked neatly inside the lapel of his black cashmere overcoat. He held a pair of expensive-looking black leather gloves in his other hand.

"Mr. Stephanos!" Alice remarked, surprised to find him suddenly in front of her.

"Hello, Alice, ladies," Emil responded, holding the door open and nodding to the women. "Alice, when are you gonna come work for me? You know I'd make you a hostess. No more waiting tables."

"That's very flattering, Mr. Stephanos, but I love my job, and love the gals I work with," Alice told him quickly as she maneuvered her way around him, adding, "but thank you, anyway," and headed out of the door. Emil held the door open for the women as they hurried past him and stepped outside. The last waitress scurried out the door saying a quick "Thank you" without looking up as she crossed the threshold. Emil closed the door behind her and walked toward the dispatch window to speak with Gino, who'd been observing him from behind the glass.

"Hello, Gino," Emil said respectfully through the small opening while reaching into the breast pocket of his overcoat and pulling out an envelope.

"Hello, Emil," Gino responded generously. "What brings you here today?"

"I have a donation. For your charity drive," Emil casually explained, pulling a check made out for one hundred dollars from the envelope and placing it in the small tray opening on the counter. As Gino reached toward it from the other side, Emil pressed his fingertips down on the check and purposefully added, "This donation is from Emil's Restaurant. You know where we're located—Sixty-second and Second Avenue, right?"

"I'll make sure all the drivers know this address, Emil," Gino sincerely reassured him, picking up the check as Emil released his fingers.

"Thank you. Stop by yourself sometime. Bring the wife."

"Thanks, Emil. I will."

Emil nodded and headed back across the garage toward the side door. Gino watched him exit and made sure the door closed behind him before turning to Willy and handing him the check.

"Here, put it with the others," he instructed Willy, who placed Emil's donation on a small stack of other checks.

"That's a lot of addresses these guys are gonna have to remember," Willy commented.

"They only gotta remember one address," Gino reassured him. "My cousin Enrico's place on Fifty-third."

Another group of waitresses, happy to be off work and in from the cold, made their way toward the dispatch window. Gino greeted the bubbly group and thanked each waitress personally as, one by one, every woman placed her individual tips in the window counter tray to help City Cabs' cause. On the phone behind Gino, Ben was trying to understand what Joe Martinez, who'd called from the air cargo hangar at Indianapolis Airport, was telling him. Ben covered his right ear with his hand, attempting to block out Gino's boisterous exchange with the waitresses and Willy's conversations with an upsurge in customers needing a cab.

"Joe, are you saying you've got it?" Ben asked, loudly, adding, "We're good for the money."

Inside the cargo hangar in Indianapolis, Joe mirrored his buddy on the other end of the line, with the phone up to his left ear and covering his right ear with his free hand, trying to muffle the sound of whirring prop engines and forklifts whizzing past in the background. The phone base rested on a cluttered metal desk that was covered with various folders and weather reports. A badly cracked brown leather chair on a metal base with wheels had rolled near the right side of the desk. Joe stretched toward the hangar opening as far as the phone cord allowed, checking the progress of his cargo and aircraft outside.

"They're loading it right now, and we'll be set to take off. And Sam Weinberg, with the iron lung company, is coming with us," he told Ben in a robust voice, hoping to be heard clearly. Then, thinking he detected a hint of concern in Ben's voice, added, "Everything okay on your end?"

Joe listened intently as Ben assured him a cashier's check would be waiting at the airport for Mr. Weinberg when they arrived in New York. Ben paused for a moment, then told Joe it was beginning to snow in

New York City and asked if that could become a problem. Joe listened patiently as Ben fired off, "What if LaGuardia gets closed? Will Idlewild stay open? Where else could—?"

"Hold your horses, Ben!" Joe gently directed his friend, "Let me get Hank." Joe covered the receiver's mouthpiece and spotted his pilot, Hank McGoran, on a phone near the hangar bay doors. Wearing a pilot's cap and a worn brown leather bomber jacket, Hank couldn't be mistaken for anything other than a pilot.

"It'll be just a minute," Joe told Ben. "Hank's on another phone with somebody."

Hank's weathered face beamed with the pleasure that comes from talking to a good friend, a fellow pilot, someone like himself, someone who's got the solution before you have to explain the issue. His friend Rick Marshall was just that guy. Rick was a test pilot for Hank's former employer Republic Aviation and was based at its manufacturing plant and airport in Farmingdale, Long Island. He and Hank had flown missions together in the Army Air Forces in Europe during the war. They shared a special bond, and they had each other's back. That came in handy in the Air Forces, because as young hot-shot pilots, they also knew how to get into trouble. And, more importantly, how to get the other guy out of trouble, both in the air and on the ground.

Rick looked like the quintessential test pilot in his navy flight suit with its Republic Aviation patch over his left chest pocket. He had the phone up to his ear as he stood next to a desk just inside the wide, open doors of Republic's hangar. He'd taken off his aviator shades and stowed them in one of the jumpsuit's numerous zippered pockets. He wasn't quite as tall as Hank but made an impressive figure in his stance, his feet planted firmly shoulder-width apart, his left hand anchored on his hip while holding the phone with his right. His dark hair was combed to the side, and despite it being December, his face was tan, which accentuated his blue eyes. They brightened as he listened to his friend's voice, and his white teeth flashed with each laugh.

"If you and Joe are gonna be here overnight—hell, yes, we'll get together!" Rick told Hank over the phone. "Uh-huh. I see. Your 'backup' here? Might as well. We can't fly the new bird out of here. Runway's too short, and this damn politician's been opposing plans to extend it. No, I'm not shittin' you, man. Hank, we build fighter jets here. The government wants them faster and more powerful. That requires a longer runway. Get this: we just had to truck the Thunderstreak down to the field at Westhampton Beach to test it. Can you believe this bullshit?"

Rick's eyes moved back and forth as he listened to his friend on the phone. He checked the time on his watch and leaned toward the hangar bay, looking up at the sky.

"Yeah, they might. They're gonna be over-cautious, what with everything at Newark earlier this year," Rick suggested, "but, Hank, this is Republic. We're not gonna flinch. I'll keep an eye on the weather reports for you."

Rick picked up a clipboard from his desk and scanned the top page, then looked straight out the hangar doors. As he listened to his friend, the wheels turned behind Rick's eyes, assessing a need, speculating scenarios, outcomes, and benefits, and developing a solution—well before an actual problem might arise.

"You say you're delivering an iron lung? Emergency, for a little girl in the hospital?" Rick confirmed. "Let me give the operations manager a heads-up. This, actually, might even be kinda helpful for us. It'll be just a skeleton crew—most of the staff goes home by five, five thirty—but we can handle it. If it were to become necessary."

Rick laid the clipboard back down on the desk and listened to Hank, taking in every word with purpose. He knew Hank as a pilot's pilot and one he would trust in any situation, should the going get dicey.

"I'll be here, Hank. Don't even worry about it. If it looks iffy, I'll head up to the tower and be available there," Rick reassured Hank, adding, "I'll find some of the old crew; they'll be happy to help out. Yup. Still is. And, hey, this could be a good thing for us, being a resource for a medical emergency. All right. Safe flight. See you tonight—one way or another. Bye."

Hank set the receiver back in the cradle and started walking toward the C-47 for his pre-flight inspection when he heard Joe call him.

"Hank! Can you come 'ere a minute?"

Hank turned mid-stride and headed toward Joe, soon followed by Sam Weinberg, who jaunted briskly to catch up with Hank.

"What's up?" Hank asked.

"Ben says they're getting some snow up there. He's concerned about closures," Joe explained.

"Did you say snow?" Sam asked, worried.

Hank looked toward the C-47 parked outside the hangar and back toward Joe, then told him, "Yeah. When I made out the flight plan, they indicated snow might impact the commercial flights. There's Newark, and I've got a few cards up my sleeve. Always gotta have a Plan B. Tell him not to worry," Hank added, then headed back to the plane to complete his walk-around.

"Newark?" Sam asked Hank, walking quickly to keep up. "Didn't they close that down?"

"It's back open," Hank reassured Sam. "We'll be fine."

"Yeah, Ben, don't worry. We're coming," Joe told Ben over the phone, hoping to quell his concerns. "These planes made it over the Swiss Alps. Hell, they made it over the Himalayas. They can make it through a little New York flurry. If LaGuardia's closed, there's Idlewild, and Newark's right across the river. Listen, Hank flew these things all over Europe in conditions you don't even wanna know about. We'll be there." Joe looked at his watch and assured Ben, "We're scheduled to leave in forty-five minutes. We should be there by 18:00 at the latest. Let's hope that little girl can hold on."

CHAPTER 13

RECONNAISSANCE

David was staring at the few first lines of text he'd managed to wrench out for the "Holiday Spirit" article his assignment editor wanted for the special section. *Just do it; just get it done*, he told himself. But there it sat, the pristine white sheet, stuck in his Remington and only three lines of copy to show for itself. Maybe he could just use the "Yes, Virginia" editorial with a nice introduction and then run the whole piece. That would take up at least thirteen or fourteen inches. *It's done every year, right? Why not our paper? Could add a pull quote, some nice artwork. Yeah. Good idea.* David had just about convinced himself when he was startled by the sudden loud voice of Dan Kalman.

"WHAT THE HELL ARE YOU DOING HERE?"

The young reporter spun around frantically, thinking, *What the hell is the assignment editor doing at my desk?*

"Uh, I—I—" David stammered, "was working on that article for the holiday section. Just—a—a—just got it nailed down."

"I WANT YOU ON THE STORY WITH THE CABBIES! The iron lung! Coming to the rescue of the little girl!"

An "oh" slipped out of David's mouth before he could prevent it.

"Yeah. I was gonna head over to the hospital later, be there when it arrives," David said sheepishly.

"Get over to City Cabs garage! NOW!" Dan told the young reporter. "We *own* this story! I want you attached at the hip to that cab driver! What's his day like? How many drivers are there? What are their names?"

Dan paused for a moment, thinking every driver had relatives and every relative was gonna want a copy of the paper, see the name in the *Telegraph*.

"Look, kid, you gotta find out who these drivers are," Dan instructed David and took a softer tone when he realized the young reporter looked scared shitless. "Ask them questions: Why did they choose to do this? What makes them tick? Are people donating enough tips? Are the drivers anxious? Worried?"

Dan coached the young reporter, then took a few bills out of his wallet and handed them to David, adding, "Here. You take a cab—a *City Cab*—over there yourself. Ask the driver how it's going. Find that Ben guy and stick to him like glue. Got it?"

"Yes, sir," David answered and abruptly left the holiday story wanting in his typewriter.

Five-year-old Rachel Hall, critically ill from the onset of polio, lay on her back in a bed inside the isolation ward at New York General Hospital, unaware that on an airstrip 700 miles away a life-saving machine was strapped aboard an airplane about to take off, headed her way. Her entire focus was concentrated on trying to inhale each thimble of air she could draw into her mouth and nose and into her lungs. Hoping for a relief she couldn't comprehend, she moved nothing but her wide-open eyes, which anxiously scanned the room and found the masked nurses around her. One of the nurses leaned an ear close to Rachel's mouth, listened to her breathing, then rose back up when she saw Dr. Neill Friedman, in a mask and gloves, enter the small room. The nurse shook her head, "No," indicating to the doctor that Rachel's breathing hadn't improved. Dr. Friedman moved close to Rachel to examine her as the nurse backed away.

"Rachel, I'm Dr. Friedman," Neill told the little girl. "We know you're having trouble breathing. We're going to get you some special oxygen that's going to help. Right away."

Rachel was too sick, too weak, and too afraid to sacrifice her desperate breathing efforts to summon any visible response.

"Set up an oxygen tent," the doctor instructed the nurses. "Immediately."

Outside the room, down a long corridor and beyond the nurses' station, Virginia Douglas headed toward the Respirators Post-Isolation Recovery Room. The heels of her pumps made a *click-clack, click-clack, click-clack* sound on the tile floor and announced her arrival as she approached the room's double doors. She rose up on her toes to look inside the small windows before heading inside. As soon as the door was cracked open, the pulsing sounds of bellows spilled out from the room. The *sswhee-swoosh, sswhee-swoosh, sswhee-swoosh* filled the air and muffled the noise of Virginia's footsteps as she passed between two long rows of functioning iron lungs supporting the lives within. She looked down the row to her right and spotted John's dark hair, his head resting on a pillow and the tray that supported it. She considerately let him know she was nearly there by calling to him from a bit of a distance.

"Hey, John! Ready to go round-for-round with me?"

John rolled his eyes, annoyed but not ready to offend, and responded with a sarcastic "Yeah, right. Get my boxing gloves." Virginia moved close, supporting herself with her left arm on the respirator, leaned in toward John's face, and spoke in hushed tones.

"And what about getting out of here?" she asked earnestly, looking at the respirator and back at John. "I heard you were able to turn this thing off for five hours yesterday."

"Yeah, but, uh, they—they want me to take it slow. It's—"

"That's fine, John," Virginia interrupted, sensing John's apprehension. "Just remember what we talked about. A few more minutes each day. Before you know it, you'll be out of there for good. And in time for your eighteenth birthday. You know what that means?"

"I can join the army?" John remarked with an acerbic bite. "Hmmm. Don't think I'm the candidate they're looking for."

"That you'll be your own boss," Virginia batted back, unruffled. "That you can decide the direction and course you want your life to take."

"I think that's been decided for me."

"Seems to me you have a choice." Virginia pressed onward, telling John that he could decide to let the situation control him or he could control the situation, none of which John wanted to hear, let alone accept. He fired back with venom.

"I DON'T HAVE ANY CONTROL! WHAT AM I GONNA DO? CONTROL *THIS*? CONTROL A JOB? CONTROL WHAT PEOPLE THINK WHEN THEY SEE ME?"

Undeterred, Virginia stayed the course and told John he had more control, more power than he realized. She was upfront with him, stating that she would not sugarcoat his road ahead, that he was too old and too smart for that. She pointed to her temple and reminded him, "John, real strength, real power, comes from here.

"Did you get handed a bad deal? No doubt," she admitted and added, "But what are you going to do about it? When you got knocked down on the basketball court, did you give up? No! You fought back."

"That's not this," John feebly stated.

"No, John, it's not," Virginia concurred. "But what it *is*, is this: fight back. Don't expect somebody to do it for you. Take control. Over you; over your future. And here's a novel idea—think about doing something for someone else while you're at it."

John was taken a bit by surprise, particularly by Virginia's last remark. No one had suggested anything like that to him—certainly not in the last ten months, anyway. Virginia stood upright and resumed a regular speaking voice.

"Think it over, John. I'm headed to an appointment. Oh, and John, you can't hide in there forever."

John listened to the sound of Virginia's footsteps fade as she walked away, her distinct *click-clack, click-clack* disappearing as she passed through the doors and the sound of the bellows gained ground. John looked straight up toward the ceiling and was overcome with an unexpected surge of emotion rising inside himself. He tried to hold back a swell of tears, but one escaped his left eye and rolled downward just above his ear. He hoped no one noticed.

Murray Dolan was waiting in his cab outside the iron gates of Columbia University on Broadway. He'd positioned his cab just south of 116th Street so he could spot his passenger when the businessman passed through the gates and out onto the sidewalk. Murray was considerate with his passengers that way, always making it a point to drive with his passenger's comfort in mind. He wasn't one for rabbit starts and stops, always took the corners slowly, and didn't believe in the frantic in-and-out lane-change method to try to shave a few seconds off a drive. He knew the city and its traffic patterns in commute times, through construction zones, inclement weather, and during holidays and summer vacations, when tourists would invariably mix things up. He was upfront and frank about realistic drive times with his passengers, particularly to the airport, a trait that was recognized and noted by Ed Bauer.

Murray enjoyed his job and was glad to have it. He'd seen his parents, Jack and Kate Dolan, struggle during the Depression and remembered the fear he'd seen in his father's eyes when Jack lost his job. He remembered the confusion when everything changed so abruptly, when no one knew where he was going to live, how he was going to eat, and how he was going to pay for any of it. Murray had often watched his mother take stale, discarded bread and create a meal with it for him and his sister, Arlene. His mother would moisten the outside of a loaf with water, then wrap it in a towel and place it in the oven to let the bread warm and soak up the moisture. He loved the smell of the warm bread. She'd slice it thick and place a slice in a bowl, one for him and one for his sister. Then she'd pour milk over it. When they had sugar, she let them each have a spoonful to sprinkle on top. It was his favorite meal. He tried to find odd jobs wherever he could, delivering this, cleaning that, digging whatever needed to be dug. He was absent from high school more often than not, and by the end of his sophomore year it just made more sense to drop out and earn whatever money he could.

When the economy finally started to pick up again, his dad got his old construction job back, and the family moved back into the small house they had in Brooklyn. Shortly after that, just when things were beginning to get comfortable, things suddenly went to hell. His mother died. They said it was a brain hemorrhage. Two years after that, when Murray was in the army, he received word that his father had suffered a heart attack and was in the hospital. Murray never got to say goodbye to him. His sister stayed in the house, renting rooms and serving meals to make ends meet. She never married. After he came home from the army,

Murray married his childhood sweetheart, Mary McLaren. With the help of the GI Bill, they bought a small house down the block from Murray's parents' home. They soon had a daughter, Katherine, named after Mary's mother, and then a son, Gabe. Murray enjoyed singing and would often croon lullabies to his children, who loved every minute of it. He could be counted on to break into an impromptu request at a neighbor's birthday party or sentimental gathering in a pub. He never bothered to learn how to read music but could belt out an aria as well as any tenor at the Met. Each Christmas Eve it was expected by Monsignor James Connelly that Murray would be at Midnight Mass to perform Schubert's "Ave Maria."

While waiting for his passenger to return, Murray read what he could of the rest of his paper, but always with a diligent eye to spot his passenger. He'd trained himself over the years; after every four or five paragraphs, look up and check to see if the passenger had come out of the bank or office or store and was looking for him. He wanted to keep himself informed and on top of the latest news, but not at the expense of his customers, who seemed to appreciate it. Certainly, Ed Bauer did when he saw Murray roll up and stop in front of him. The cab driver jumped out and quickly ran around to open the door well before Ed reached the car. It was cold outside, and Murray was glad he'd kept the engine running and heater turned on for his passenger.

"Hop in, sir. It'll be warm in there," Murray let his customer know.

Ed didn't need to be convinced. It *was* cold, and the occasional snowflake on his walk across campus reminded him the temperatures could drop further. He tucked himself into the backseat with his briefcase on his lap and settled in as Murray pulled away from the curb and headed into traffic.

"How long do you think the drive to LaGuardia will take?" Ed asked.

"This time of day, not bad, under thirty minutes, but…" Murray replied, hesitating a bit before adding, "I think I'll wait for you at the curb. If you'd like to check inside just to make sure your flight isn't going to be delayed or cancelled."

"You think that's a possibility?"

Murray leaned over the steering wheel and peered up at the dense gray clouds that had filled the sky, then noticed the specks of soft white snowflakes landing on his windshield, occasionally sticking for a moment longer than he'd like.

"Well, I've seen it like this before and, to be honest, it doesn't look good. But I'm not a scientist, so how 'bout if we play it by ear, and I'll just stick around at the curb for a while after I drop you off?"

"That'd be fine. Thank you. I'd appreciate that," Ed said genuinely, suddenly remembering he didn't have a hotel room booked for the night. Though he sure as hell wasn't going back to the ostentatious Waldorf Astoria.

Murray kept checking his rearview mirror to see how his passenger was faring and thought the man looked somewhat anxious. Murray wanted to lighten things up by sparking a little conversation.

191

"Well, hope your time here was good. You visiting us for business or just a pleasure trip?"

"Oh, strictly business this time," Ed replied.

"Business on Wall Street? Or—"

"Oh, no. In manufacturing. Not here. Down in Atlanta. My company makes exhaust fans. And air conditioners."

"Air conditioners! Might not need them today, but boy, they sure come in handy in the middle of July!" Murray offered in what Ed could see was a genuine attempt to compliment.

"Yes, and I'm very fortunate most people feel that way," Ed responded.

On the way to LaGuardia, Ed scanned the report he'd picked up at Columbia, noting some key areas he'd delve into, hopefully, on the flight back to Atlanta. As he examined the contents of the report, the thought kept occurring to him that his driver was actually rather considerate, offering to wait while Ed checked to see if the flight was cancelled or leaving as scheduled.

"You sure it's not a problem to wait?" Ed asked. "I wouldn't want to prevent you from grabbing a good fare."

"Not a problem, sir. Besides, the doorman back at the Waldorf said you requested a City Cabs taxi, and with the tips charity drive today, it'll be hard to get one of our cabs here at the airport," Murray explained. "Most of ours are staying in Manhattan today because so many people are asking specifically for City Cabs."

"Well, if things go south at the airport, would I be able to hire you—for the day?" Ed asked. "Is that possible? Are you even available?"

"Um, well, I'm available, sir, though I'd need to check with my boss about the day fare, but I don't think it should be a problem," Murray replied, finding his passenger in his rearview mirror.

"Fine. My name's Ed Bauer. May I ask what your name is?"

"Name's Murray Dolan."

"Thank you, Mr. Dolan."

The men got their names and how they would address each other squared away, along with the where-are-you-from and the where'd-you-grow-up, by the time the cab pulled into LaGuardia airport and up to the curb at the terminal entrance. Ed let himself out as Murray retrieved Ed's suitcase from the trunk, handing the worn cognac-leather case to Ed with an "I'll think positive thoughts" statement of encouragement. Ed paid Murray for the fare and added a ten-dollar tip for the donation.

"I'll loop around and be right there, just in case," Murray told Ed, pointing to a spot on the curb several yards behind them.

Ed put on his fedora, thanked Murray, and headed inside the terminal entrance, carrying his briefcase and suitcase. As Murray was just about to pull away from the curb, Bobby Nolan popped out of the City Cabs airport dispatch booth and ran up to Murray's cab, making quick, small circles with his forefinger to get Murray to roll down his window.

"Where ya goin', Murray? Your light's turned off. I need you."

"I'm doing a loop. My passenger's gone inside to check if his flight's on or cancelled."

"Trust me, it's cancelled. They're not taking any chances. Not with that mess at Idlewild this year. I think it's overkill—this isn't a blizzard—but it ain't my decision to make."

"Well, I'm just circling and headed back to pick him up. Hey, what'd Gino charge if this guy wants to hire me for the day?"

"I dunno—forty, fifty bucks? Your guy doesn't want one of them cars with a driver? Ask Gino. Are you gonna take him back downtown?"

"I guess so. He didn't say."

"Check it out with Gino first. This guy okay?"

"Yeah. Strictly business, but a nice guy. Not a jerk. Gave a nice tip for the drive, but not a show-off. Let me loop around before he gets back out here."

"Go on. Get outta here!" Bobby told Murray, rubbing his glove-covered hands together, trying to warm them as he headed back to his dispatch booth.

The snowflakes began sticking to Murray's windshield as he pulled back up to the curb. Within five minutes, sure enough, there was Ed Bauer, walking out of the terminal and looking for his cab and driver. Murray jumped out and waved, catching Ed's attention. Ed shook his head to indicate "no go" and headed toward the cab.

"It's cancelled. Mine and everything else that was supposed to take off," Ed said as he handed his suitcase to Murray and climbed back into the cab.

After Murray got in, Ed asked him how to arrange for the day hire and assured Murray that City Cabs would be paid upfront for the service. Murray explained he'd need to contact his boss, Gino Ruganni, to get the fare amount, but that it would be easy to do. Ed asked if he could meet Mr. Ruganni and added he didn't mind driving to the garage to do so. Murray explained that once they crossed the bridge, he'd pull over at a call box and give Gino a heads-up to make sure he'd be there when they arrived.

On the drive back to Manhattan, Ed looked out of the front window, intrigued by how the falling snow seemed to part in front of the cab as it whizzed over the bridge. He wondered about the streets being drivable if the snow continued. Murray reassured him the snowplows would be out in full force to keep the streets open, especially so close to the holidays. Ed was thinking about his wife, Bonnie, and wanted to let her know about his flight being cancelled. He didn't want her to worry. Then feelings of guilt began to bubble up. Why hadn't he taken the time to get something for her and for his daughter? All he'd wanted to do was get in, take care of business in New York, and get out. Return to his home and business in Atlanta. Why did the women always want to come to New York? Why couldn't they be happy with what Atlanta had to offer? When Murray pulled over to use the call box, Ed told himself he'd call his wife as soon as they reached the garage. Find a phone booth. The agents at the airport seemed confident things would open up in the morning. She needn't worry. He'd be home tomorrow in time for dinner.

When Murray pulled into the garage, he was glad to see Gino was waiting for them outside the office. For some reason, Murray had thought it would be awkward to have Mr. Bauer speak to Gino through the small round opening at the dispatch office window. Murray pulled the cab in just past the office and parked. He and Ed got out of the car at the same time and approached Gino, who was ready with an outstretched hand to greet the passenger and driver. Murray made the introductions, then took his cap off and clutched it with both hands while he explained to Gino about Ed's cancelled flight and the request to hire Murray's cab for the day and tomorrow morning to get him back to the airport. Gino inquired if Ed was visiting New York on business or for pleasure.

"Strictly business," Ed answered.

"You're sure you don't want a driver and one of the town cars?" Gino asked sincerely. "We could arrange that for you, if you'd like."

"No, thank you. Don't need it. Wouldn't want my employees to think I'm riding around in some fancy limousine," Ed answered matter-of-factly.

"Mmm-hmm. Okay. We can take care of you. It'll be forty dollars for the rest of today and twenty for tomorrow morning. Plus a five-dollar charge for the driver's meals," Gino detailed.

"That's fine," Ed said. "Speaking of which, you must be getting hungry, Mr. Dolan. I know I am."

Murray looked at Ed, then Gino, and acknowledged he was. Gino asked if Ed would like a recommendation for lunch or if he just wanted to be driven to his hotel.

"Would you like me to take you back to the Waldorf?" Murray asked.

"No! Uh—no, thank you," Ed answered. "Not my cup of tea. I will need to find something, but I don't need to be in Buckingham Palace. Just need clean, quiet, simple."

Gino had been sizing Ed Bauer up during the brief encounter and pegged Ed as a man about the same age as himself, probably former military, hardworking, successful, but self-made and with simple needs. He didn't bother to hesitate and asked Ed, "Were you in the 'Great' one?"

Ed simply answered, "Yes."

"Army?" Gino asked.

"Marines."

"Mmm-hmm. I was army," Gino shared. "You hungry? I'm headed to a good little place just around the corner. Great turkey club and homemade soups."

"Sounds good. Uh, is there a phone booth nearby? I want to call my wife and let her know I'll be coming home in the morning. And I'd like to take care of the day hire fee for today and tomorrow morning," Ed added. "If we could do that first."

"You can use the phone in the office here, and I'll write out a receipt for you," Gino told Ed, gesturing behind him, then turned to Murray and said, "Let me get Mr. Bauer squared away with the phone."

Gino took Ed into the office and introduced him to Ben Wilson and Willy, who had a receipt ready for Gino to sign. Ed handed Gino a fifty and three twenties, explaining the extra twenty was for the driver, and asked if Murray would be available the next day as well, as he'd prefer him. Gino signed the receipt, handed it to Ed, and asked Ben and Willy to step out of the office while Ed made his call. Willy already had an operator on one of the phones and handed the receiver to Ed with a "Here you go, sir. A long-distance operator is on the line." Ed relayed his request to the operator as Gino, Ben, and Willy headed into the garage to huddle with Murray.

While Ed explained flight cancellations and weather predictions to his wife, Murray provided the group with a brief rundown on his passenger. Gino was genuinely interested, but his mind was racing ahead to something else. His instincts told him that Ben might become a concern if the weather became problematic. He knew Ben had pinned so much personal need on saving the life of the young girl in the hospital.

Ben had come by the office earlier to wait for Joe's call from Indianapolis, then offered to stay and help manage the unexpected surge in customer phone calls. It seemed as soon as the *Telegraph* hit the newsstands, the phones were ringing off the hook with people gushing over "the tips donation article in the newspaper!" and wanting to hire a City Cabs taxi. Though Gino and Willy could manage the calls just fine, Gino saw the writing on the wall with Ben. If things with the transport flight went downhill, Gino wanted him within arm's reach.

"You stay by the phone, Ben. We'll get you guys something to go. What do you like, Ben? Willy? The usual? Grilled ham and cheese. With fries and a bottle of Coke?"

Willy nodded affirmatively.

"BLT on toast. Yeah, a Coke sounds good," Ben added, then asked, "Did I just hear him say all flights are cancelled?"

"Not sure about that, and let's not get worked up yet," Gino urged, then abruptly changed the subject, turned to Murray, and asked, "You think your sister has a nice room available? For the night? I'm thinking this guy might prefer something like that."

"You think so?" Murray questioned.

"I'd bank on it," Gino stated emphatically. "Why don't you go in and call her when he's done? Then, come join us. Tell me what you want. I'll order it."

"BLT sounds good. And some soup. It's freezing out there. And coffee."

With all the commotion, no one had noticed David Lindsey walk up behind the group. He himself wasn't really sure how to make his presence known and now felt awkward overhearing the men in the middle of their lunch orders and, feeling hungry himself, even thought about leaving to get a bite and coming back. Gino noticed the bob of curly dark hair and black-framed glasses popping up behind Ben and caught David's eye.

"Hi! Can we help you?" Gino stretched to get David's attention.

Ben and the others turned around to see David, pen and pad in hand, hurriedly trying to introduce himself.

"Hello. Hi. David Lindsey with the *Telegraph*."

"Hey! Hi!" Ben reached out his hand to shake David's and enthusiastically introduced him to the others. "This is the reporter I told you about! He wrote the story!"

"Oh, great! We can blame you!" Gino joked. "No, no, seriously, great story. Really appreciate it. Take it you're here to find out what's going on?"

"Yeah, but don't let me keep you from your lunch," David answered, secretly hoping he'd be asked to join them.

"Just ordering for these guys. What can I get you?" Gino asked in a way that made David feel almost comfortable accepting the gesture. Besides, nobody here was going to tell his boss that the cab dispatch manager had paid for David's lunch.

"Uh—burger. And a cherry Coke? Thanks."

"Got it. Ben, come on over in ten to get you guys' food. I'll order it first."

Ed finished his call and joined the men outside the office. Ben, Willy, and David headed inside the office with Murray, who, Gino explained to Ed, would join them shortly.

On the short walk to the restaurant, Gino assured Ed that Murray was one of his most reliable drivers, had an excellent record, and was a very decent man. He also shared that Murray had served with the US Army, 47th Infantry Regiment, 9th Infantry Division in Tunisia during World War II. He didn't have to tell Ed it was a cluster; both men understood. Inside the restaurant, the two found an open booth near the lunch counter and sat down. Gino gave the waitress the to-go orders for Ben, Willy, and David, then asked about the day's specials. The waitress talked up a meatball sandwich with marinara sauce and the homemade minestrone and New England clam chowder soups. She gave the men a few minutes to decide while she put the to-go orders in for the others. By the time Gino and Ed had shared what infantry, battalion, and divisions they'd served in, the waitress was back to take their orders. Gino knew Murray would want the clam chowder; Ed went for the minestrone.

"And ours was supposed to 'end all wars,'" Gino mentioned after the waitress left.

"Well, at least these younger guys were treated a little better when they got home. The GI Bill, some veterans' benefits," Ed added, "though we had to fight and scrape for that too."

"Yup. That's why I try and make a point to hire the veterans when I can," Gino said. "They served. They sacrificed. They deserve a job."

"The young man you introduced me to back in the garage, Ben…"

"Ben Wilson?" Gino asked and answered.

"Was he the one I read about in the article this morning about your 'tip' drive? He put it together with a buddy of his, the owner of the new—well, somewhat new—air cargo company. Is he, uh…?"

"That'd be Ben. His buddy Joe Martinez and another guy have the cargo company they're trying to get off the ground—no pun intended," Gino said, then described how Ben came to him with the idea for the iron lung transport. He told Ed about City Cabs' annual charity drive during the holidays, explaining that the drivers donate their tips from one day toward a cause the men have chosen.

"You see, the whole idea of tips for cab drivers is still—sometimes people do, sometimes they don't. The tips donation day is a way for people to see it's not all about 'taking' for the guys," Gino said. "It's also about giving. The newspaper article really helped, though. I'll say that."

As the waitress bagged the to-go orders, Ben walked in the door and was headed to the counter when Gino flagged him over to the table.

"Everything good?" Gino asked Ben.

"Yeah," Ben answered. "So far."

"Uh, Mr. Wilson, your friend," Ed inquired, "who has the air cargo company—"

"Joe Martinez?" Ben asked.

"Yes, him. Uh, is he going to be around later? Is he staying in New York tonight?" Ed asked.

"Yeah. His pilot got a place by the airport, but he's staying with me, and he planned to come to the hospital with the unit so he can see our old teacher, Mrs. Douglas," Ben said, adding, "if all goes well."

"Any idea about what time that might be?" Ed asked.

Ben took a deep breath, trying to remember what Joe had told him, then recalled, "They should land sometime around five thirty, six, hopefully. Figure some time to unload, then a forty-minute drive to the hospital."

"You guys got your work cut out for you," Ed commented.

"Thanks, Ben," Gino added. "Enjoy your lunch. Tell Murray to get over here before his soup gets cold."

The waitress set down a freshly made turkey club sandwich in front of Gino, then one for Ed, along with a steaming bowl of minestrone soup, which brought a smile to Ed's face. He appreciated the rich combination of vegetables and was happy to see it included Swiss chard and parsnips, all soaking in the savory broth. The silence that ensued echoed the bliss of enjoying the taste of fresh, honest, made-from-scratch food. Halfway through the sandwiches, Gino asked Ed about his business in New York and if he was working with Columbia University. Ed explained that he had a manufacturing plant in Atlanta, made exhaust fans and, recently, air conditioners, and that he'd been invited to New York by a banker and financier who wanted to talk to him about expanding his business.

"My lawyer back home checked them out and said they were fairly well known, but not to sign anything," Ed said. "Expand my business—like hell! They wanted to buy my business! At least take a major holding in it. To hell with that nonsense! Couple of fast-talking lawyers and financiers with their fancy offices and flashy cars."

"Crooks and shysters," Gino commented, shaking his head.

"Those idiots don't know the first damn thing about me or my business. I don't need their cash to expand. Take care of that myself," Ed stated, finishing his last spoonful of soup.

"Yup. That's the way to go," Gino agreed. "Don't need some outsider telling you how to run things."

"No, sir."

"So, uh, you have a son or daughter at Columbia?" Gino asked.

"No, and my wife and I have just the one daughter, Julia. She went to a small women's college just outside Atlanta," Ed shared. "I was at Columbia to pick up a report."

Ed could see that Gino's intention wasn't to grill him but that Gino was genuinely curious. And Ed got a bit of a kick himself from being able to share what he was up to at Columbia. He explained that he'd stopped by the university to pick up a report from a graduate student who'd done some work for him. He'd met the student a year earlier in New York at a symposium on population shifts and migration patterns in post-World War II America. Being the founder and owner of an exhaust fan and air conditioner manufacturing company, Ed had seen the value in understanding the impact population clustering and dispersal had on the commercial building, construction, and housing industries, all of which would need exhaust fans and air conditioners. The student had researched data for Ed and appreciated the generous stipend he received for his work, as well as the experience gained.

Ed could see that Gino was impressed with the broad picture Ed had shared of his business and his foresight in using data information in decision making. In fact, Gino was more than impressed; he appreciated Ed's generous sharing of business tactics with someone like himself. Gino imagined the bankers and financiers who'd met with Ed a day earlier were fools for not finding out who this guy was and doing whatever it took to make things work with him. *Idiots*, Gino thought to himself.

Murray snuck through the door, hung his jacket on the coatrack, and slid in next to Gino in the booth. He wasted no time and dug into his sandwich and clam chowder. The bacon was extra crispy, almost crumbly, and the tomatoes sliced thick. And just enough mayonnaise where a small dab or two clung to the curly green lettuce leaves peeking out between the layers of lightly toasted fresh white bread. They'd nailed the clam chowder. The steaming, creamy, thick broth had just enough salt, just enough clam juice, and just enough butter and pepper. And coated in the middle of the heavenly creamy broth—chunks of potatoes, caramelized onions, and tender, fresh clams. The waitress brought him coffee and asked Ed and Gino if they'd like some too. After Murray had swallowed sufficient amounts of food to curb his hunger, he mentioned his sister's place and that she had a nice room available, nine dollars for the night, breakfast and dinner included, if Mr. Bauer was interested.

"And she's a good cook too," Murray added. "Said to tell you she's making herb roasted chicken with roasted potatoes and carrots for dinner tonight."

"I'll vouch for her cooking," Gino offered. "Best pot roast this side of Chicago. Her place is neat, it's clean, and it's quiet. Best part is, Murray lives just down the block, so he can be there any time you want tomorrow morning."

It was the roasted chicken that sealed it; Ed said he would take their suggestion for accommodation. Now that his room for the night was taken care of, Ed had another item he needed to check off his list.

"I would like to pick up something for my wife and daughter this afternoon; I know the weather's not helping. Any suggestions? Are the streets going to be open to drive?" Ed asked, looking at Gino, then Murray, who looked back at Gino for recommendations.

"They'll keep the streets open. What were you thinking for them?" Gino asked.

"Oh, maybe a nice scarf," Ed replied. "A pair of gloves?"

Gino reached into his back pants pocket for his wallet, pulled out a small white business card, and handed it to Ed.

"This is my niece, Ellen Passanisi. She works in the ladies' furnishings department at Bonwit Teller. She'll help you find something just right for them," Gino offered.

"That'd be a great help," Ed said, relieved. "Is that—downtown?"

"Right downtown," Murray jumped in. "Fifty-Sixth and Fifth Avenue. Easy."

"It's a nice building," Gino added. "Bonwit Teller. The ladies will know you did your homework."

CHAPTER 14

PLAN B

As the sun set behind the Falcon Air C-47, the horizon ahead began to fade to twilight. Inside the plane's cockpit, instrument lights cast a soft greenish-white glow on the pilots' faces. When the plane started to pass through turbulent weather, Hank and Joe kept a steady hand on the control wheels; the two men took each bounce in stride. Sam Weinberg discreetly tightened the strap on his seat belt and kept his eyes on the two pilots, hoping for some small sign of reassurance.

Joe contacted the control tower at LaGuardia and learned the airport was considered closed for landing now, as well as takeoffs.

"Copy that. Let me confirm with the pilot and I'll come back."

Joe looked over at Hank and told him the news. "LaGuardia and Idlewild are out. Snow on runways. Newark's a no-go."

"To each his own call. They're dealing with passengers. And they want to show they're ahead of the game, not taking any chances, what with this past year," Hank said.

"Will—are—do we have to turn back?" Sam asked, concerned.

Joe informed Hank that the next-closest major airport was at least another hour south of them, which Joe estimated could add another three hours of drive time to deliver their cargo to the hospital.

"My buddy at Republic said he'd be working late," Hank remarked, prompting Joe to retrieve a binder of airport maps from his pilot's case.

Gino, Willy, and Ben had been holding down the fort inside the dispatch office, keeping things under control while they waited for news from the airport. David was hammering away on a typewriter Gino had made available for him, drafting the first part of his follow-up story on the cabbies and their tip drive to help the young patient.

Gino was intentionally appearing busy for Ben's sake, pretending to be involved with a deep search in a filing cabinet so Ben would continue to answer the ringing phones. Anything to keep Ben busy. Gino could see the writing on the wall and sensed the worst when Willy handed the phone to Ben, and told him, "It's Bobby out at LaGuardia." Gino knew the news wasn't going to be good, which meant it would be particularly difficult for Ben to hear. David stopped typing and turned to observe the call.

"Hey, Bobby! What's the word?" Ben asked, his heart racing.

Gino watched Ben's eyes shift anxiously as the cabbie listened to Bobby on the phone. He knew when

Ben looked at him that any hope of landing at LaGuardia was gone.

"Idlewild too?" Ben asked, his concern mounting.

Willy and Gino looked at each other and back at Ben.

"Shit! I don't believe it!" Ben blurted. "And no to Newark? You're sure?"

Ben's eyes kept darting, looking at some obscure mark on the floor and then up to Gino, who knew well the look of despair. Gino had a ringside seat to watch as hope receded from Ben's eyes. And in its place, desperation—seeking from Gino an alternate idea or last-ditch solution for a game plan to somehow salvage the chance of saving the young patient's life. And Gino had neither. Ben saw the look of concern on Gino's face as he placed the phone's receiver back in its cradle.

"How they gonna land?" Willy asked, breaking the silence in the small office.

"Yeah," David quickly interjected. "What do they do now?"

"We came so close—and *snow*?" Ben lashed out, looking aimlessly around the room. "DAMN IT!"

"Hey, Ben," Gino cautiously remarked. "Get a grip. They can't land if it isn't safe."

"That little girl deserves—everybody's donated, worked so hard," Ben stammered, his frustration mounting as he gestured with his open hand toward the stack of donated money and checks. "How—how are we gonna explain—all *this*, and for—for nothing!"

"Ben—" Gino began, but quickly realized Ben needed to vent his disappointment and held back. But Ben said nothing. Instead, the cabbie exhaled a heavy sigh, walked to the office window, and took down one of the "Tips for Iron Lung" posters and then the other. He stared at the posters for a few seconds, then calmly tossed them into a wastebasket and walked out the office door. David looked at Willy, who looked at his boss. Gino called out to Ben, but the cabbie didn't, or wouldn't, respond. Gino watched Ben walk through the garage and storm out a side door. David started to get up, but Gino extended a hand, palm up, to him—and David sat back down. Willy gave David a look, which David wisely interpreted as "Don't even think about following him. Stay put. Gino's got it handled."

The cold blast of air hit Ben smack in the face. He didn't care; in fact, something cold was just what he needed. But then again, maybe not cold. Maybe straight up. Yeah. That sounded good.

Not a goddamned thing I can do about the fucking weather. Who gives a shit, anyway? Not the airport. Not the weatherman. Not the hospitals that didn't buy enough machines in the first place. Not the doctors and scientists who can't seem to come up with a cure for polio but sure as hell can invent an atomic bomb.

And, for reasons Ben didn't want to pretend to understand, obviously not God, either. So what the hell? Ben headed across the street and into Ernie's Bar, a neighborhood favorite.

After examining several different maps depicting geographic terrain and airfield configurations, Hank and Joe identified an airstrip on a map from the binder. Joe looked at Hank and asked, "You thinking what I'm thinking?" A smile grew on Hank's face and he answered, "Going to Plan B."

The plane lurched abruptly, which continued to worry Sam. The three men were jostled in their seats as the turbulence mounted. Hank and Joe held their control wheel loosely, while Sam strengthened his grip on each side of his seat.

"What's going on?" Sam asked, nervously.

"Plan B," Joe answered, giving a wink to Sam as he called the Republic Aviation Tower on the radio. "Republic Tower, this is Douglas two-niner-two-Bravo-Papa."

Only crackling static was heard in the headphones of Joe and Hank.

"Republic Tower, this is Douglas two-niner-two-Bravo-Papa."

Again, only static came back over the radio until, finally, "Two-niner-two-Bravo-Papa, we're awake."

"Requesting approval to land at Republic Field. Diverting from LaGuardia," Joe relayed over the radio.

The plane continued to lurch sharply, and Sam again tightened his grasp on his seat. Once more, only static was heard over the radio.

"Give 'em a few more minutes," Hank suggested. "We're pretty far out."

Static sputtered over the radio as the plane continued flying east. Joe waited a few more minutes before attempting to contact the tower again, when suddenly a voice came back with "Yeah, we got word that LaGuardia and Idlewild are out. Newark as well. You with Hank McGoran?"

"Affirmative. Falcon Air. Strictly a cargo flight. No commercial passengers. Medical airlift of an iron lung for a critical patient in New York General," Joe confirmed.

Static crackled again for a few seconds, then dead silence. Sam looked anxiously toward Hank, then to Joe, for some kind of indication, a look or word that would put him at ease. Another few seconds of dead silence passed, which seemed way too long for Sam to be comfortable with. Finally, a voice came back and affirmed, "Roger. You're good to land here. We'll stand by for your next contact."

"Roger. Confirming change of flight plan to Republic," Joe replied.

Hank nodded affirmatively to Joe, who returned it with a "got it" nod.

"Guess everything's gonna be okay now, right?" Sam asked, but quickly assumed he made a mistake and added, "I shouldn't have said that. Don't want to jinx—"

Sam abruptly stopped talking. He concentrated on taking slow, measured breaths and tried to focus on a row of metal rivets on the cabin floor. Joe and Hank looked at each other and shook their heads.

"Sam," Joe said calmly, leaning toward the nervous Kerner representative, "it's not our first time doing this kind of thing. We're good here."

Gino had given Ben a few minutes—enough of a lead, he thought, to provide Ben some breathing room, but Gino wasn't going to let his man go down in flames. Not alone, anyway. And no matter the resistance, outbursts, below-the-belt punches, or excuses Ben was going to launch at him, Gino was going to be there for Ben. When he opened the door to Ernie's, the first thing that hit him was the warm smell of beer and spirits that had been poured for years over the long, dark mahogany bar. Sure enough, there was Ben, seated by himself on a stool down at the far end of the bar. As Gino walked up, the bartender was pouring whiskey into a shot glass placed directly in front of Ben.

"Hey, Gino!" the bartender called out with a welcoming voice.

Gino nodded to the bartender and sat down on the stool next to Ben, then slid the shot glass away from his cabbie and toward himself.

"Make his a coffee," Gino told the bartender. "He's got more driving to do."

The bartender read Gino loud and clear and moved down the bar as Gino leaned in toward Ben.

"What are you doing, Ben?" Gino asked, his voice hushed. "What the *hell* are you thinking?"

Ben didn't look up, but simply folded his hands on top of the bar.

"I thought I could help her," Ben said. "Well, I guess I was wrong."

"So *this* is gonna make things better?" Gino asked, pointing with his thumb to the shot glass of whiskey.

"Nothing—nothing makes it better," Ben replied stoically.

Gino leaned away from the bar for emphasis and nodded his head.

"Ohhh, I see. So all of this back there," Gino stated, waving his arm in the direction of the garage, "all of the phone calls, the fundraising, finding the

213

machine—it was really all about *you*? You were thinking, '*This*—this is gonna make it all better'? 'This is gonna make up for the past'?"

"No," Ben stated, finally looking at Gino. "It—it was—"

"So that's what this was all about?" Gino asked candidly.

"I just wanted to help them—her," Ben replied, frustrated.

The bartender returned with a cup of hot coffee, set it down in front of Ben, and left the two men to themselves. Gino knew all too well the demons his driver was battling; he could see the pain in Ben's eyes, but as his friend, Gino knew he had to pull Ben out of himself and back into the world. Gino exhaled a deep breath and leaned close to Ben to speak.

"Let it go," Gino said discreetly but earnestly. "It was war. You were in active combat. There weren't supposed to be any civilians in that building. Only the enemy."

"Yeah, but I—"

"But nothing," Gino came back, taking a stronger stance. "Wallowing in self-pity, remorse, doesn't do anybody any good. Ben, you can't change the past. It's not about changing the past. It's about changing the future."

Ben didn't say anything, and Gino gave him a moment to contemplate and process what had just been said. The quiet was suddenly broken when Willy stormed in the door and shouted to them both.

"Gino! Ben! You gotta come take this call!" Willy exclaimed, out of breath. "They're gonna try and land at Republic Airport!"

Ben sat frozen on his stool, then slowly looked at Gino, back at Willy, and back again at Gino, who gave Ben a look of "What the hell are you still doing here?" Ben jumped up and ran out the door, with Willy following close behind. Not wanting a fine whiskey to go to waste, Gino downed the contents of the shot glass and headed toward the door, calling to the bartender on his way out, "Put it on my tab!"

"Yup!" the bartender answered with a nonchalant wave of his arm.

Behind the glass windows of the dispatch office, Willy listened intently to Ben, who was on the phone with an assistant administrator manning the telephone inside the control tower at Republic Airport. David scribbled notes on his pad as fast as he could to capture Ben's conversation. Gino had walked in and was checking a map on the wall, where Willy pointed out Republic Aviation's private airport, about thirty-five miles east of Manhattan.

"Uh-huh, but how are—if they can't—?" Ben stammered. "IL—what—?"

Ben listened intently, his brows tensed with anxiety as he tried to ascertain how problematic the flight and landing might be for his friend Joe, and delivery of the iron lung uncertain. Ben covered the mouthpiece of the receiver with his free hand and shared what the caller had told him.

"The plane's just over an hour out, but this guy says they're getting snow out there now too," Ben conveyed. "But the problem is, Republic's plant closes at five. Most of the staff has gone home for the day. They got one guy operating one snowplow. He's not gonna be able to keep up with it. They're trying to call another guy in—"

"What'd you say?" Gino asked.

David whispered to Willy, "Where's Republic Airport?"

Willy whispered back that it was pretty much in the middle of Long Island and pointed again to the map on the wall.

"The next-closest open airport is over an hour south of here, but that would mean another three-hour drive, at least, to get the respirator here. They'll have to—" Ben tried to explain.

"No! The thing about—you said they need one runway?" Gino interrupted Ben and added, "Just the one?"

"What?" Ben asked Gino.

"Ask them!" Gino repeated to Ben. "That they need just one runway cleared."

Ben took his hand off the mouthpiece and asked the caller, "Uh, you guys need just the one runway cleared, right?"

Ben nodded affirmatively to Gino, who quickly instructed Ben, "Tell 'em to hold the phone. My brother-in-law's with Public Works. They got extra snowplows all over the city. Let me get on the horn."

Gino picked up another phone and started dialing as Ben jumped in to inform the tower assistant there may be a solution. David wrote furiously on his pad, trying to keep up with the series of events unfolding in front of him, thinking to himself, *Man, there's a lot of pieces to this puzzle.* He thought about calling his assignment editor to update the man, but pictured his boss's usual aggravated reaction and decided against it. The rookie in David couldn't appreciate that if his editor had a clue of what was actually happening and the story's potential, the man would be doing backflips to get David whatever he needed.

"Hey, hold on, we're gonna see if we can get some city snowplows out there, pronto," Ben hurriedly conveyed on the phone, while looking at Gino for confirmation.

"Hey, Tony! It's Gino. Yeah, the commercial airports are closed, but they're gonna try and land at Republic out on Long Island," Gino said loudly into the receiver, hoping to be heard above the noises of the Public Works Yard on the other end, "but they could use some help clearing the runway. They only got one guy out there right now. But this is a—it's an official medical emergency airlift. Can you help 'em out?"

Ben watched Gino's eyes, looking to see a trace of hope—and then it came; a strong thumbs-up signal and a huge smile that lit up Gino's face. Ben's expression and voice shifted from worried to assured as he informed Republic Tower on the phone, "When the pilot radios you—just tell 'em—just tell 'em the runways will be cleared!"

Ben hung up the phone. His mouth opened, but the words didn't come out. David had been watching Ben, then looked at Willy and Gino. No one uttered a word. Gino looked at Ben for a few seconds, then broke the silence.

"Well, what the hell you standing around here for?" Gino shouted heartily. "Get a few of the guys and head out to Republic Airport! And follow the snowplows; they'll clear the way for you!"

Ben snapped out of his daze and looked at Gino, then Willy, then back at Gino and said, "Yeah!" and sprinted out of the office toward his cab.

"I'm going with him!" David shouted as he threw on his jacket, grabbed his pad and pen, pulled his half-written article out of Gino's typewriter, and ran out the door after Ben.

Gino jokingly threw his arms up and asked Willy, "Do we have to orchestrate everything around here?"

Willy said nothing—no need for a response—then he and Gino looked out the office window toward Ben, whom they heard calling to a couple of his fellow cabbies in the garage. The two drivers walked quickly over to Ben and David, where the four huddled and just as quickly dispersed. The other two drivers jumped into their cabs, backed out of their stalls, and followed behind Ben's cab as it headed out of the garage and into the night.

High above the ground, inside the cockpit of the Falcon Air C-47, Hank had just one word for Joe.

"Beautiful!"

"Nothin' like it," Joe concurred.

It was the treasured sight of millions of stars sparkling in the night sky. And with no moon in sight to impede its display, every star, no matter how small, dazzled the dark space it occupied.

As Hank and Joe observed the weakening front pass beneath them, an occasional break in the clouds exposed the lights of the cities on the ground below.

"We'll continue east just beyond the edge of the front, drop down, continue to the coast, and circle back," Hank said confidently to Joe, looking out of the windshield.

Inside the cabin, Sam Weinberg winced with each lurch of the plane as it flew through another patch of turbulence; nothing new to Hank and Joe, but Sam continued to worry with each bump. Keeping a relaxed hand on the plane's control wheel, Hank looked out of the window over the instrument panel and then out of his side window toward the ground. He took in a deep breath and slowly exhaled. An easy, relaxed smile grew on his face.

In the darkness above the Public Works Yard, the gentle snowfall was illuminated by several pole lights. Floating unseen from the blackened sky overhead, the feathery white puffs would suddenly appear as they breached the light beams hovering above the yard. Dump trucks, street sweepers, and snowplows were parked within a tall chain-link fence that was rimmed at the top with strings of barbed wire—a half-baked statement meant to dissuade adventurous youths. The fence had a wide entrance with two gates, broad enough for the heavy equipment to move in and out unimpeded. A yard office, not much more than an elaborate shed, painted a dark brick color with white-framed windows, stood at the right side of the entrance. The lights were on inside the little shack, and a small column of smoke rose from a narrow metal chimney on its flat roof. In the center of the yard, a group of eight or ten working-class men, truck drivers dressed in heavy jackets, knit caps, and work gloves, stood facing each other in a circle. Their breath was evident in the cold night air as they rubbed their hands together and balanced themselves from foot to foot, first right, then left, then right, then left, to keep themselves moving and stay warm. The yard supervisor was standing in the middle of the circle, addressing the group.

"I need volunteers. We got a medical emergency airlift. There's a plane in the air trying to bring an iron lung for a little girl at New York General," the supervisor explained. "LaGuardia, Idlewild, and Newark are closed, so they're gonna try to land at Republic Airport. But everybody's gone home. They got one guy out there to clear the runway, and they can't land until it's cleared. They need help. Snowplows and a small transport truck. Who's in?"

The truck drivers looked quickly from side to side at each other, then each raised a glove-covered hand.

The yard supervisor nodded his head to the men and shouted, "Let's go! We ain't got much time!"

The men turned and headed toward their respective trucks, climbed into their cabs, and one engine after another was engaged and revved up. The heavy snowplows began to lumber over the thin layer of snow covering the gravel-and-asphalt yard. The fresh powder emitted a dense crunching sound as it compressed under the weight of the machines and the mammoth tungsten tires. The thick tread of each heavy wheel imprinted a wide, patterned trail in the snow when the vehicles moved forward. The trucks began to pick up speed as they cleared the gate and headed out onto the street—a convoy of massive machines and humble do-gooders.

As evening settled inside New York General's Post-Isolation Recovery Room, *the sswhee-swoosh, sswhee-swoosh* pulse from the rows of respirators continued unnoticed. The rhythm was broken only by the occasional clank of a stainless steel plate cover being placed back inside a meal cart. Dinner or a drink concoction had been served earlier to those who could eat or ingest, and orderlies were helping nurses clear away any remnants that remained. John Williams had finished eating some time ago and was lying compliant on his back inside his respirator, his head protruding from the end facing the aisle. The nurse who'd fed him earlier had remarked to John that he'd eaten rather quickly tonight—or seemed to be in a hurry, anyway. She even asked if he was extra hungry for some reason. "No. I just want to be done," he'd told her in his usual cocky, indifferent manner. And the truth was, he wanted to be finished early to get on with his intentions, to go forward with his plan. If he didn't move forward, didn't maintain his momentum, he might change his mind. He was the master of his speed and timing at the moment and he didn't want to chance losing that control by having second thoughts—however rational they might be. And never mind that odd feeling pushing downward on his chest. Drive forward.

John turned his head from side to side, looking for a nurse. Finding none in sight, his first reaction was to call out, but instead he hesitated for a few minutes and gave hope one last chance to guide a nurse past his respirator, but no luck. He waited patiently for what seemed to him to be a reasonable amount of time and anxiously looked again, to his right, then his left, and back up toward the ceiling. He let out a loud sigh of frustration, his nostrils beginning to flare a bit, then erupted with a snap decision to shout out.

"Hello! Nurse!" John called out. "Can someone help me?"

John's voice echoed off the ceiling and hung over the heavy rhythmic hum from the respirators occupying the room. He listened intently for a response or the sound of approaching footsteps but heard nothing. The impetus to push forward drove him to forego patience, and he tried again.

"Nurse! Can you help me?" John yelled, hoping not to sound angry. "I need some help over here!"

Sswhee-swoosh, sswhee-swoosh, sswhee-swoosh drummed around him. He fought the pressure his own respirator forced down on his chest as he tried to inhale. He forced the air out of his lungs as he attempted to call out again, "Nurse—I—" But he stammered without air, and his voice trailed off. For a moment, he began to wane from his goal and felt the pull of defeat, always waiting in the wings with its seductive lure of comfort. His eyes looked down and his vision was filled with the sage-green metal disc circling the rubber collar around his neck. It sickened him. He raised his eyes up toward the white ceiling and found a small tan stain almost directly above him. He could focus on that, he thought to himself, and allowed himself the opportunity to regain strength by deliberately syncing his breathing with the machine's timing. The small round stain. Maybe the size of a quarter. Had he ever noticed it before? *Doesn't matter*, John thought to himself. He'd fought the machine and outsmarted it. *It doesn't rule me*, he realized. *It's a timing thing. I can anticipate and react. It can't.* John lay on his back, intently focused on his breathing, now gaining strength with each drum of the bellows feeding the rows of respirators around him. The air filled his lungs and centered his focus as oxygen seeped into his system, igniting his will. He felt stronger. Stronger in his chest. Stronger in his torso. And, suddenly, stronger *there*. It felt good. Whoa! It felt *great*. To feel *that* again.

He called out once more with renewed determination. And confidence.

"God*DAMN* it! CAN I GET SOME HELP OVER HERE?"

"Calm down, John!" he heard a nurse call out. "I'm coming!"

Shit! It was the young nurse. Why this time? On second thought, this might be fun.

John listened for her footsteps and realized she was approaching quickly. He attempted to restrain the wicked smile forming on his face, but he enjoyed anticipating what the young nurse's reaction might be. When she reached John's respirator, her eyes rapidly scanned his face and assessed his breathing, which seemed okay. She swiftly moved to the midsection of the iron lung to peer inside the two rectangular glass windows on its upper side. Immediately, her eyes widened, her jaw dropped, and she quickly backed away. Her cheeks flushed as she stood motionless and composed herself. She didn't look at John before she ran off to get a senior nurse.

John couldn't help but laugh, even if it was at her expense. He just couldn't help himself. It felt good, and in more ways than one. He knew he was gonna catch hell, but it was worth it. He tried to stifle his laughter when he heard the voice of an older female within range. Wait. Was she—*singing*? Lefty Frizzell's song?

"If you've got the money, honey, I've got the time—"

John didn't know whether to laugh or—but he knew this was too good to miss.

"We'll go honky-tonkin' and we'll have a time—"

The woman's voice was getting closer and closer and John tried, as best he could, to muffle his own laughter. He was practically spasming trying to hold his mouth closed, each laugh forcing short bursts of air out his nostrils. For some reason, he hoped whoever she was, she would appreciate his half-assed attempt to restrain himself.

"Well, howdy, cowboy!" Ruth Hoffman declared when she arrived at John's respirator, then added, "Is that a Colt .45 in your pocket or are you just happy to meet the new Nurse Supervisor of Post-Isolation Recovery?"

John laughed out loud.

"I'm Ruth Hoffman. Why don't you tell me who you are?"

John couldn't contain himself and managed only a "John—" before he burst out laughing again.

The senior nurse looked on top of the respirator and found the patient identification card, then stepped back closer to John and asked, "You ready to get back in the saddle, Mr. Williams? Well, now! This is your lucky day! I'm here to help you! Me and Clyde, the orderly, that is. What can we do for you?"

"No. I just—" John stammered, not able to keep himself from laughing. "I just—"

The seasoned nurse put her fists on her hips and planted her feet squarely. She wore a white nurse's hat that capped her short, curly reddish-blonde hair. The buttons on her white uniform dress were straining against her ample breasts, waist, and hips. Her short sleeves fitted tightly around her heavy upper arms. Her girth alone would have caused the toughest combat soldier to think twice before challenging her. She gave John a "look, buddy, my patience is limited" deadpan stare, then slowly scanned his respirator and the rows of respirators surrounding John's while she waited for him to pull himself together. When John's laughter subsided she looked him straight in the eye and asked, "What do you want?"

John relaxed his brow but not his tone, as habits are sometimes hard to break.

"I want you—" he rapidly fired, but then paused as he saw the look of resentment on the nurse's face. He reframed his statement.

"I—I need you—to help me," John said almost gently, then added, "please."

John watched the nurse's expression dissolve into one of understanding. She even smiled at him and reassured him, leaned in close and softly told him, "Okay. Hold on. I will." She moved to the right side of his respirator, scanned the readings on the pressuriza- tion dials, then looked John in the eye and nodded. He smiled back, and she began adjusting dials and levers down on the iron lung. The clink and clank of metal clips was faintly heard as the drumming of bellows rippled down the row of respirators, past the nurse's desk, and up against the two doors at the entrance. There, the rhythmic sound was muffled and subdued by the heavy wood before its pulse squeezed its way through the small space between the doors and seeped into the hospital corridor.

CHAPTER 15

IN SIGHT

Sam Weinberg looked at his watch, and at his shoes, and down the middle of the long, open cabin of the C-47, where the pediatric iron lung stood by itself, securely strapped down in the middle of the fuselage. He thought about unloading the machine, getting it back up on a truck and finally installed at the hospital. He ran the setup procedures through his mind, even imagining the sound of the bellows forcing the rise and fall in air pressure. As the pilots maneuvered the plane over the coast, turned, and descended below the clouds, Sam continued to calm himself with slow, purposeful breaths. He'd just about succeeded, as the turbulence had abated some time ago, but he was soon to be unnerved by a different jolt.

"Looks like the power's out in pockets down there," Hank remarked to Joe.

Joe looked out of his side window, checked the ground below, and replied with a simple "Yup."

"Look over there—no lights," Hank commented, pointing with his left hand toward a darkened area on the ground below.

Sam's uneasiness ramped up and he stretched forward in his seat, leaned toward the cockpit, and anxiously asked, "No lights?"

As he unwrapped a stick of gum, Hank turned to Sam and Joe and, with a smile, asked, "Where's Rudolf when you need him?"

"Republic Tower, this is Douglas two-niner-two-Bravo-Papa," Joe called over the radio.

Sam watched Joe's face as the copilot waited for a reply. Sam didn't like the fact that it always seemed to take so long to receive one.

"Republic Tower, this is Douglas two-niner-two-Bravo-Papa," Joe called again over the radio. "One thousand feet over Long Island for landing, Republic."

"Two-niner-two-Bravo-Papa, we've been expecting you. Wind is one-eighty at ten runway nineteen make right traffic," came back over the radio, followed by, "And just a heads-up, we're moving to generator power. It'll be up before you make your turn. You have the runway in sight?"

Sam watched as Hank and Joe craned their necks peering out of their respective windows, looking forward and back behind the plane as if searching the ground below, when, matter-of-factly, Hank stated, "Well, look at that, will ya? They got the runway lit up with—are those—car lights? Trucks?" he asked, turning to Joe for confirmation. "This oughta be interesting."

"Car lights?" Sam asked, nervously.

"Uh, something like that. I'll be damned," Hank answered coolly. "Let's say hello."

"Sam," Joe said calmly, turning toward the fidgety salesman, "we got this."

On the frosty ground below, the headlights from six snowplows, two large dump trucks, and three City Cabs were in place, facing the runway on both sides, lighting runway 1-19 to be seen clearly from the sky. Several of the men had stepped out of their vehicles, leaving engines revving, lights on, exposing their frosty breaths in the cold night air. Dressed in thick wool jackets snapped up to their necks, the men hunched their shoulders up to their ears, trying to keep themselves warm in the bitter cold blowing across the open airfield. Some waved their arms back and forth across their torsos, trying to keep the circulation flowing in their limbs. Every head was covered in a tweed flat cap, fedora, or knit beanie, pulled down over the ears as far as it would go. One of the men suddenly spotted the Falcon Air cargo plane as it flew low overhead, making its pass above the runway. He pointed his gloved hand toward the sky, yelling out, "There it is!" The men broke into a cheer and waved to the plane above as Joe blinked the wing lights, signaling the crew's "thumbs-up" to the men's unconventional and resourceful lighting of the runway. Inside the cockpit, Hank and Joe smiled at each other as they headed northeast and began the bank into the turn.

"Two-niner-two-Bravo-Papa," Joe called into the radio. "Those are some unusual runway lights."

"Complete your turn and head due south to runway one-nineteen," a female voice came back over the radio. "You'll see the lights back on when you complete your turn."

Hank's jaw dropped, which didn't slip past Joe, who shot his pilot a quizzical look.

"A female?" Sam blurted out. "Was that a female?!"

"Y-y-y-yeah," Hank answered, slowly, then told Sam, "Uh, Republic Aviation hired a lot of females—during the war—still does in its plant. They, uh, had women in the control towers—some of the best—"

Hank turned to Joe and asked, somewhat bewildered, "Was that—*Charlene?*"

"Charlene?" Joe asked over the radio, then added, "South to one-nineteen."

"We've got you in sight," the female voice stated over the radio. "The tower will be on your right. I'm sure Hank remembers."

"Roger," Joe replied, looking quickly at Hank, then added, "he remembers."

Joe gave the raised eyebrow look to Hank, who took a deep breath, sighed, and told his copilot, "Let's take her in."

The C-47 completed its wide turn south, Joe lowered the landing gear, and Hank headed the plane toward a sweet spot inside the approach end of the runway.

"Two-niner-two-Bravo-Papa descending to five hundred feet," Joe stated to the tower, "and those approach lights look beautiful."

"Copy," Charlene replied. "You're looking good. Right where you should be. Just keep coming."

On the ground below, Ben and another cabbie, Phil Morton, stood outside Ben's cab, parked at the other end of the runway near an open hangar. As the C-47 approached to land, Phil looked at Ben and told him, "You did it, Ben!"

"*We* did it," Ben told Phil, and the two men embraced. "I'm gonna run inside and call and tell 'em it's here!"

Ben ran off into the hangar as Phil, wiping his nose with a handkerchief, watched the cargo plane land. At the sound of tires skidding on the runway, the truck and cab drivers broke into another throng of loud cheers and whistles. The sound of the mighty engines roared past them as Hank masterfully brought the awesome force and forward speed of more than 20,000 pounds of metal, rubber, and fuel to a smooth, picture-perfect landing. Simultaneously, he engaged the brakes to bear down, and the C-47 began to wane in speed and force as it progressed down the runway. Too excited to hesitate, the truck and cab drivers jumped into their vehicles and headed out, one after another, behind the plane as it continued the final leg of its journey.

Hank and Joe brought the aircraft to a stop, then taxied it for several hundred feet, bringing it to a parking position on the tarmac outside the lighted hangar. Sam finally released a heavy sigh of relief just as Hank turned and wished him "Happy Hanukkah!"

"Hank," Sam stated slowly and deliberately, "that was a good landing."

"Any landing you walk away from is a good landing," Hank replied, still chewing gum, and shot Joe a knowing wink.

"Hey, I'm gonna go with Ben to the hospital," Joe told Hank and Sam. "You both wanna ride with us?"

"That's fine with me," Sam answered. "I just wanna make sure they get the machine strapped down in the truck before we head out. Okay?"

"Of course," Joe said. "So do we. What about you, Hank?"

"Uh, I'll go take care of the flight report, and, uh, I think I'm gonna check on some of the guys, uh, here," Hank answered Joe. "You know, catch up on old times."

"Yeah," Joe replied, then asked wryly, "Any of them guys named Charlene, by any chance?"

Hank figured the cat was out of the bag, and a smile emerged as he shut down the engines and stowed his radio headset.

"Come on, Sam, let's grab our gear and get this show on the road," Joe suggested, then turned to Hank and asked, "You'll file the flight plan for tomorrow morning, right? We gotta be in the air by eight if we're gonna get back to Florida on time."

"You got it," Hank assured him. "I'll be here, bright-eyed and bushy tailed!"

"Be sure you get a good night's sleep, will ya?" Joe suggested.

"You betcha!" Hank assured him with a big smile.

Dr. Neill Friedman was standing outside the nurses' station on the third floor at New York General Hospital when a young nurse leaned over the counter and handed a telephone receiver to him. She explained the caller was Ben Wilson, "calling from the airport." The nurse sat back down at her station but watched the doctor's face light up when he learned the news from the caller on the phone. Neill covered his right ear to better hear as noisy carts and gurneys were wheeled up and down the hospital corridor behind him. He looked down the hallway to his left, and saw Virginia Douglas approaching, and motioned to her to come quickly, mouthing the words, "They landed!" Elated, Virginia clasped her hands together, raising them in the "victory" sign. She and the nurse exchanged joyous smiles in silence, listening earnestly to hear the doctor's conversation with Ben.

"I don't know how you did it," the doctor told Ben, exuberantly. "Not in this snow, when everything's closed. It's a miracle!"

Dr. Friedman covered the mouthpiece with his right hand and told Virginia and the nurse that the respirator was being unloaded and they would head out soon.

Virginia gently shook her head in gratitude and said to herself under her breath, "Benny. Imagine that."

The doctor listened intently to Ben and couldn't help but gush, "Great! Ben, I—I don't know what to say. What you and your fellow—it's—"

Dr. Friedman paused and listened while Ben estimated the arrival time at the hospital. He took a deep breath and exhaled, then told Ben simply, "Okay. We'll be ready for you."

The doctor handed the telephone receiver back to the station nurse, then, smiling with obvious excitement, told Virginia, "I'm going to go prep our patient!"

The young nurse sat patiently until the doctor walked away, then stood up and leaned discreetly over the counter toward Virginia, who immediately picked up on the nurse's signal.

"Mrs. Douglas?" the nurse whispered.

"Yes?" Virginia answered, moving close so the nurse might speak freely.

"What did you say to John Williams?" the nurse inquired, genuinely impressed. "He's—he's like a new patient!"

Virginia allowed herself a small laugh and quietly told the nurse, "Sometimes you have to speak to teenagers in their own language. I wonder if he's met the new nurse supervisor down there. He'll have met his match." The two women raised their eyebrows and exchanged an understanding glance.

Fred Cromwell, a longtime aircraft mechanic at Republic Aviation, had stayed on after work, wanting to be a part of the excitement and to offer his help in any way he could. He answered the phone at the desk inside Hangar 21 and told the caller that the iron lung was being unloaded off the plane as he spoke. He was explaining to the caller about the generators being up for maybe another hour when the caller interrupted and asked if Fred could locate someone—one of the cab drivers.

"Ben Wilson?" Fred confirmed with the caller, quickly adding, "Sure! Let me check."

Fred spun his chair around and wheeled it a few feet to a better vantage point to see the hangar entrance. He held the telephone receiver away from his face and called to someone who had just walked out of a phone booth outside the bay doors.

"Hey! Your name Ben?" Fred yelled. "Ben Wilson?"

Ben spun around but continued walking backward away from the hangar as he called back, "Yeah! I'm Ben!"

"This guy says he needs to talk to you!" Fred shouted across the hangar.

Ben stopped, feigned a sigh of frustration, and headed inside the hangar to take the call. As he approached Fred, the mechanic stretched out his arm and handed Ben the receiver, telling him, "Says his name is Gino, that you know him." Ben grabbed the receiver with gusto and beamed as he relayed the good news.

"Hey, Gino! It's here! They made it!" Ben enthusiastically told his boss. "You wouldn't believe what these guys did, but it's great! Just great! They're loading it now and we'll be heading out."

As he turned back to the paperwork on his desk, Fred couldn't help sensing the elation in Ben's voice; it was a good feeling to know the hard work of so many had paid off, especially when it meant the life of a child could be saved. And then, just as the excitement had lifted his spirits, he noticed Ben had stopped talking, and Fred began to feel the silence—the odd and distinct sensation when the surrounding air suddenly becomes heavy with disappointment. He sensed Ben was being hit with the type of letdown that takes hold before the unprepared poker face can calibrate, and he wanted to give Ben a moment before turning back toward him. Fred waited another minute, then slowly rotated his chair and looked up at Ben. The frustration, a hint of pain, was evident in the cabbie's eyes as Gino's words gurgled from the phone's earpiece. Ben caught Fred's stare for a second but quickly turned away and focused on the truck parked just outside the hangar, engine humming and ready to roll, with the iron lung secured safely inside.

"But I—everybody's set to go," Ben tried to tell Gino. "I was gonna drive with—"

As he listened to Gino on the phone, Ben watched the men outside giving each other the high sign as they prepared to depart. Fred observed Ben and saw the look of disillusion on his face. He looked away as he heard the enthusiasm drain from Ben's voice, disheartened into compliance.

"All right. Okay, Gino, I got it," Ben acquiesced as he turned away from the hangar opening and began searching under his jacket, in his flannel shirt pocket, for a pen. "Gimme a second. Let me grab a piece of paper."

Anticipating the need, Fred had pushed a small yellow notepad toward the corner of his desk. The gesture was accepted and appreciated by Ben.

"Okay, Gino, go ahead," Ben said stoically as he cradled the phone receiver between his left ear and shoulder and began writing. "Five twenty-six Sycamore, apartment eight, but pickup at the back door. In the alley."

Fred saw that Ben was expressionless as he continued holding the phone to his ear and patiently processed Gino's instructions. He watched Ben close his eyes in defeat—perhaps it was even despair—as the cabbie absorbed the words he was hearing. When Ben opened his eyes, he took a deep breath, letting the air in his lungs escape slowly, and with it, any delusion of self-achievement. Fred read it as the look of discouragement—or, worse, the loss of hope.

"Hey. Gino. Don't worry about it," Ben reassured his boss, his voice flat. "I'll be there."

Ben was about to place the receiver down, but for some reason he held it for a few seconds just above its cradle and exhaled a small cynical laugh before setting it down. Fred had already peeled the top sheet of yellow paper off the notepad and quietly handed it to Ben. He didn't want to say a word before Ben did.

Ben stared at the black phone on the desk while he asked Fred, "Um—would you mind telling the pilot, Joe Martinez, when he comes in here looking for me—" Then Ben raised his eyes, looked directly at Fred, and added, "Tell him I had to go pick up a fare and for him to catch a ride with somebody else. I'll meet him at the hospital right after."

"Sure thing," Fred assured Ben. "Don't worry about it. Joe Martinez. I'll make sure I let him know."

"Thanks. I gotta get in my cab," Ben said, then turned and, without fanfare, walked out of the hangar and disappeared in the darkness.

CHAPTER 16

FIGHTING DEMONS

At the nurses' station near the Polio Isolation Ward, Dr. Neill Friedman and Virginia Douglas were cautiously weighing the outlook for the young patient, Rachel Hall. Hospital staff hurried along the corridor behind the doctor and Virginia; orderlies rolled gurneys and a noisy cart along the speckled tile floor. Two nurses seated at the station were carefully verifying patients' prescription charts. All of that activity was merely background noise to Virginia, who, at the moment, had only one concern.

"Is she going to make it?" she asked Dr. Friedman directly.

The doctor took a deep breath and exhaled before crossing his arms across his chest.

"To be honest, she may not," he answered frankly. "We've put her in an oxygen tent, but her diaphragm is barely functioning."

The frustration of being so close to a life-saving solution but unable to abate the progression of the disease was left at a quiet understanding between Virginia and the doctor. They both had enough years under their belt, seen enough children fade away before their eyes, and understood that polio would pick and choose its own victims. There was no cure, only treatments. Drama and anger wouldn't change that fact, at this moment, in this hospital. There was—only hope. As if administering an order with a dose of optimism, Virginia confidently stated, "She's just got to hang in there."

"You can tell her I did," Megan's voice called out from behind them.

Virginia and Dr. Friedman turned around and, to their surprise and delight, saw Megan standing upright and Valerie behind the empty wheelchair. Megan began walking, albeit struggling, but walking, for several steps toward them. The sense of accomplishment, bolstered with both surprise and relief, beamed from Megan's face; her eyes were wide with pure joy, even astonishment, at her own efforts being realized.

"I don't know if it will help," Megan continued, her own achievement reinforcing her hopes for the little girl. "But tell her to—to try—and be strong. Because— it's—so many people are rooting for her—to succeed. She just has to—to try."

Leaning into each forced step, Megan moved closer to Virginia and Dr. Friedman, who instinctively extended his arms to support the triumphant student. Megan grabbed the doctor's forearms and laughed out loud with pleasure, pride, and that special sense of joy when will triumphs over fear.

"I'll do you one better, Megan," Dr. Friedman told her. "When Rachel's out of isolation, you can tell her yourself. She'd much rather hear it from you than an old fuddy-duddy like me."

"Ohh—kay," Megan said, gladly and somewhat out of breath, as Valerie and Virginia moved in to help her back into her wheelchair. Virginia and Valerie exchanged a "life is good" look with each other as Megan repositioned herself.

"Congratulations, young lady! I look forward to seeing more of that," Dr. Friedman told Megan, then addressed the group. "Ladies, I'll leave you to celebrate amongst yourselves."

Virginia and Dr. Friedman gave each other a positive nod before the doctor turned and headed down the hallway. Virginia leaned down and hugged Megan tightly, then whispered in her ear, "Well done, Megan!" The two women held the embrace, understanding the significance of the milestone for Megan. As the noise and bustle of the busy hospital emerged from the background, Megan and Virginia released their grasp. Virginia stood upright, beaming with the contentment that comes from witnessing a student's success. Valerie sensed the moment to open the conversation.

"She wanted to surprise you," Valerie revealed. "She's been working on this diligently."

"This is fantastic news, Megan!" Virginia exclaimed, then asked, "Does your mother know?"

Megan shook her head to indicate "no."

"But she will," Valerie interjected. "She'll be here soon."

Virginia noticed a fast-moving orderly with a loaded meal cart coming up quickly behind Valerie and Megan and gently guided the women to the other side of the hallway. The orderly whizzed past with the cart, wheels jiggling and plates and utensils clanging, and headed toward another wing.

"Megan, you did say that nice cab driver—what's his name?—is going to be here too, didn't you?" Valerie asked.

"Yeah, he is. His name's Ben," Megan answered and pointed out, "He's the one who got the iron lung here."

"We found out he was a former student of yours, Mrs. Douglas," Valerie remarked. "Didn't we, Megan?"

"Yeah! You've been teaching a really long time, Mrs. Douglas!" Megan shot back. As soon as the words left her mouth, she abruptly realized her faux pas and sheepishly sank back in her chair while Virginia gave her a sharp raised eyebrow.

"I think she's ready to go home—*now!*" Virginia joked to Valerie. "I don't know if I can take much more of her."

"Oh—Mrs. Douglas, I didn't mean—" Megan woefully offered, trying to recover. "I— I—"

Virginia just shook her head and rolled her eyeballs in jest.

"Come on, Megan," Valerie jumped in. "We'd better get out of here before we're thrown out!"

Virginia cracked a smile, to the relief of Megan, who couldn't help release a little laugh herself as Valerie began to wheel her away.

A few miles from Brooklyn, on a dark two-lane road, two police vehicles escorted a procession of snowplows, trucks, and two City Cabs toward New York General Hospital. Occasionally, the lead police vehicle sounded its siren, emitting a lonesome, shrill wave over the blanket of newly fallen snow covering each side of the roadway. The siren repeated, announcing the urgency of the mission of the small, robust band of vehicles bouncing and plodding its way into the city.

Joe and David rode in the cab with one of the truck drivers; David in the middle and Joe riding shotgun. The three men had been quiet for a few minutes when the word "shit" rolled out of David's mouth. It had suddenly dawned on the young reporter why Ben had chosen to pick up a cab fare rather than drive to the hospital with the group.

"What?" Joe asked him, concerned.

"Damn! I just realized what Ben's doing," David replied, somewhat humbled.

"Figured," Joe remarked, not surprised. "It's what he does, man."

"Yeah, but he worked so hard for this," David emphasized. "He should be here—when it arrives at the hospital. He should—oh man!"

"He's doin' what he needs—what he *wants* to do," Joe pointed out. "Like he said, he'll meet us at the hospital."

David stared out the front window, letting out a sigh of disappointment for a guy he barely knew, a man he reasoned had to be feeling confused, frustrated, and—*shit!* David reprimanded himself. *What am I doing?* He shrugged it off and reestablished the safe boundaries of the reporter-interviewee separation. *Fine. Guy's gonna do what he's gonna do. Don't get involved. Just report it,* he instructed himself, forcing the self-survival impulse to override the desire to give a rat's ass about someone else. The cheap, quick-fix act of conjured justification, always at the ready to defend doing the less-than-noble thing. Always there, always handy, always available to convince—and so effective at keeping dormant the lifelong seed of regret.

"Hey, look! It's stopped snowing!" the driver of the truck called out to Joe and David.

"Naturally!" Joe remarked jokingly. "Couldn't have done this an hour ago, when we needed to land, huh?"

Ben steered his cab cautiously as he made his way along a quiet, darkened street in Brooklyn. His hands held the oversized steering wheel purposefully as he maneuvered the icy streets, his tires crunching and compacting the newly fallen snow. Up ahead on the left, the lights inside a small neighborhood store brightened the corner of the street. Ben slowed down and looked at the store's window, where a neon sign with rounded, glowing letters spelled out the word "Liquor." Just before he reached the corner, Ben brought the cab to a stop and pulled over to the curb. He looked over at the sign and its soft, inviting pinkish-orange hue. He hesitated for a brief moment, thinking he shouldn't get out, but quickly convinced himself—*I could use a little help, so what the hell?*—and threw his door open. He ran across the street, almost losing his footing in the slippery snow, and dashed inside the store. In less than five minutes, his dark figure appeared, silhouetted from the store lights behind him. He pushed the door open with his forearm and was out on the icy sidewalk, his frosty breath caught in the glow from the streetlight above. He was clutching a small brown bag at its neck. He hurried back across the street to his cab and shoved the bag into his jacket pocket as he opened the car door. The twisted neck of the bag protruded from his pocket as he jumped back in behind the wheel. He slammed his door shut and took off, his tires skidding in the snow as he gained traction, trying desperately to make up for lost time.

At the next stop sign Ben realized he'd pulled up a little too fast when he abruptly applied the brakes and the cab started to slide on the snow and ice through the intersection. Luckily, the streets were empty, but that didn't make him feel any better. He slowed down a bit, at least as much as he felt he could, though he needed to get to where he needed to be. A few more blocks, then left, then down the alley. He approached the next intersection a little more gingerly. And the next. And the next, where he turned left. Halfway down the block, on his right, he saw the alleyway where he needed to turn. He brought the cab to a slow stop and turned into the narrow lane. It wasn't much wider than his cab, and any decent-sized truck would have difficulty squeaking past a garbage can if it had to do so.

The alleyway was lit up by a single, lone light on a pole; not a streetlight, really. More like an ordinary household door light someone had rigged up and attached to a telephone pole that had been there for some time. Ben rolled the cab forward until he reached the back side of the apartment building where his fare resided. The building's rear door was made of metal, painted a dark forest green, and was recessed a few feet from the side of the building. The doorway was dimly lit by a small single bulb. It looked as if its glass covering had gone missing quite a while ago. Ben turned off the car's motor and stared at the door; both his hands were gripping the steering wheel. He didn't notice his breathing becoming anxious, but as his heavy, deep breaths flooded the inside of his car, the warm, humid air began to fog up the cab's cold windows. It made the light in the alleyway appear to have a fuzzy halo surrounding it. Ben's heart was beating against the inside of his chest in rapid fire—*pow-pow, pow-pow, pow-pow, pow-pow!*—as he withdrew into the quiet cocoon the cloudy windows had created around him.

Ben closed his eyes and in it came—the faint sound of gunfire popping, then mortar fire ricocheting in the distance. He saw the cloud of smoke rise in front of him, wisps of gray dust floating away gradually, in slow motion, as if giving time for the viewer to prepare for the horror behind the veil. The face of the young soldier stunned by remorse, wailing. The raw voice of the other soldier screaming.

"HOLY CHRIST!"

"OH MY GOD, SERGEANT! THEY'RE KIDS! AND THEIR MOTHER! THEY'RE ALL DEAD!"

Ben remembered shouting back at the young infantrymen.

"SOLDIERS! GET AHOLD OF YOURSELVES! YOU WERE ORDERED TO DO IT! IT'S ON ME! NOT YOU! GO AROUND AND SECURE THE BACK OF THE BUILDING! BOTH OF YOU! NOW! I'LL DEAL WITH THIS."

Ben remembered the sight of the two young men, unable to move—then suddenly snapping out of it, nervously nodding and shaking their heads to affirm his order, then watching them turn and run behind the building. After they were out of sight, he remembered turning slowly back toward the hallway. Black powder burns shot up both sides of the narrow corridor. An abstract circle of blood, about the size of an orange, was plastered on the wall on the right, about a third of the way up, the pattern reflecting the velocity of the impact. Some of the blood had begun to run down the wall; it stood out against the black. There was a stunning amount of blood strewn on the opposite wall. Splattered on the floor. Everywhere. Bits of shredded flesh. A small hand with only a thumb. He wanted to believe the mother had tried to shield her young son, a boy, who couldn't have been more than five or six. His stomach had been ripped open by the blast. He was splayed on his side and bowels were hanging from the bloodied waist area of his pants. There was a baby. The mother must have turned away with the baby, who'd been thrown ten feet farther down the hallway by the blast, its head covered in blood. Ben remembered squatting down next to the young mother's body. She was wearing a pale blue apron and blood was pooling in it. He noticed her light brown hair was pinned into a loose bun when he checked to feel her neck for a pulse. There wasn't one. He checked the boy's. He knelt down next to the baby and placed his hand on the infant's chest. And knew all of it was pointless. He couldn't stay. He had to lead his men. The carnage around him, and its author, forever seared into his memory.

A single heavy drop of moisture formed on the inside of the windshield, near the top, and slowly trickled down the glass, leaving a clear transparent line, allowing the light from the pole in the alleyway to shine into Ben's eyes. He used the fingers on his right hand to rub the windshield in a quick circular motion, wiping away the fog and giving him a clear shot of the alleyway, the apartment building, and its back door. He talked himself through measured, purposeful breaths to slow down his breathing and leaned back in his seat, cracking the driver's window open to inhale and fill his lungs with crisp, fresh air.

The rush of the cold had a sobering effect and the flashback faded. Ben took hold of the cab's door handle and was out of his car, headed toward the apartment building. When he reached the door, he noticed it was dented on the lower half, as if a heavy piece of furniture or a vehicle had hit it by accident. He hesitated before turning the handle and instead rapped with his knuckles on the metal sheet. The *ping, ping, ping* of his knock echoed in the doorway, and before he could put his hands on his hips, Ben heard it being unlocked from inside. The bulb overhead revealed the face of a frightened young mother, maybe in her twenties, holding a young boy, listless, in her arms. The image made Ben's heart sink. He'd seen it too many times this year.

"I'm Mrs. Lewis—uh, Amy," the woman said. "I need to get my son, Scott, to the hospital. He—he's—he's really sick."

Ben figured the mother had been waiting for him for a while; her coat was on and she was wearing a hat. Her young son was wearing cowboy-print pajamas under his coat. His mother had managed to put a pair of moccasin slippers on Scott's small feet. His short blond hair was pressed flat against his head, as if he'd been sleeping. He wasn't moving.

"Right. That's where we're going. Here, let me take him while you climb in," Ben told the young mother.

Amy Lewis followed as Ben instructed, opened the back door, and scooted herself toward the center of the rear seat. For some reason, she noticed the seat's black leather was worn and slightly cracked near the edge. Ben lifted the boy into the seat, laying him so his mother could hold him in her lap, then closed the door. He ran around to the driver's door, jumped in behind the wheel, and headed carefully out of the alley and toward New York General.

CHAPTER 17

IN THE AIR

Inside the emergency room in New York General Hospital, the intense bright lights oddly emphasized the sharpness of the room's angles, equipment, and noise. A white curtain, somewhat dull from age, hung from the ceiling and hovered just about a foot from the floor. The curtain cordoned off a small area where six-year-old Scott Lewis lay on his back on a bed. The bed had wheels and was equipped with metal safety bars; one had been lowered on one side. Two nurses in masks and gloves moved around the bed and were focused on taking the boy's vital signs. Scott's mother sat anxiously on the edge of a single chair, leaning from side to side to keep an eye on her son as the two nurses moved back and forth. She thought that Scott would have been afraid of, or would have at least protested, the poking and pulling by strangers. What she failed to understand was that her son, at this stage of the virus, was far beyond the ability to experience fear. The effects of the disease rendered Scott too exhausted to care about what was going on around him or to him. The poliovirus now inside the young boy had taken the attention away from his body's instinct for concern about surroundings. The six-year-old's small body was now focused on one internal effort: a frantic attempt to produce enough antibodies to outpace the more powerful, more committed virus from rapidly multiplying itself. The sobering reality was that Scott's young immune system was no match. The potent, intelligent invader had already made its way toward specialized cells in Scott's intestines, successfully breached his bloodstream, and was engaged in an unstoppable systematic assault on his central nervous system.

"Mrs. Lewis, we're going to have to remove these now and discard them. We'll put a hospital gown on him now," one of the nurses informed Scott's mother, who watched as the masked and gloved nurses removed her son's pajamas, underwear, and slippers and placed them in a covered metal bin. Amy Lewis didn't think they would take Scott's little coat as well, and she quickly caught herself, keeping an instinctive wail in check with a sudden deep inhale, as she watched the nurse fold it, place it in the bin with his other clothes, and seal the lid shut. The panic of fear forged its way up her back as she sat in her chair, her lips quivering between short, deliberate exhales of air as her brain allowed the processing of measured doses of reality.

The nurses quickly removed their gloves, discarded them, washed their hands, and put on new gloves. One of the nurses dressed Scott in a fresh children's hospital gown, turning him on his side to tie the gown in the back. The other nurse readied a syringe on a white porcelain tray, laying it carefully next to several small medical instruments, a bottle, and several puffy white cotton balls. The nurse who was dressing Scott positioned him on his side, using a bolster to hold him in place, and raised his knees up toward his chest. Amy thought about how small and helpless her son appeared in the stark bed and noticed the metal bar near Scott's back was now lowered. She looked at her son, who was lying perfectly still, and thought, *He's not complaining, not crying, not resisting in any way. Scotty's like this only when he's sleeping. But he's not asleep. His eyes are open. Oh God, oh God, oh God, please help him!*

And the negotiations began.

The curtains were quickly pulled aside by Dr. Sean Morrow, in his early forties with round wire-rimmed glasses, who looked at Mrs. Lewis first, then Scott, then the two nurses. He seemed hurried, Amy noticed, as he quickly scooted around the side of the bed where Scott's small back had been exposed by the nurse.

"Go ahead," he instructed the nurse closest to Scott and nodded to her.

The nurse used one of the white cotton balls and wiped a small area on Scott's back. She placed the cotton ball in a small bowl, then stepped back. The doctor picked up the first of two syringes on the tray and moved close to Scott.

"You might feel a little pinch, Scott, but just for a moment," the doctor told the boy. "This will take only a second."

Mrs. Lewis watched from her chair, straining to observe her son's face to see how painful the procedure was for him, but his eyes were closed. He emitted a small sound, not quite strong enough for a whimper; just a small, faint sound that his mother would recognize as Scott being too weak to object. The procedure seemed to be taking a long time, she thought, but soon realized it was over quickly.

"All done," the doctor said as he raised the second syringe and handed it to the nurse, who placed it back on the tray and covered it with a neatly folded sterile cloth. The other nurse unwrapped a small bandage and affixed it over the site where fluid had been withdrawn from Scott's spine, reassuring Scott with another "all done" and telling him she would move him to his back, where he would be more comfortable. Mrs. Lewis realized the doctor was standing in front of her. In the brief second their eyes met, she couldn't identify if his look had any shred of encouragement in it. He quickly half smiled, but was that encouragement? Or was it nervousness? Or was it just what doctors did at this time? In these cases? *I should stand up*, Scott's mother thought and instinctively stood up, hoping for some signal or clarification, perhaps guidance, or even a social clue from the doctor of what her next move was supposed to be.

"It'll be a while, Mrs. Lewis," the doctor informed her. "You'll have to wait outside now."

The other nurse was already waiting at the doctor's side and escorted Amy Lewis out of the room. She heard the doctor behind her tell the nurse at Scott's bedside, "Get him in isolation. Tell them I'll be right in."

In the bitter cold, under the glare of the hospital's entrance lights, a noisy caravan of police vehicles, trucks, and cabs lumbered its way onto the driveway at

New York General and came to a stop at the curb. An anxious group of newspaper reporters, photographers, and hospital staff, shivering in the wintry night air, converged on the drivers as they emerged from their cars and stepped down from their truck cabs. Flashbulbs popped and spontaneous cheers and applause erupted from the crowd when the back doors of the transport truck opened to reveal the iron lung inside. David Lindsey found a photographer from his paper, then spotted Mike Reilly at the front of the herd. Joe Martinez and Sam Weinberg were joined by an ad hoc group of cabbies, snowplow drivers, and orderlies eager to offload the respirator. Another cabbie got out of his vehicle and walked over to one of the policemen who was watching the iron lung roll down a ramp from the truck.

"Who sent you guys?" the cabbie cheerfully asked the officer.

"Captain Ruganni, Gino's younger brother," the cop answered.

"Huh! Figures. Tell him thanks!" the cabbie suggested, then, out of the corner of his eye, spotted Ben Wilson walking up the sidewalk behind the officer and called out to him.

"Hey Ben! They made it!" the enthusiastic cabbie shouted. "Where've you been? The thing's here!"

Ben nodded, forced a smile, gave a thumbs-up to his fellow driver, and headed to join Joe and the group unloading the iron lung. Ben's appearance on the scene was soon observed by David, who couldn't resist the urge to feel a little relief when he saw that the main subject of his story had made it to the hospital.

"Hey! Ben!" David shouted as he hurried toward the cabbie. Ben gave David a nod and a flat "hey" and the two walked together toward Joe and Sam. David was charged up, and as soon as he and Ben reached the group, he couldn't help but blurt out, "You guys did it! How does it feel?"

Joe put an arm around Ben and pointed at him with his other hand, remarking, "Here's the guy who did it, right here: Ben. He did it!"

"I didn't do anything," Ben said somberly. "Come on. Let's get this thing inside."

The sound of pops and bursts of light from photographers' flashbulbs flooded the group as several men rolled the iron lung toward the hospital entrance doors, held open by two orderlies. The bright lights from the lobby illuminated the metal respirator as the large, cumbersome dolly was maneuvered through the open double doors. Ben, Joe, Sam, and David followed the unit inside, along with Mike Reilly from the *Times*.

Inside the entrance lobby, hospital staff cheered and applauded as the device rolled past them. Virginia Douglas observed the procession from the far side of the lobby, along with Rachel Hall's parents, who watched anxiously—and hopefully—as Dr. Friedman joined Sam for the last segment of the respirator's journey. Mike Reilly spotted Virginia from the entrance and joined her, along with Ben and the others. Virginia seized the opportunity to showcase her former students.

"Ben, Joe—these are Rachel's parents," Virginia indicated, gesturing toward the Halls. Mrs. Hall hurried toward Ben and embraced him, then Joe.

"Thank you—words can never—" Rachel's mother tried to say, fighting back tears.

Joe took a small step back, took one of Mrs. Hall's hands in both of his, and told her, "Don't worry about—it's—it was—we're happy we could help," then turned to his buddy and said, "Right, Ben?"

"Yes, ma'am," Ben reassured her.

"Thank you, Mr. Martinez," Mr. Hall told Joe, shaking his hand, then turned to Ben and added, "Thank you, Mr. Wilson. We're so grateful for what you've done to help save our daughter."

Ben nodded and pursed his lips, unable to say what was in his heart. Mr. Hall seemed to understand what was left unspoken and put his arm around his wife, guided her to turn, and followed the iron lung as it made its journey down the long hallway. Virginia beamed with pride over her two former pupils and warmly remarked, "It's been quite a day." All in the group were smiling, obviously happy with the day's outcome—with the exception of Ben, though he made a noble effort to temper his disappointment and frustration for the benefit of everyone around him.

"So, Mr. Martinez," Mike spoke up, "your company flew the iron lung up here? On your dime? Is that correct?"

Ben felt a flash of relief, thinking he was off the hook for answering questions at the moment.

"Hey—the credit goes to Ben and his fellow cabbies—and a lot of waitresses! They helped out too," Joe answered, then turned to his buddy. "Right, Ben?"

Looking down, Ben nodded affirmatively, accepted there was no getting around answering reporters' questions, and responded graciously. "They did. A lot of different people, from all over the city, came together to help."

Mike had been around long enough to quickly sense this wasn't the time to press Ben, and he turned his attention back to Virginia, asking, "Mrs. Douglas, I understand that both Mr. Wilson and Mr. Martinez are former students of yours?"

"Yes!" Virginia acknowledged with gusto. "I'm very proud to say they are!"

Mike looked at David as if to say, "What are you waiting for?" David took the cue and asked, "So, uh, Mrs. Douglas, Mr. Wilson—so, uh, this little girl's gonna make it now, right?"

Ben didn't say anything, and his silence prompted Joe to jump in with, "That's my understanding."

"We hope so," Virginia told David and suggested, "Why don't you follow us upstairs? You can speak with the doctor in charge."

"Thanks. Appreciate that," Mike replied, then gestured toward Virginia with an, "after you," and the group followed her down the hospital corridor.

Inside a small isolation room, the pediatric iron lung was wheeled into position adjacent to Rachel Hall's bed. The undercarriage of the respirator stood about three feet off the floor, counter-top level, allowing doctors and nurses easier access to treat the patient within. Sam Weinberg, covered in a hospital gown, mask, cap, and gloves, quickly plugged the device's electrical cord into a nearby wall socket, then flipped the respirator's On/Off switch to On briefly, confirmed there was power, then quickly turned the motor back off. He moved swiftly to the front end of the iron lung and forced open the two large silver hook clasps, one on each side, and released the large disk-shaped plate that sealed the circular chamber near the patient's head. The round plate was attached to two metal legs on wheels, which rolled along the floor and supported the iron lung's inner bed table as it was extracted or reinserted into the cylinder. The large circular plate had a smaller circular opening at its center through which Rachel's head would protrude from the metal chamber. The small opening was fitted with a rubber collar, which would be adjusted to wrap snugly around Rachel's neck to sustain positive and negative air pressure within the respirator once her body was sealed inside.

Nurses in masks and gloves hurried to prepare a pad and sheet for the narrow, flat bed table of the iron lung. Dr. Friedman continued to encourage Rachel, whose eyes displayed the panic and purpose of saving one's last gram of energy for breathing only.

"Rachel, we're going to move you into the iron lung now. It might seem scary at first, but I promise you, it will help you breathe. Right away. I promise."

Dr. Friedman nodded to the nurses, who immediately assisted him in lifting Rachel from her hospital bed and placing her onto the respirator's bed tray. The nurses then maneuvered Rachel's head through the small opening in the end disk and placed a stack of folded towels for a pillow on a small headrest tray attached to the outside of the disc-like plate. The nurses quickly adjusted the rubber collar, pulled it close around Rachel's neck to form a secure seal, then pushed the undercarriage of the disc back onto the chamber and secured it by closing the metal hook clasps on each side of the disc.

Sam turned the respirator's motor back on and began adjusting dials and monitoring pressure gauges to bring the respirator online. The nurses looked at Dr. Friedman, Sam, and Rachel as the *sswhee-swoosh, sswhee-swoosh, sswhee-swoosh* of the respirator's bellow began. The effect of the air moving into and out of Rachel's lungs was immediate, but Dr. Friedman monitored it and hoped its impact had been in sufficient time for the patient. Sam made a minor adjustment to one of the dials on the side of the iron lung, then stepped back; he said nothing, but appeared satisfied and at ease with his efforts and with his machine.

Dr. Friedman noticed Rachel's eyes close, then, to his relief, reopen. Her lids relaxed. The fear in her eyes was gone, her body allowing itself to relax, to feel merely exhausted, and soon to give in to sleep. Visibly moved, the doctor took a deep breath and held his emotions in check. He gently stroked Rachel's forehead and told her, "You're gonna be all right, Rachel. This will help you get better now."

The nurses began stripping Rachel's hospital bed, then placed the sheets and pads in a sealed metal container within the room. Dr. Friedman thanked both women, then turned to Sam, who told the doctor matter-of-factly, "Works like a champion. Every time."

Inside an adjacent room, Emergency Room physician Sean Morrow, covered in an isolation mask, cap, gloves, and gown, bent over Scott Lewis, straining to hear the little boy's shallow breathing. The effects of the poliovirus combined with less oxygen entering Scott's bloodstream rendered him unable to protest verbally or physically as he lay motionless on his back; only his big brown eyes could attempt to plead, to scream, at the doctor, "Get away from my air! Go away! My air! Please, go away!"

Two isolation nurses stood on either side of Scott's bed, ready to erect an oxygen tent when the doctor ordered them to do so. Dr. Morrow stood upright and lifted Scott's right arm upward at the wrist.

"Scott! Scott, listen to me, Scott," the doctor loudly instructed the boy. "I'm holding your right arm. I'm going to let go of it and I want you to hold it up by yourself. Got that? Okay, I'm letting go—"

Scott's small arm fell like a dead weight and landed with a soft *thud* on the bed.

"That's okay, Scott. Now we're gonna try your left arm."

Another *thud*.

"This may seem like a silly exercise, Scott," the doctor reassured him, "but don't worry. This is all very normal."

Scott didn't understand why the nurses were so quiet. He wished one of them would cover him with a blanket or just hold his hand.

"Scott, we're going to try the same thing now with your legs, first with your right and then your left. Okay? Here goes. Can you hold your leg up for me, Scott?"

Thud.

"How about this one, Scott? Hold it—"

Thud.

"Okay, Scott. Not to worry. This is all very normal. Just what we expect," Dr. Morrow told the young boy, convincingly. "We know you're having trouble breathing, Scott. So we're gonna set up a small oxygen tent around you—to get you more air. It'll help you breathe a little easier. It'll be like having your own fort. You'll be able to see through it. And these two very nice nurses are gonna stay with you the whole time. I have to go out for just a moment, but I'll be back in to see you shortly."

Dr. Morrow warmly patted Scott on the leg and nodded to the nurses, who began draping the oxygen tent behind the head of Scott's bed and up and over the boy's torso. The nurse near the door caught the doctor's eye as he headed toward the hallway. Without words, the two conveyed to each other, "He's got to get into a respirator," but the doctor quickly looked away, not wanting to reveal his frustration, and walked out the door.

Virginia had noticed that Joe was trying to answer the questions Mike Reilly and David Lindsey were tossing at both him and Ben. Sensing that Ben wasn't quite up to engaging, Virginia steered the conversation toward Joe and his young company. Joe welcomed the opportunity to focus on his business and remembered his wife telling him, "Be sure and talk about Falcon Air Cargo whenever you get the chance!"

"Uh, Mike, right?" Joe asked the reporter.

"That's right," Mike answered. "What's up?"

"Uh, any chance you'd be able to mention Falcon Air Cargo in your story?"

"Hey!" Ben piped in. "We couldn't have done any of this if it wasn't for Joe and his company!"

"Is that right?" Mike asked knowingly, pushing his fedora backward on his head.

"No way," Ben reiterated.

"I think we could get that in there somewhere," Mike acknowledged.

"Really appreciate it," Joe told him. "And I know my wife sure will."

"You're based out of Florida, right?" David asked.

"That's right. Gainesville. It's in the northern part of the state."

"Got it," David noted, jotting down the name of the city on his pad.

"Must be nice this time of year," Mike remarked to Joe, adding, "Warm. Sunny."

"Oh yeah," Joe emphasized. "It is. And, hey, thanks."

Joe turned toward Ben and noticed the top of the twisted brown paper bag sticking out of his buddy's jacket pocket. He almost asked Ben about it but stopped short when he saw the strange look on Ben's face. He followed his friend's gaze toward a group of three women who were approaching. Virginia had already assessed the situation and eagerly welcomed the women to join her and the others.

"Hello, Mrs. McGuire!" Virginia greeted Megan's mother. "It's so nice to see you again."

Nora McGuire was glowing as she pushed Megan in the wheelchair, accompanied by Valerie, toward the group.

"Thank you, Mrs. Douglas," Nora replied, then turned her eyes to Ben and said, "Hello, Ben. Nice to see you again."

She remembered my name.

"Hello," Ben said, worried he'd hesitated a bit long to reply. "Good to see you too."

Joe had to nudge his buddy to arrest the momentary lapse of intelligence Ben appeared to be having. Joe gestured toward Nora and gave Ben an exaggerated facial stare which emphatically asked, "Are you going to introduce me or just stand there with that stupid look on your face?"

Ben snapped out of his trance and introduced Joe to Nora, who extended her hand, which was met by an enthusiastic shake and smile from Joe.

Eager to share the promising news on young Rachel, Dr. Neill Friedman jogged up to the group. Joe was anxious to learn if their transport of the machine had made a difference and didn't hesitate to ask, "How'd it go?"

"Joe, Ben, I could kiss you both!" the doctor exclaimed, unconcerned about his own exuberance. "She's breathing regularly. It saved her life. *You* saved her life!"

Joe and the others broke into comments of "Great!" "Wonderful news!" and "Fantastic!" all of which were fastidiously recorded by Mike and David in their reporters' notebooks. Ben forced a half smile, which both Virginia and Valerie noticed. Each woman was very familiar with the look on his face. They'd seen it many times on the faces of many parents when the light of hope in their eyes faded to discouragement.

On his way to a lab, Dr. Sean Morrow was about to walk past the group when Dr. Friedman spotted him. Dr. Morrow quickly looked away and kept walking, passing the group as Neill turned and called out to him.

"Sean! Dr. Morrow! Did you hear? The respirator? It's here! The patient's in it and she's breathing—fine!"

Neill was caught off guard by Sean's lack of response and again called out, "Dr. Morrow!"

Neill took off to catch up with Sean, who finally paused and turned around to listen to his colleague. It was then that Neill noticed the frustration on Sean's face. He didn't need to ask what was wrong, only what the status was.

"How far along?" Neill asked, transitioning straight to the point.

Sean let out a huge sigh and began to relay Scott's status and circumstances.

"They just brought the boy into isolation. His diaphragm isn't moving; he can't swallow. It's as if he's suffocating in front of me and there's nothing I can do to stop it. Not without a respirator," Sean relayed, then added, "He's six years old."

"Damn it!" Neill cursed under his breath. "And oxygen? It's not—?"

"You know everything I've tried, Neill. You've tried them all before yourself," Sean answered flatly. "This boy deserves more. We're gonna lose him— without a respirator."

"He can have mine," a strong voice called out from across the hall.

The two doctors turned to find John Williams, seated in a wheelchair, being pushed toward them by nurse Ruth Hoffman.

"John!" Dr. Friedman couldn't help exclaim. "This is—when? When did—?"

"Today!" Ruth replied. "He's out today. I think he must have heard I was coming, and he just wanted to get the heck out of there."

"I don't care what his reason was!" Dr. Morrow blurted out. "That's terrific, John! This means—" The doctor paused, his mind quickly calculating the options for young Scott Lewis.

"We'll get it up to—" Dr. Friedman attempted to say, but Ruth was well ahead of him and interjected, "It's already been prepared and being moved into the isolation room as we speak."

Dr. Morrow started to rush back toward the Isolation Ward but turned and called back to John and Dr. Friedman. "John—I owe you one!"

John, Ruth, and Dr. Friedman watched as Dr. Morrow turned and picked up his pace.

"No," Dr. Friedman added, then turned and looked John directly in the eye and said, "His *patient* owes you his life."

"He doesn't owe me anything," John replied sincerely.

Dr. Friedman reached to shake the hand of John, who offered his strong left hand to the doctor, who quickly adjusted and shook hands, telling the young man, "You're okay in my book, John."

"Thanks," John offered genuinely and, for the first time in what felt like a long time, accepted the compliment—and even allowed it to linger.

Mike Reilly and David Lindsey had left the group and planted themselves at the bank of phone booths on the far end of the hall to call in and secure space for their stories. It finally gave Joe a chance to lean over to Ben and, with a concerned look, ask him, "Hey, buddy, what's in the paper bag?" as he looked discreetly toward the twisted-up neck of the brown bag sticking out of Ben's pocket.

"What? Oh man! I forgot—" Ben remarked, somewhat flustered in front of the group, but wanted to clarify for his friend. He quickly added, "It's not what you—hold on."

Ben slowly pulled the bag out of his pocket as the others looked on, then carefully opened it, gingerly reached inside, and drew out two small Whitman Sampler holiday chocolate boxes, much to Joe's relief. Ben handed one of the boxes to Megan, then the other to Nora, and explained, "You—you two didn't get to have your chocolate hearts last Valentine's. I, uh, found these and thought you could, you know, have a do-over."

"Oh, Ben, that's so sweet of you," Nora exclaimed, with a look that conveyed she was genuinely moved. "I can't believe you remembered."

Virginia and Valerie couldn't help repeating Whitman's famous slogan and, not missing a beat, chimed together, "Whitman Samplers. A woman never forgets—the man who remembers!" and broke into laughter with the others.

"Wow! Thank you," Megan declared as the four women shared their appreciation with Ben and Joe.

"Whitman Samplers. They used to send these to us overseas—in Europe, during the war," Joe remarked. "Some of them even had little notes or messages inside the box—from the women at the plant where they were made. It was really cool. Made us feel good. A real morale booster!"

"I read where some of them even got married," Ben blurted out, explaining, "I mean—the guy who got the message came back and looked up the girl. You know that kind of thing."

"Imagine that," Joe stated with a hint of suggestion, looking Ben square in the eye.

"I love it! Thank you, Ben," Nora gushed, holding the small yellow box with its colorful needlepoint motif close to her heart, a gesture which allowed Ben a sigh of relief and a brief moment of joy.

Murray Dolan had succeeded in getting his passenger, Ed Bauer, up from his sister's dinner table, into his cab, and driven to the hospital in short order. He wasn't sure how long Joe Martinez would stay at the hospital after dropping off the iron lung and wanted to make good on his promise to get Ed there before Joe left. He was impressed Ed could keep pace with him as the two men walked briskly from the cab to the hospital entrance, through the lobby, and into the elevator. After several nurses followed them inside the elevator, Murray felt obliged to remove his cap, and clutched it in both hands, as usual. The senior nurse in the group sized

Murray and Ed up and sensed their urgency wasn't driven by a patient, which prompted her to ask, "You two here with the people who brought the iron lung tonight?"

"Yes, ma'am," Murray replied. "I was told to look for them on the third floor."

"That's correct," the nurse offered as the elevator ascended. "One more up. We're getting off here. And congratulations."

"Thank you, ma'am," Murray replied as both he and Ed smiled, somewhat reassured, somewhat buoyed by the words and tone of the nurse.

As the doors opened to the third floor, Murray was downright relieved when he spotted Ben and a guy who looked like a pilot among the group, just down the hallway ahead of them, and turned quickly to Ed, assuring him, "I believe that's Martinez, Mr. Bauer, straight ahead, with that group."

"Oh, good. Thank you, Mr. Dolan," Ed replied in a way that let Murray know Ed was pleased with the cabbie's efforts.

Murray and Ed were quickly recognized by Ben, who greeted Ed Bauer and wasted no time introducing him to Joe.

"Hello, Mr. Bauer, Murray," Ben said, pushing Joe in Ed's direction. "This is Joe Martinez, who flew the iron lung here on one of his cargo planes."

"Pleased to meet you, Mr. Martinez," Ed said directly, extending his hand to Joe.

"You as well, Mr. Bauer," Joe responded, shaking hands with the no-nonsense Ed Bauer.

"I wanted to meet you, Mr. Martinez—"

"Please call me Joe."

"Thank you. I wanted to meet you, Joe, in person and find out a little bit about your air cargo company."

"Falcon Air, yes, sir," Joe interjected, quickly adding, "We're small yet. Two planes right now—C-47s."

"The stalwart," Ed commented.

"That they are," Joe agreed.

"Falcon Air, yes," Ed continued. "Your friend Ben tells me you're based out of Florida and are flying up and down the East Coast, and even looking at the Midwest."

"That's right, sir," Joe said with confidence.

"I understand you and your pilot served with the Army Air Forces—that right?"

"That's correct," Joe affirmed. "My copilot's Hank McGoran, a great pilot. Flew a hell of a lot of missions."

"Mmm-hmm," Ed acknowledged, then added, "Well, it seems to me if you two can safely land and deliver a critical piece of equipment to New York when all the airports are closed, well, you're just the fellows I'm looking for—for my business."

Virginia and Valerie were listening intently to the men's conversation and gave each other an impressed, exaggerated raised-eyebrow look. Megan was listening to the various grown-ups, hoping something exciting might actually happen, but didn't get her hopes up. Down the hall, Mike had observed Ed and Murray walk up to the group and sensed that something newsworthy might be brewing. He shot a look at David, signaling there might be something the rookie reporter should investigate. With a quick nod toward the group, Mike indicated they should head over to join them, posthaste.

"I—we'd welcome the opportunity to transport your equipment, Mr. Bauer," Joe quickly offered, "and I'm available to talk specs and fees whenever it's convenient."

"I'll have my operations man, Tom Hainsworth, call your office. Is there someone he should talk to?"

"Um, that would be my wife, Brenda. She manages the offices," Joe confessed.

"A woman?" Megan asked somewhat boastfully, unable to resist the opportunity to highlight the fact that a female was managing the office of an up-and-coming air cargo company.

"She's real good with the books," Joe quickly offered.

"She must be a very smart woman," Megan emphasized.

"You're a lucky man, Joe," Ed added.

"That I am, sir. And, yes, she is, Megan," Joe acknowledged.

Mike and David, pens and pads in hand, joined the group, prompting Virginia to introduce the two reporters to Ed and Murray. Just as they were about to ask the businessman a few questions, Megan hijacked the group's attention.

"*John?* What's *he*—when did—?" Megan blurted out, taken by surprise when she spotted John Williams down the hall. He was sitting in a wheelchair being pushed by the new nurse supervisor, Ruth Hoffman. Dr. Friedman was with them. Megan noticed John was out of a hospital gown and wearing jeans. And loafers. And a tan short-sleeve shirt with flap pockets on the chest. Without forethought, a softly spoken, apprehensive "Oh God" escaped Megan's mouth when she realized they were headed her way. Mike, David, Joe, Ben, Murray, and Ed all turned to see what had grabbed Megan's attention. Nora, Valerie, and Virginia shared a moment of women's intuition, and didn't need to guess.

In a fraction of a millisecond, Megan's mind processed the pros and cons of doing nothing or being boldly assertive and intercepting John's group. She'd dreamt about this moment, meeting John again, in person. She'd imagined it wouldn't be in front of her mother. It would be somewhere normal, like school or a football game or—but if it had to be here, it wasn't going to be stolen from her. She looked for assurance from Valerie, who shot her the "what are you waiting for?" look, which gave Megan the confidence to act immediately. She wheeled as fast as she thought she could get away with without appearing too eager, too obvious—and suddenly regretted wearing her lame navy pleated skirt and matching cardigan with a white blouse. She thought she must look like a Catholic schoolgirl, not a cool sixteen-year-old. Why hadn't she put on some of the makeup her mom brought her? Thank God she'd washed her hair, but why had she put it in a ponytail? And *today*—of all days? And there was that one stubborn little bump of hair popping up on the left side of her head in between the smooth hair, refusing to cooperate when she'd hurriedly twisted the rubber band on. At least her bangs weren't too short.

Dr. Friedman, John, and Ruth came to a halt, uncertain if Megan would be able to stop herself in time to avoid an outright collision. Megan, however, was well adept at maneuvering her wheelchair and stopped just in front of them, strategically blocking their path before they could get any closer to the other group.

"Hello," John said matter-of-factly, followed by a tentative, "Megan?"

"Yes. I'm Megan," she answered somewhat smartly. "I can't believe you're out of—I mean—when? How?"

"Hey, I asked Santa for some new lungs," John replied, feebly attempting to play it cool.

The banality of John's wit went unnoticed. With Megan's brain circuitry abruptly compromised, she heard only clever, interesting words flow from his mouth. She giggled, even blushed. The idea of being close to a boy, this boy, had suddenly washed over her. It felt wonderful. Heavenly. And she didn't want the feeling to end. Ruth sensed the opportunity for John and Megan to have a moment alone and nodded to the doctor, indicating they should leave these two to themselves. Ruth and Dr. Friedman excused themselves to join the group down the hall, allowing the young adults to have a conversation in private.

"You—so you—you're out of the respirator now, right?" Megan asked, instantly questioning herself why she asked something so obvious.

"Yeah," John answered with seriousness. "Feels good."

"So—so, what are you going to do, now? How long will you—?" Megan asked, concerned.

Dr. Friedman beamed as he approached the group with the news about John Williams and was eager to let others know what it also meant for the young polio patient, Scott Lewis. He told the group he had "great news!" and gestured toward Megan and John down the hall, sharing that John was officially out of his respirator. "Done! No longer needs it!"

"It happens just like that?" David asked. "I mean—a patient can stop using it—needing it—?"

"Not exactly," the doctor replied, explaining, "We—we refer to it as 'weaning' the patient off the iron lung."

The doctor described how patients may need to retrain their diaphragm and chest muscles, depending on how long they've relied on a respirator to breathe. He shared that John had been in the iron lung for nearly ten months, which was unusual but sometimes happened in cases where patients didn't recover as expected, for a variety of reasons. Sometimes a patient found the idea of having to think through each breath too frightening. That's why it was a lot easier for the youngest patients, he explained. "They don't think about it. They just breathe."

"In John's case, a bit longer," Neill pointed out. "It takes time to strengthen the diaphragm, but he's been working hard with breathing exercises. And not a moment too soon. His machine is being put to good use this very moment."

Ben listened intently as Dr. Friedman told the group about the six-year-old boy who was admitted earlier and diagnosed with polio. He relayed how the sudden availability of John's respirator saved the life of the young boy, who had been unable to breathe on his own. The words "saved the life" hung in the air for Ben, who finally allowed himself to feel almost okay about the circumstances.

"Was that the fare you picked up tonight, Ben?" Joe asked.

"Could be," Ben answered quietly.

"Scott Lewis? Mother's Amy Lewis?" Dr. Friedman asked.

"Sounds right," Ben answered humbly.

"You helped save his life—getting him here in time," the doctor told Ben. "Not everybody will do that— knowingly place a child infected with polio in their car."

"My mother had polio as an adult," Ed Bauer boldly shared with the group, and added, "And the iron lung saved her life too. I was a grown man. Never thought about something like that happening to her. So, Joe, Ben, you've done something really important here."

"Indeed you have," Virginia reiterated to her former pupils.

"Yeah, so did your daughter Megan," Ben said, turning to Nora. "She was the one who told me about the girl who needed an iron lung in the first place."

"That's true," Valerie affirmed.

"She got the ball rolling," Ben told the group.

"And you ran with it!" Dr. Friedman pointed out.

"And Joe flew it," Ben added, sounding upbeat.

"You've all helped in different ways, directly and indirectly," Virginia added, "and often behind the scenes. You've all helped someone today."

"And that's what I call a good day at the office," Valerie emphasized with a smile.

Ruth Hoffman returned to check in with John, thinking he might be tired or hungry or both.

"Yeah, I am," he told her, then turned to Megan and asked, "You hungry or something? I could really use a burger. I hear they got 'em in the cafeteria downstairs."

The thought of eating almost made Megan nauseous, but the words "Yeah, I could eat something" slipped out of her mouth without effort, and more kept coming.

"I eat there a lot—well, obviously—I'm here. Duh," she said, rolling her eyes to appear nonchalant and trying to recover from her perceived loss of "cool," then quickly added, "Yeah, I'm okay to go."

John looked at Ruth, who nodded and began pushing his wheelchair. Megan spun her wheelchair around to roll alongside John's. That's when she noticed his shirt was open. Somewhat opened. She could see part of his chest. His nipple. *Oh my God! Oh my God! Heart beating faster. Breathe.* She looked away slowly and suddenly realized they'd need to pass her mom and the group on the way toward the elevator, and hoped they wouldn't notice. Megan kept pace in her wheelchair but, intimidated to feel awkward by John's silence, brought up his therapy for conversation.

"So, you can start physical therapy now?" she asked.

"I have to. Every day."

"They're forcing you?" Megan questioned.

"Yeah. Every day. Twice a day."

"*Twice* a day?" Megan asked, concerned.

"Yeah. They said I have to," John answered, adding with a straight face, "If I want to take that pushy McGuire girl out New Year's Eve. You know, ponytail? The one who's always in everybody's business?"

Megan was processing John's words when she was blindsided by the awareness that he meant *her*. The fickle teenage ego kicked in and Megan, not wanting to appear childish, came up with a sound that was somewhere between a laugh and a "huh?" followed by "Wha—what makes you think I don't already have a date for New Year's?" *Oh God, oh God, oh God!* She couldn't believe what she had just said, that she'd actually uttered those words. And with such confidence, driven by excitement and hope.

John didn't say anything and, again, the silent void had to be filled by something.

"Or if I'd even want to go," Megan continued. "Maybe I have plans already. Maybe I—"

"Don't you ever stop talking?" John asked as they wheeled past the group.

Virginia and Valerie chuckled as the teenagers headed toward the elevator. Joe watched them for a moment, then asked Virginia, "We were never like that, were we, Mrs. Douglas?"

"No!" Virginia said emphatically. "You were much worse!"

The rest of the group enjoyed a laugh, and Joe and Ben had to as well. Nora's eyes followed her daughter wheeling into the brightly lit elevator with John and Ruth and watched as the doors closed.

"Now *that's* a Christmas present," she remarked to Virginia and Valerie.

The adults stood around awkwardly for a moment, not talking but not wanting the uplifting mood to end. Nora didn't see any reason it should and asked if anyone would like to get a cup of coffee or a bite to eat.

"But—I thought you were having dinner with Megan?" Ben blurted out.

"I think she has more interesting plans right now," Nora suggested, "than dinner with her mother."

Joe nudged Ben, who finally got the hint but stumbled with his delivery.

"Oh, yeah, I see. That *would* be more interesting" came out of Ben's mouth, and instantly he regretted his gaffe. "I—I mean—for *her*! For a teenager. For them, I mean."

"He'd love to! We'd all love to!" Joe quickly announced, rescuing Ben.

"There's a cafeteria right here in the hospital," Nora told Ben and, not wanting him to feel embarrassed, added, "and Megan can join us later, if she likes."

"Yeah, yeah, that'd be good," Ben stuttered, then collected himself to manage, "Can you wait here for me for just a minute? I need to call Gino back at the garage. Just want to let him know that everything worked out okay here. With the iron lung, I mean."

"Of course," Nora told him. "Take your time."

"I'll be right back," Ben told her and started to walk away but turned and looked back at Nora and asked her, "Don't leave."

"I won't," Nora assured him with a warm smile, then watched Ben turn and head down the hallway.

"We've already eaten," Murray chimed in, looking at Ed, "but we'll join you for a cup of coffee—or something. I think Mr. Bauer here would like to speak with Joe a little more, right?"

"Absolutely! Great idea!" Joe jumped in.

"Good. I can give you some numbers about weight and dimensions," Ed suggested.

"Yeah, and I'd like to hear about your needs around schedules, timelines," Joe added.

"It's simple. I need to get my fans and air conditioners where they need to be before my competition does," Ed explained.

Willy had stayed late at the dispatch office; he knew his help would be appreciated, particularly on this day. Gino was standing just outside the door, talking with a couple of drivers in the garage who'd returned from their shifts. Gino's white shirt looked like it had seen a full day, perhaps a day and a half; his sleeves were rolled up midway on his forearms, and with those wide black suspenders and baggy black pleated pants, for some reason Willy thought Gino looked more like a bartender tonight than a dispatch manager.

Gino had told Willy he wanted to treat him to dinner to thank him, and the young clerk was trying to get the ride sheets organized and tallied before they left. Willy's energy and drive had been fueled throughout the afternoon and evening by soda pop, and there were four empty Coke bottles lined up on his desk to attest to it. He was hungry and looked forward to eating a nice meal. A bottle of Seagram's 7, half full, stood on

Gino's desk. Willy had just poured a shot for his boss when the phone rang.

"Hey, Gino! Call from the hospital!" Willy shouted through the glass window to his boss, who told the two cabbies he needed to take the call, as it would be Ben on the phone.

"Hey, tell Ben 'great job, buddy!' from us, Gino!" one of the men shouted as Gino ran into the office, eager to speak with Ben. Gino signaled with a thumbs-up to assure the men as he grabbed the phone with his other hand.

"Hey, Ben! I just heard the machine got there A-okay. How's things going?"

"Actually, pretty darn good," Ben had to admit. "The doc says the machine saved the little girl's life."

"That's great, Ben! That's absolutely great! Everybody's gonna be glad to hear that!"

"And—and even that little boy you had me bring in tonight—he got a machine too," Ben shared. "An older patient, he—he was able to give up his machine today! And just in time for that little guy—they said it saved his life."

There was silence on the phone for a moment, and Ben understood. Willy looked away from Gino, not wanting him to feel self-conscious. Gino forced a cough, took a deep breath, and exhaled.

"Two lives saved, Ben," Gino said, his voice cracking despite his best efforts. "Not a bad day."

Ben finally released a little laugh, then echoed, "Not a bad day at all."

"So, go celebrate! You've earned it! What are you guys gonna do?"

"Uh, actually, remember I told you about Megan's mother, Nora?"

"Yeah?"

"Well, gonna have dinner with her tonight!" Ben told Gino and actually started to smile.

"Where ya takin' her?"

"Oh, we're just going to the cafeteria in the hospital," Ben answered.

"Really romancing her, eh? Are you NUTS! THE HOSPITAL CAFETERIA!" Gino exclaimed. "Do I have to teach you guys everything?"

Ben realized how cockamamie it may have sounded to Gino and reassured him it was Nora's idea and that the whole group was going and that it was okay and that he would do better next time.

"Look, you take her to my cousin Enrico's place next week. Make a date," Gino told him. "Impress her. He'll save a real nice table for you."

"Okay, okay. I will. Look, I, uh, gotta get back to her."

"I don't know what you're doing flapping your gums on the phone to me."

"Hey, Gino," Ben said, pausing a moment to express his sincerity. "Thanks."

"Ya did good, Ben," Gino said warmly. "Now get the hell off the phone!"

Gino placed the receiver back in the phone cradle and picked up the glass of Seagram's Willy had poured him. He exhaled a small laugh and smiled, savoring the day's remarkable success. Worthy of a drink, he thought, and it felt damn good going down. He looked at Willy and thought about his drivers. He knew he had good men on his team.

As if resigned to his role, Gino gently threw up his arms and softly reiterated, "I gotta teach these guys everything," then grabbed his overcoat and told Willy, "Come on. Let's get something to eat. I'm hungry."

Mike and David were wrapping up their interviews and comparing notes for the stories they were about to write. Mike attempted to compliment David, telling the young reporter what a good thing he'd done with the cabbies' fundraising story. Mike also pointed out how good things often seemed to orbit Virginia. David suspected Mike was not only quite fond of Virginia but surmised his colleague respected her immensely as well.

"So, do you see?" Mike suggested to David. "There's a lot of positive things that happened besides just getting that iron lung here. Looks like even Martinez is gonna get some help for his new company with that Bauer guy throwing some business his way."

"Yeah. The power of the press," David said with a little too much self-assurance.

"No," Mike said slowly and with purpose, "the power of good people doing the right thing."

David realized at once his arrogance had again exposed his inexperience. Mike saw it in David's eyes and saved him from total humiliation by adding, "And it's our job to make sure it gets reported."

"Right," David acknowledged humbly. "And thanks for the reminder."

David looked over at Virginia, who was talking with Joe, Nora, Dr. Friedman, Valerie, and Ben, who had rejoined the group. David studied Virginia's face; she seemed so happy—or was it contentment? He wondered how she managed to be so upbeat while working in a place that saw its share of sorrow—most likely daily. Virginia noticed David looking at her and thought he and Mike might be signaling they needed to get back to their offices. She excused herself from the group and walked over to the two reporters, greeting them with, "Well, gentlemen, you certainly have a lot of good news to write about today."

"A nice change," Mike quickly offered, then let Virginia know he was going to head out. Tipping his hat, he excused himself, then added, "Merry Christmas, Mrs. Douglas."

"Merry Christmas to you, Mike," Virginia replied, then turned to David and asked, "Well, Mr. Lindsey, do you have your story now?"

"I believe I do. I think I even understand what Mr. Church meant."

"Even in these *modern times?*"

"Even in these modern times," David said sheepishly but genuinely.

"I'll look forward to reading your story," Virginia told David. "Happy holidays, Mr. Lindsey."

"Same to you, Mrs. Douglas."

Virginia smiled, and David knew it was with approval of what he'd said. He watched her walk back toward the group, then watched as she, Ben, and the others walked down the hospital corridor and headed toward the elevator. Just plain folks, he thought, doing some incredible things with little or no concern about self-glory. They seemed so happy.

David had finished his piece on the cabbies' successful fundraiser. The story was slated for the main section of the paper, and he had turned it in to his editor. He knew it would be in the morning paper—maybe not on the front page this time, but it would definitely get in— his boss knew readers were anxious to learn about the outcome of the cabbies' efforts. David's focus now was on the story he'd previously dreaded: the Christmas content article for the special holiday section. Who knew he'd actually enjoy writing it? He quickly pulled the finished copy out of the typewriter—he always enjoyed the unique whirring sound that made—and scanned the words for inch count. It looked good, and a head shot of Virginia would be included.

Satisfied, he leaned back in his chair and held the sheet in his hands, quietly reading his words aloud to himself.

VIRGINIA SPREADS SANTA'S GOODWILL
By David Lindsey

Yes, Virginia, there is a Santa Claus. He exists as certainly as love and generosity and devotion exist, and you know that they abound and give to your life its highest beauty and joy.

Those were the words written by Francis P. Church, a senior editor at *The Sun*, back in 1897 that affirmed the existence of Santa Claus to a young girl who asked the newspaper a question which many young girls and boys might have asked: "Is there a Santa Claus?" The affirmation was part of a longer commentary that also gave a nod to the political and religious climate of the time. Church may have been tasked with crafting the reply because he was well respected among his peers for taking on controversial theological topics from a secular point of view. The editorial became an overnight success and was reprinted every year in newspapers across the county and across the globe, establishing itself forever in American tradition.

Virginia O'Hanlon Douglas, the once-eight-year-old girl who wrote to the newspaper, is now a principal at P.S. 401, a hospital school in Brooklyn for children who are too ill to attend regular classes. Mrs. Douglas encourages helping children whose resources are limited, particularly during the holidays.

"In the harsh realities of today, many children are faced with unpleasant circumstances," Mrs. Douglas stated. "There is a great need for us to ensure these children know the joy of the holiday experience."

Mrs. Douglas is keeping the spirit of Santa Claus alive and well among all those she encounters, demonstrating that the immortal words of Francis P. Church are as meaningful today as when he wrote the famous reply to her question more than fifty years ago. Church ended his editorial with the following commentary:

No Santa Claus? Thank God he lives, and he lives forever. A thousand years from now, Virginia, nay, ten times ten thousand years from now, he will continue to make glad the heart of childhood.

Afterword

In the first half of the twentieth century, poliomyelitis, commonly known as polio, was considered one of the most feared diseases in America. The Center for Disease Control (CDC) reports that polio outbreaks in the United States in the early 1950s caused more than 15,000 cases of paralysis each year. The year 1952 marked the height of the polio epidemic in the US, with more than 58,000 cases reported, resulting in more than 21,000 paralytic cases. After the Salk vaccine was licensed in 1955 and the commercial use of the Sabin oral poliovirus vaccine in 1963, the number of polio cases dropped dramatically. Polio originating in the US was eradicated in 1979. The campaign to eliminate polio across the globe continues to this day. The World Health Organization works in partnership with the CDC, UNICEF, Rotary International, and the Bill and Melinda Gates Foundation to eradicate polio worldwide. At the time of this book's publication, polio remains endemic in two countries: Pakistan and Afghanistan. Nigeria was declared polio-free in 2020. There is no cure for poliomyelitis, only treatment. The polio vaccine is the only method of prevention.

During the polio epidemic of 1916 in New York City, many young children who were ill were forcibly removed from their homes and their parents by ill-informed and overzealous members of the Sanitary Squad, sanctioned under the New York Board of Health. Families living in tenements often could not meet the strict sanitary conditions imposed, which meant their ill children would be removed and sent to hospitals. The Board of Health passed resolutions requiring isolation of such patients for eight weeks. Often, children of more affluent parents with larger living accommodations were allowed to be cared for within their own homes.

Throughout her life, Virginia O'Hanlon Douglas was frequently interviewed by newspaper reporters who sought her opinion of the famed "Yes, Virginia, There Is a Santa Claus" editorial and its relevance in modern times. Reporters were also drawn to her teaching career and where she chose to practice it. *The New York Times* reported that Virginia began teaching in New York City schools after earning a bachelor's degree from Hunter College in 1910. An article in the *New Yorker* stated she earned a Master of Arts degree from Columbia the following year and that she chose to work in some of the city's most disadvantaged districts. After earning a PhD from Fordham, she became a junior principal in 1935. Prior to retiring, she was a principal at P.S. 401, which *The New York Times* reported "held classes in hospitals and institutions for chronically ill and crippled children." She retired in 1959 after serving forty-three years with the New York City Public School System.

Virginia died on May 13, 1971 at the age of eighty-one. The following day, *The New York Times* ran a story, "Virginia O'Hanlon, Santa's Friend, Dies," on the front page.

The editorial, as published in *The Sun*, September 21, 1897:

We take pleasure in answering at once and thus prominently the communication below, expressing at the same time our great gratification that its faithful author is numbered among the friends of *The Sun.*

Dear Editor,

I am 8 years old. Some of my little friends say there is no Santa Claus. Papa says, "If you see it in *The Sun,* it's so." Please tell me the truth, is there a Santa Claus?

Virginia O'Hanlon 115 West 95th Street

Virginia, your little friends are wrong. They have been affected by the skepticism of a skeptical age. They do not believe except they see. They think nothing can be which is not comprehensible by their little minds. All minds, Virginia, whether they be men's or children's, are little. In this great universe of ours man is a mere insect, an ant, in his intellect, as compared with the boundless world about him, as measured by the intelligence capable of grasping the whole of truth and knowledge.

Yes, Virginia, there is a Santa Claus. He exists as certainly as love and generosity and devotion exist, and you know that they abound and give to your life its highest beauty and joy.

Alas! how dreary would be the world if there were no Santa Claus! It would be as dreary as if there were no Virginias. There would be no childlike faith then, no poetry, no romance to make tolerable this existence. We should have no enjoyment, except in sense and sight. The eternal light with which childhood fills the world would be extinguished.

Not believe in Santa Claus! You might as well not believe in fairies! You might get your papa to hire men to watch in all the chimneys on Christmas Eve to catch Santa Claus, but even if they did not see Santa Claus coming down, what would that prove? Nobody sees Santa Claus, but that is no sign that there is no Santa Claus. The most real things in the world are those that neither children nor men can see.

Did you ever see fairies dancing on the lawn? Of course not, but that's no proof that they are not there. Nobody can conceive or imagine all the wonders there are unseen and unseeable in the world.

You tear apart the baby's rattle and see what makes the noise inside, but there is a veil covering the unseen world which not the strongest man, nor even the united strength of all the strongest men that ever lived, could tear apart. Only faith, fancy, poetry, love, romance, can push aside that curtain and view and picture the supernal beauty and glory beyond.

Is it all real? Ah, Virginia, in all this world there is nothing else so real and abiding.

No Santa Claus! Thank God he lives, and he lives forever. A thousand years from now, Virginia, nay, ten times ten thousand years from now, he will continue to make glad the heart of childhood.

Francis P. Church, Columbia College, New York City, 1859

Photo: Preservation Department, Columbia University Libraries, New York, N.Y.

THANKS

My deepest gratitude to Susan Coddington, Sandy Peterson, Torv Carlsen, Irene Cook, Marian Prentice Huntington, Moira Heddy, Kathleen Emrey, Mary Connell, pilots Al Coddington, Howard F. Hall, and Dan Heddy, Sr. Aaron Winkelman, Prof. Carlos Rodriguez, my sisters Kathy Poggi and Debra Parks, and to Mom. Your tireless encouragement, genuine support, and valuable guidance are immeasurable. My sincere thanks to the staff at the Preservation Department of Columbia University Libraries, the Archives and Special Collections of Hunter College Libraries, the Baker-Cederberg Museum and Archives, the New York Public Library Astor, Lenox and Tilden Foundation, and the Library of Congress.

ABOUT THE AUTHOR

Patricia P Goodin is an award-winning writer who grew up in Virginia, Illinois, and California. She also lived in Queens, New York City. She was honored with a First Place Award for Editorial Commentary by the California Newspaper Publishers Association and is the recipient of a USA Today Hot Site Award for her cyber-soap, "Moms Night Out." She earned an MA from Dominican University in Northern California, where she lives with her husband.

The Santa Claus Girl is her first novel.

For a reading group guide, visit
www.thesantaclausgirl.com